# A Mind Prone to Evil

P S Lynch

Stairwell Books //

Published by Stairwell Books
161 Lowther Street
York, YO31 7LZ

www.stairwellbooks.co.uk
@stairwellbooks

This is a work of fiction, based on fact. A few names have been changed. Most other characters, businesses, places, events, locales, and incidents are as close to the truth as possible, though some may have been used in a fictitious manner.

ISBN: 978-1-917334-11-2

"All things can corrupt when a mind is prone to evil."
*Ovid*

For Laetitia & Camille.

# Unique in the History of Jurisprudence

Like a cityscape of cinders in the grate of a fireplace, broken buildings flounder in grey ash.

She picks her way diffidently through the rubble, grateful for the flat-soled brogues she is wearing on the advice of an American serviceman.

"Heels? You ain't bin there in a while, have you ma'am?"

Her beige couture suit is garnering the wrong kind of attention, especially for a woman accustomed to working in the shadows. She is stared at by two small boys trying to fill a tin bucket with grimy water that spews from a pipe.

She clutches a redundant street map, now six years out of date. It bears no resemblance to the fractured wasteland that stretches in every direction; the streets are impossible to differentiate. Picking her path across the bombed-out city has been an arduous game of hopscotch over rubble and misshapen slabs of pavement. Exasperated and perspiring, she stops to ask for directions from a middle-aged man on crutches who refuses to acknowledge her. A little further on, she passes the concrete entrails of a department store, and is absorbed by the vision of a rouged mannequin in bra and panties teetering on a high ledge, the lonely remnant of the third-floor lingerie department. The sight of the impassive dummy is haunting; a suicidal coquette smirking inanely at her own misfortune. Her plastic rictus face is the most expressive she has seen all day.

Rounding a corner, it is a relief when she sees it at last. Incongruous in the midst of wretched destruction, the Nuremberg Palace of Justice has remained almost completely unscarred. Perhaps that's how God wanted it, she wonders before blinking the idea away as dust is thrown into her eyes from a passing US army jeep. The courthouse is the largest of its kind in Bavaria and comprises eighty courtrooms. Today, there is only one room she is looking for: Courtroom 600 in the east wing, on Bärenschanzstrasse.

Find that, and she'll find him. The man Hitler once called 'as cold as ice'.

She makes her way along Fürtherstrasse, unable to take her eyes off the towering building behind the wall. It is crowned by a steeply pitched roof with burnt orange tiles, under which are dozens of square windows yawning black silence. She has no idea where she should be going, but spotting three photographers hurrying in the opposite direction, she pursues them on the assumption that the press always follow a story, and this morning, he is the story.

There is a queue at the entrance. Approaching the steps, from her purse she withdraws the *Ausweiskarte* and panics. Is it valid? Will it gain her access? She hands it hesitantly to one of the American guards who gives the image of Fräulein Gisela Weschler the most fleeting of glances, before passing it back as his eyes move to the next in line. She enters the darkness of the main hall and is struck by the beautiful paneling which immediately puts her in mind of those heady days at Carinhall. She casts the thought from her mind and walks on towards the courtroom.

Within, she feels a sense of disappointment. She was expecting an expansive vaulted hall, a huge canvas upon which he might paint vivid depictions from the last thirteen years to enthrall the jury and the world beyond. The space is too small for an artist of his stature. The entire room is dressed in dark varnished oak and walls have been removed to accommodate additional space, enough for almost four hundred people. Down and to the left, she sees where the twenty-one will sit on long benches. She stands looking down over the courtroom with a feeling of dread beginning to gnaw. She takes a deep breath and whispers to herself.

'Come on old girl,' he'd surely say, 'pull yourself together.' Smoothing her skirt, she shuffles along one of the rows and takes a seat. She begins fussing nervously at her hairpin, its gold and rhinestone detail catching the light as she does so.

Over the next thirty minutes the room slowly fills. It's mostly press people with too much bluster and too little respect. She pays close attention to what is unfolding around her in the gallery, catching whispers and mutterings that float on the air. There a *frisson* of excitement as she hears his name muttered around her. An imperious British journalist lights the spark with a reference to the Reichsmarschall followed by something about his foul temper.

The flame of conversation catches light as two Americans behind her are talking about 'great snaps' of Göring in the dailies.

The fire spreads and soon she hears tell of him all around her.

He was once a dashing fighter pilot – a hero of the Great War, says an elderly German man to his wife.

He was one of the boys, says a young man in a wheelchair. Always a stein of beer in one hand and that walnut pipe of his in the other.

Yes, she concedes quietly to herself, certainly he could play the Rabelaisian well.

Behind her a Bavarian sniggers about The Fat One and she flushes, wanting to scold him for being so beastly. If only they'd borne witness like her, seen how his health suffered. The drugs that poisoned his mind and bloated his body came later, only when the pain was too much to bear.

An older lady behind her speaks in reverent tones about the great military strategist.

Yes, she thinks, that's surely how we will all remember him, Paladin of the Third Reich.

Does she imagine it or did someone in the front row say 'Carinhall'?

She is desperate to shout out that she was there with him, that she knows the Reichsmarschall personally. But she resists the urge. She knows that the quality he always valued most was her discretion, and it is that same quality she must possess now above all others.

She listens on and the fire ignites again: one of the French journalists has heard a story about exotic animals that ran wild in the forest at Carinhall.

Not just animals, says another, women too – cavorting in the woods, no less. A harem, he's heard.

There's talk of wild parties. Didn't the Americans find all that booze in his cellar in Berchtesgarden?

There were orgies apparently, one woman says with a sneer. Her husband guffaws and is rewarded with a glower of disdain.

She shuts her eyes and tries to close her mind to it all, just as she has been doing for the last five months. This is precisely why she doesn't read the newspapers any longer. Why she lives in quiet solitude.

What nobody sitting in the gallery mentions because none of them know, is the secret that she shares with the Reichsmarschall. It is the special bond that binds them – art. His collection. The Inventory.

Suddenly from below, the room is flooded with an infantry of court officials. Clerks, bailiffs, marshals, interpreters and stenographers sweep efficiently into position. It's then the turn of the legal teams to filter into the courtroom, surveying their surroundings, taking the temperature of the room. Next the judges, like a murder of crows in pleated black gowns, noiselessly process through a door and take their places. The nine, led by the ruddy-faced Sir Geoffrey Lawrence, move slowly and noiselessly to their seats. Finally, an oak panel opens and an altogether different group – the final one – materializes. Somewhat disheveled and graceless, the defendants emerge one by one from the corridor that leads to the prison. Does she imagine it or are they emaciated? Perhaps it's the intensity of the lighting. For the purposes of the cameras, powerful spotlights have replaced the soft glow of chandeliers and now cast each man in a pallid glow. She scans each face, her eyes darting from one to the next, but it's difficult to see them as they bow their heads and shuffle in a disorderly fashion. The people around her point and whisper. With this perceptible change in atmosphere, she shifts awkwardly, flushing. Suddenly she wonders if this was a mistake, wonders if she will be recognized. 'Come on old girl, pull yourself together.'

Now settled on the benches in two rows, the twenty-one defendants look like old men. It's hard to believe that only a few months ago they governed a towering nation. Slumped in dark, crumpled, ill-fitting suits they look like pensioners adrift at a tea party, sitting on the margins, lost and wondering when it was that the world changed and why nobody bothered to tell them. Most of all they look like the past, sagging and exhausted; a past that nobody wants, and everybody is now suddenly desperate to be shorn of. All except one. One of the men looks younger than she remembers, and certainly slimmer (how baggy his Luftwaffe tunic looks). She's heard rumours that he has been cured during his incarceration, that he's feeling better, sharper than ever. She looks down and watches him sitting there, taking it all in. His eyes dart this way and that as he observes first the interpreters, then the judges, then the prosecutors – his quarry. The quick movements of his head remind her of a raptor, his slicked hair glistening like silky feathers under the light. Everything is being observed and evaluated. Everyone is a potential foe, and everyone is prey.

Sir Geoffrey Lawrence peers over his spectacles and leans towards the microphone, blowing softly to check the sound. Bearing the lofty title of President of all the Judges at Nuremberg, one might expect him to sound more animated as he opens the proceedings. However, forty years' experience have imbued him with a dispassionate rhetorical style.

"The trial which is now about to begin is unique in the history of the jurisprudence of the world," he says casting his eyes across Courtroom 600 and reading from the eighteenth draft of his opening address, "and it is of supreme importance to millions of people all over the globe. For these reasons, there is laid upon everybody in this trial a solemn responsibility to discharge their duties without fear or favor in accordance with the sacred principles of law and justice. It only remains for me to direct that the indictment shall now be read: 'The Tribunal shall ask each defendant whether he pleads guilty or not guilty.'"

As the most senior ranking of the defendants, Reichsmarschall Hermann Göring is summoned to begin. He stands slowly, holding several sheets of paper. Sir Geoffrey sees them and frowns, surmising that each one spells trouble.

"How do you plead, guilty or not guilty?"

Holding the sheaf before him, Göring begins with characteristic bombast.

"Before I answer the question of the Tribunal whether or not I am guilty – "

"I informed the Court that defendants were not entitled to make a statement," Lawrence interjects irritably. "You must plead guilty or not guilty."

Göring drives on, undaunted.

"Before I answer the qu – "

"No, no, no," with three raps of the gavel. Sir Geoffrey flushes. "You must – "

"I declare myself in the sense of the Indictment, not guilty," Göring snaps, then resumes his seat.

The trial, which is apparently unique in the history of the jurisprudence of the world, has begun.

# The Charlatan

Inventory of the Art Collection
of
Reichsmarschall Hermann Göring

Collection: David David-Weill
Artist: Gabriel de Saint Aubin
Medium: Works on Paper
Title: *The Charlatan*
Measurements: 6.8 cm x 10.5 cm

Note:  From a recently obtained collection. Please
find herewith an etching by Gabriel de Saint-Aubin, a
French artist of good pedigree.*
Entitled *The Charlatan*, this particular item is
emblematic of Saint-Aubin's social commentary,
preoccupied as he was with social scenes, often
sketching as he wandered the streets of 18th Century
Paris. It captures the gullibility of the public and the

cunning of imposters who exploited it. Central to the image is the raised platform or stage. It's where our attention is focused, and from where he commands the crowd. Typically flamboyant, he represents deceit and manipulation. His posture – note the grand gestures – suggests confidence and showmanship. Meanwhile, the gathered public are easily swayed by spectacle and promise, posing here as they do in various states of engagement and susceptibility. Historian Grete de Francesco explains that: 'The charlatan always was the foe of education…in its place he offered propaganda…He does business best when people are suffering, when they are hopeless, or rather have only the hope of a miracle to right their fortunes'.

B.L.

* * *

*Victor's justice.*

*Give it your best shot you little prick.*

With a snort of indignation, he sinks his bulk into the chair, shoulders nestling into the supple brown leather. He inhales deeply. His pearl-grey uniform swells, the brass buttons shimmering in the light from the bulbs overhead. His hand smooths over his left breast, feeling the small cotton hooks where an array of insignia and emblems of rank and service once hung. He counts off each honorific one by one in his head. Today there are no adornments to proclaim his greatness, no fanfare to his accomplishments. It's up to him.

*In fifty or sixty years there will be statues of me all over Germany. Little statues, perhaps, but one in every home.*

The gentlemen of the press are watching, flashbulbs prepared. He's reminded of a movie premiere once. He adjusts the black polaroid sunglasses, and turns his face towards the glare of the spotlights. A swansong.

*Who was it Carin said I reminded her of? Same dark eyes, she said. Willy Fritsch, yes, the slicked back hair. 'The Last Waltz'.*

There is fidgeting in the gallery. Amid the hubbub, he preens.

His defence counselor, Dr Otto Stahmer, looms.

"They're saying another five minutes," he says, adding gloomily, "More technical problems, I'm afraid."

*Victor's justice.*

*With technical problems.*

*Technically, victor's justice is problematic.*

Suddenly, the cavernous room is plunged into darkness and a small voice calls out 'Power cut,' followed by groans across the courtroom.

Above him in the gallery, the woman calling herself Fräulein Gisela Weschler stands and leaves, edging past the crowd of onlookers. She promised herself just a few minutes in his company and no longer, she knows that to tarry is to put herself at risk. She had hoped that perhaps by sharing the same air for a moment he might subconsciously draw strength from her loyalty, be reminded of her devotion and know that she was with him. A soldier opens the door and she exits towards the light of her counterfeit life.

Below, momentarily distracted, the Reichsmarschall looks up to see the back of an elegantly dressed middle-aged woman leaving the gallery. Her hair is tied in a French twist. He thinks of Linnie.

Suddenly, at Dr Stahmer's prompting, Göring reaches for his headset: IBM's Hushaphone Filene-Findlay System. A flimsy mass of wires, metal, plastic and leather earpieces, connected to a panel with two features. The first is a dial that controls the language: Channel 1 is the verbatim proceedings in the original speech. Channel 2 is for English, 3 for Russian, 4 for French, and 5 for German. The second feature is a monitor with two flashing lights. A yellow one blinks if a speaker needs to slow down to be interpreted, while a red one flashes to indicate that the proceedings need to be interrupted to replace an interpreter or if a phrase is inaudible. Göring hates wearing the headphones. His primary objection to them comes from the fact that he believes they make him look ridiculous and therefore tarnish the debonair public image he is trying to cultivate for the world's press. One recent article in the American press described 'his Martian ears that sprouted silver antennae.' Notwithstanding their aesthetic limitations, the headset has come to serve a more useful purpose. Sporadically, he removes them as exaggeratedly as possible as a public statement of disinterest or disrespect. It's juvenile, but keeps him entertained.

To his right, sitting in glass-walled booths, are the ladies and gentlemen of the Court Interpretation Branch of the Translation Division, in three teams of twelve. Everything being politic, the Russians fought to ensure that their booth is positioned in front of the German one, even if it means they are next to the British. The French are relegated to the second row next to the Germans. It is a source of frustration to the Reichsmarschall that Margot Bortlin is translating him into English. He would rather that the world hears his words delivered by someone with more gravitas and import. "Whom?" asked Sir Geoffrey upon hearing this, "Orson Welles, perhaps?"

Göring considers it most ungallant that a lady should be tasked with listening to the more unsavoury details that will be disclosed during the trial. He needn't worry about sparing her blushes, she is a highly experienced translator with an average lag of only five seconds behind the speaker. She is known affectionately as 'the Passionate Haystack' because of her expressive style and her blonde hairdo, especially coiffed to accommodate the headset. Bortlin has become adept at interpreting the euphemisms that are indicative of Nazi obfuscation. Evidential documents describe 'expulsion' and 'debarment' rather than 'extermination' and 'liquidation'.

Now, the bespectacled American prosecutor, Justice Robert Jackson, leans over the lectern, rocking gently back and forth and chewing the corner of his bottom lip. He is an engine revving, his head is bowed and he is awaiting a signal from the interpreters to begin. When it finally comes, he looks at Göring and taps the headphones to say "Channel 5", and with an abrupt cough, begins.

"Upon coming to power, you immediately abolished parliamentary government in Germany?"

"We found it to be no longer necessary," replies Göring indifferently.

"The principles of the authoritarian government which you set up required that there be no opposition. You also considered it necessary to establish concentration camps to take care of your opponents?"

"They were set up as a lightning measure against those who were attacking us."

"And you also had certain organizations to carry out orders, did you not? If you wanted certain people killed you had to have an organization that would kill them, didn't you?"

"Yes," he confirms blandly, before feeling obliged to add, "This is just the same in other countries, whether it is called the secret service or something else."

Jackson is trying to goad, prodding the Reichsmarschall with emotive references to the Gestapo, the camps, the absence of democracy. So why, he wonders, is the man so nonchalant?

"And there was nothing secret about the establishment of the Gestapo as a political police, about the fact that people were taken into protective custody, about the fact that there were concentration camps? Nothing secret about those things?"

"Nothing secret about them at all," Göring replies casually, leaning back now and squinting under the glare of the overhead lights.

"In fact, part of the effectiveness of a secret police and of concentration camps is that the people know that there are such agencies, isn't it?"

"This is true." The Reichsmarschall leans in, speaking slowly, teaching a lesson. "It is useful for everyone to know the consequences of their actions," he adds ominously.

"So how did you manage to persuade the German people to accept Nazism?"

"It was very easy." With a pause, he invites his audience closer and momentarily, silence fills the courtroom.

A stenographer coughs; a bench creaks up in the gallery.

"It has nothing to do with Nazism," Göring says quietly into the microphone, "and everything to do with human nature." His podgy fingers slide together and he frowns in careful, academic reflection.

*How did we do it? How did we cast our spell? Why did they let us get away with murder?*

"You can do it in a Nazi regime or a socialist one or communist one," he continues. "You can do it in a monarchy and even in a democracy. Voice or no voice, the people can always be brought to the bidding of the leaders. All you have to do is tell them they are being attacked and denounce the peacemakers for exposing the country to danger. It works the same everywhere. The only thing that needs to be done to enslave people is to scare them." He nods slowly,

12

remembering a time. "Find a way to scare people, and you can make them do anything you want."

If Jackson is expecting to extract a hint of contrition, he is mistaken.

The red light on the interpretation box blinks and there is a pause in the proceedings.

Göring sits back, eases his back into the seat and slides the sunglasses onto his face. He remains impassive, sitting there under the glare, waiting. He slowly removes the headphones, and tosses them onto the ledge of the witness box. He turns his head and stares out at the grey sky beyond the tall leadlight windows.

From Courtroom 600, his past is beckoning him to retrace steps down well-worn streets towards old haunts with familiar friends. On the way, they will try to poison his memories and tarnish a glorious past. But the truth is that the Reichsmarschall can remember it all vividly for what it was: his golden age.

# The Golden Age

Inventory of the Art Collection
of
Reichsmarschall Hermann Göring

Collection: Karl Haberstock
Artist: Cranach, Lucas the Elder, 1530
Medium: Painting on wooden panel, transferred to an oak panel
Title: *The Golden Age*
Measurements: 68 x 102cm

Note:   We have Haberstock to thank for locating and obtaining this gem by Lucas Cranach the Elder. In excellent condition.
Painted in 1530, the panel depicts an Elysian paradise: Men and women gambol naked around a fruit tree in a typical pagan ritual while others bathe in the waters from the spring and some dance gaily.

The relaxed postures and engagement of the figures with one another and with the animals suggest a unity between humans and nature, and the absence of conflict or predation.

This item is particularly of interest as an educational tool for reinforcing the doctrines of National Socialism, since within the Utopian scene we witness racial uniformity and a purity which has a reassuring absence of diversity. One caveat: even in this Utopia, there is an air of disquiet. Note how the paradisical garden is encircled by a wall. The *polis* beyond Utopia is a looming, malevolent presence and the painting speaks of the tension between the harmony of our natural state versus the madness of the civilized world beyond. Within, all is peace and sanctuary; without, chaos and catastrophe.

B.L.

* * *

'Out there, always betrayed,
the busy world rushes.
Draw your boughs
around me once more,
you canopy of green!'

*Abschied vom Wald* by Joseph von Eichendorff

Carinhall, Schorfheide Forest
March, 1944

A satyr shuts his eyes.

"I'll give you a head start. Ten…nine…eight…"

The two nymphs skitter across the lawn and leap into the darkness of the wood. The satyr gallops in pursuit, guided by the girlish laughter and the thrashing of greenery.

Behind them, an elegant middle-aged lady steps through the glass doors into an opulent room. Dozens of pairs of glass eyes stare at her from above. In her arms is a book. It has a greyish blue cloth cover and gold lettering: Inventory. The marbled vellum endpapers envelope sheets of yellow foolscap. It is a *grimoire* of sorts, for within these pages are hundreds of works of art, and art – the master always says – is magic.

The nymphs sit breathlessly under an old oak. The pair shriek with laughter as the satyr pounces from behind it and proffers a packet of *Trommlers* cigarettes.

"We shouldn't," says one, hoisting up her ivy-festooned bodice.

"Gotta get back," says the other checking her watch. "She said fifteen minutes."

They stroll towards the lodge readjusting their costumes. Like all the domestics, they are bound to conform to the fickle whims of their master, and so for the duration of the weekend all duties are being conducted in costume: satyrs for the boys, nymphs for the girls: welcome to the Spring Festival of Ostara at Carinhall. Passing the library windows now, the satyr tempts the nymphs to a quick peek through the glass. Apparently, the master has a collection of erotic sculptures that have just arrived from Paris. Not true, says a nymph who knows the maid who knows the valet. She's heard that there's a bowl of fabulous diamonds that he masturbates into. Unable to resist temptation, the three young faces press against the glass that quickly steams with their breath as they struggle to peer into the darkness. Within, they see only a Rosewood high back throne chair with Bordeaux leaf velvet upholstery. There's someone in there, giggles one nervously, her breath steaming the small windowpane.

Within, enormous shoulders spill out from either side of the chair. A right arm hangs pendulously, clasping a goblet that sways gently. It's a small cup, whispers the satyr beyond the glass. No, says a nymph, it's a bottle, a glass one. She should know, her aunt's got one just the same for her medication. All three spies instinctively lean away from the window as the shape in the chair stirs. A head emerges over the tip of the back. Wearing a crown. No, not a crown, a wreath. A gold laurel wreath.

The master is oblivious to their presence. He is in a playful mood, excited about the morning he has planned for his guests.

*You won't believe what the boys have built for me this year, Emmy. And wait till you see the costume.*

With a theatrical flourish, he is on his feet and the muslin draped on his lap comes to life, no longer a lank piece of cloth, but at once a regal toga that envelopes the bearer in a swathe of bravura. In some quarters of Berlin society, 10 o'clock might be considered *infra dig* for pre-lunch libation, but the master has always baulked at convention, so a third serving of claret sloshes into the goblet, this time spilling onto a 19th

Century Persian rug from Arak. He picks up his small glass bottle, then tips two 'jewels' into his hand, tosses them into his mouth and swallows with another glug of wine. There is a knock at the door followed by a brief pause. Robert Kropp, valet to the Reichsmarschall, peers into the room. He knows that slow and deliberate is best, lest he should catch the chief *in flagrante delicto*, a sight that the prudish valet can live without.

"Sir, your guests await. The horse and er…rest have been readied."

\* \* \*

Deep within the forest that engulfs the house a boy shivers and tugs the collar on his coat. In the distance something is stirring. His mother remembers her first visit here. She is fascinated by German woodland folklore. Tacitus noted the malevolence of the forest; Caspar Friedrich its romanticism. For Hesse it had restorative properties while for Beatrice, here in Schorfheide, beauty mingles with threat. The pair are surrounded by tall pines. The woodland is dense, and from where the boy stands, endless. The warmth of the last few days has not yet touched the recesses of the forest floor.

"Schorfheide," the woman explains "derives from a German word for sheep," reading from her crumpled yellow guidebook. "Over a thousand kilometres of reservation here. The Cistercians used to farm the land out of the monastery at Chorin."

Far off, there is a commotion that threatens the peace of the wood. After two hours trudging deeper through the trees, the boy is aware that he's on unfamiliar territory and an uneasiness begins to gnaw. Signs of strange animal life surround him and nature has unfurled a malevolence that has no business in the boy's world of Parisien society. HC SVNT DRACONES. Here Be Dragons. His mother senses his anxiety and comes to his side, embracing him while her lips gently peck his forehead in reassurance. In the distance there are men's voices.

"Where is this thing?" the boy asks.

"Not far now, Bertrand. It can't be."

Beatrice digs deep into her coat pocket and pulls out a square of baking paper. In a swift motion, she unwraps it and hands over a *röggelchen*. The boy snatches it and stuffs the rye roll into his mouth, sinking his teeth into the gouda and pickles. He sniffs, and slides a sleeve across his nostrils, leaving a snail-track down the forearm of his houndstooth jacket. The noise of the men is louder now. Bertrand can hear a horse. Perhaps a wagon.

"Wild boar," hisses Beatrice pointing to the beast foraging about twenty metres away from them. Listening, it's not the sound that Bertrand expects to hear. The animal emits a series of sonorous grunts that seem conversational, as though it is conversing with the earth, discussing the merits of every root. The beast forages oblivious to their presence − until it isn't. It stops and stares directly at the human interlopers. It grunts, tugging at the air, evaluating this odd pair smelling of sweat, damp and gouda. The boar is perhaps six feet in length with wiry red brown bristles over an impressive round bulk. Beatrice is struck by the beauty of its muscular back and shoulders, the sheer power crowned by thick yellow tusks. In contrast, the feet seem delicate, almost dainty. A stick snaps under Bertrand's foot, breaking the stalemate. The boar spins to the right and in a flurry of ferns, scampers into the distance. Beatrice watches it disappear into the dark folds of the forest.

"Run, *The Fat One*, run," she whispers after it.

"*The Fat One?*" asks Bertrand.

She smiles. "Our host − but for goodness sake, don't let him hear you say that," she warns, continuing on the trail.

A short while later, Beatrice grips her son's hand. They must be getting nearer because now the noises in the distance are clearer. There can hear cheering, revelry. They are now confronted by two imposing concrete sentinels standing at the threshold of the estate. Beyond lies a driveway that stretches into the darkness of the forest. Bertrand is gazing up at the stone pillars. He squints to make out the heroic insignia: two military batons crossed above a cluster of three *Eichenblatt* – oak leaves.

"This way," says his mother nodding in the direction of the dense woodland. "Nearly there now."

She takes long strides over nettles and under the oaks, deep and deeper still into the woods. Perhaps into the realm of the Brothers Grimm. It is not long before they reach the small clearing she has been searching for. There he is, just as Leon said he would be. *Kronenhirsch*, the Crowned Deer. He stands defiant, four metres high atop a stone plinth.

"Impressive, isn't he?" says Beatrice, grinning and slowly placing a loving arm around her son, cherishing this shared moment she has been waiting for.

"He's beautiful," says Bertrand.

"He's real, too. There once was a stag called Raufbold that lived here in these woods."

"What happened to him?"

"*The Fat One* shot him. February 1936. It was my first visit here with your father, a hunting party. I wanted to see him once more and show him to you. The sculptor is Johannes Darsow. Do you remember him? You were probably too small, but he dined with us once."

They both stand silently paying homage to the majestic creature, marveling at the patina of the bronze beast, with its distinctive verdigris. Time has seen to it that the body is enriched by shades of bottle green and dried grey rivulets that streak the muscular flanks. There is jade here, emerald there that dissolves into cobalt green, then blue. Time has weathered the proud body, imbuing Raufbold with a mythic quality. How long Beatrice has waited to see Darsow's work, and how much has changed in the intervening years. How lucky she is to be in her position, and how cruel that others like her cannot boast the same social circle.

"Come on darling, we should go. We mustn't keep our host waiting."

She turns and strides through the trees but Bertrand needs to savour the moment.

"Goodbye Raufbold," he whispers. In his ten-year-old imagination it feels proper to make an offering to this woodland king before he leaves. He searches the ground for something appropriate and at his feet he sees a perfectly round stone, white in colour. He picks it up, wipes it clean with his spittle and then ritualistically places it at the base of the plinth, careful to make sure that it sits exactly in the middle. He rejoins his mother, and the pair heads towards the house.

Somewhere up ahead of them something large is rattling through the trees at speed. Twigs shatter and small branches crack as the vibrations gets louder. Suddenly, Beatrice seizes Bertrand and yanks him to her side as a golden chariot erupts through the vegetation in an explosion of flora. There before them is a vision of Ancient Rome: Emperor Nero, sweating profusely and clad in a red toga flecked with catchweed, is desperately tugging at leather reigns harnessed to a galloping white mare. Hurtling past, Nero turns and stares at Beatrice with a look of mania that gives way to panic. He steadies his teetering laurel wreath and then as swiftly as they materialized, horse, chariot and emperor career onward, tearing through the shattered peace of the woodland. Beatrice and Bertrand exchange bewildered looks and stride off in pursuit as quickly as the undergrowth will allow.

Emerging from the verdant confines of the woodland, their feet crunch upon the gravel driveway that leads to Carinhall, Hermann Göring's sprawling idyll set in thirty kilometers of the Schorfheide forest. The lodge itself is like a vision from a fairy tale, a testament to the grandeur of its eccentric owner. The cream sandstone façade is adorned with intricate carvings and reliefs of hunting scenes, the handiwork of skilled German craftsmen. A gargantuan entrance overlooks meticulously manicured gardens. The most notable details are the Nordic rustic features comprising timber framing and a distinctive steeply pitched thatched roof. A cobblestone courtyard unfolds before them, and the soothing sound of a bubbling fountain fills the air. Well-tended hedges that bloom with seasonal flowers border the approach to the main entrance, while stone statues of Elysian figures silently pose. Beatrice tarries, intoxicated by the fragrance of roses. She didn't notice them when she arrived yesterday evening, but now the scent reminds her of the Bois de Boulogne. Beyond the courtyard, the massive wooden doors of Carinhall beckon. They are adorned with intricate bronze handles; one an eagle, the other a falcon, as if the edifice needed any more symbols of power and prowess. As she reaches out her hand towards the door it yawns open before them and they find themselves stepping into the dark jaws of the Great Hall.

At 1pm lunch is served. The assembly on the lawn consists of twenty weekend houseguests, a dozen satyrs and nymphs and Göring's beloved pair of pet lion cubs. Everyone mingles around enormous rustic tables laden with food and drink. There is much guffawing as Emperor Göring regales his guests about his brush with death in the chariot. He is gesticulating animatedly, recreating the ride while his wife dutifully picks off clumps of catchweed that still cling to his toga. Typically for a weekend at Carinhall, the guest list is eclectic. Now dressed in an elegant blue day dress, Beatrice stands holding Bertrand's hand and sipping a chilled 1940 Chateau Rabaud-Promis. She is thinking about her absent husband; how she envies Leon's ability to socialize so easily at these events. She is not entirely sure why she has warranted an invitation to the Ostara Festival at Carinhall, but before leaving for Chambord, Leon counseled her against coming here again. She knew better of course, convinced that gaining favour would be worth the effort during these straitened times. With a pat on Bertrand's elbow, she urges him to the buffet while her eyes survey the rest of the crowd. Beside her, and rather closer than she would like, stands Joseph Goebbels, drowning in a double-breasted grey worsted suit. A rictus grin hangs immobile on his pallid face while he eyes a nymph ladling soup from an enormous tureen.

"Be a good boy, Joseph, and don't feed the lions," yells Göring from beyond the jellied eels.

Priding himself on being a principled National Socialist, Goebbels has deliberately not engaged in conversation with Beatrice. He would rather stand and quietly seethe about why the bitch doesn't have a yellow star sewn onto the *haute couture* frock that she's bought on the backs of exploited German workers. Typical, Goebbels tells himself, of how Göring has retreated further and further into his own private fantasy world: dressed as a Roman Emperor one minute, hob-knobbing with a Jewess the next, and obsessing about his art collection. Bormann's right, he tells himself, Göring is no longer fit for the rank of Reichsmarschall, and the sooner the Führer sees it the better.

Moving further down the line and buffeted by the servants moving to and fro is the Papal Nuncio Monsignor Cesare Orsenigo, a regular guest of the Nazi elite. As a good Catholic, he always manages to muster enthusiasm for the pomp and ceremony of a shindig with the Görings, even if he does have reservations about the Pagan theme. To his left, he is unsure what General Ion Antonescu of Romania is saying, but his thick black eyebrows are arched in a gesture that he reads as disapproval. Further along, feted film-maker Leni Riefenstahl stands in a striking trouser suit with one hand resting on her hip while the other clasps a champagne flute. She has perfected an air of aloofness over time and, in a moment of well-honed affectation, she flicks her head, tossing her curly fringe from her face. All this is for the benefit of a young satyr with whom she has been flirting for as long as he has been topping up her glass. Opposite her, it's anybody's guess why Magda Goebbels and Emmy Göring are chatting so amiably over the *Häppchen*. According to rumour they loathe one another and spend most of their time vying for the title of First Lady of the Reich in the absence of a Frau Hitler.

"What on earth did he think he was doing?" chuckles Magda.

"Reenacting the Triumph of Bacchus," replies Emmy, brushing the remnants of foliage from the silk brocade of her dress. "On his last trip to Paris one of his art people – Lohse I think, well he found this oil painting by Moreau – *Le triomphe de Bacchus* – is that how you say it? Well, Hermann's become sort of besotted. Even had a thyros made by a chap in Frankfurt."

"A what?"

"No, I didn't know either. A thyros, a sort of spear. It's quite harmless. It's got a pinecone on the end of it, so he can't poke out an eye or anything." Emmy now turns to her husband. "Do take that thing off your head, Hermann and come and show Magda the stick."

Göring tuts. "It's a *thyrsus*. How many more times, woman!?" Brandishing the spear, he waves it under Mrs Goebbels' nose. The Monsignor, wary of being impaled, takes a cautionary step backwards and busies himself at the cheese platter.

"See? It's wrapped in ivy. It's a sceptre and also a weapon to vanquish my enemies," explains Göring with fiery conviction.

"And the er…?" asks Magda, waving a hand vaguely at his head.

"My gloriole," he says, beaming. "Got one of the carpenters on the estate to knock it up. Had a devil's job getting hold of gold paint."

"Well there *is* a war on, darling," says Emmy. Now it's her turn to roll her eyes as she leans in front of her husband to reach a *forellentaler*. She gives his tummy a loving rub in passing. He reciprocates with a fruity squeeze of her rear.

"Did you see the way my toga billows in the wind, my love?" He's still a little out of breath from his exertion. "I hope they got photographs, I asked them to take photographs." Foraging in his toga, Göring withdraws his glass bottle. Tap, tap and two pills fall out. This is followed by a swig of claret and an audible gulp.

"Medicinal," he says to Magda with a wink. But Magda knows better.

The buffet lunch continues in this fashion, with light conversation here and there, punctuated with the occasional party piece from their host, who remains in full Roman emperor garb even when rain clouds threaten. At one point he interrupts the proceedings to march out an infantry of kitchen staff.

"Ladies and gentlemen let's have a generous round of applause for the boys and girls of the Hotel Kempinski! How's that, eh? On loan to me for the day. So you know what that means – it's cabbage soup on the menu back at the hotel!"

The next moment he's waving a greasy dinner plate under the nose of Goebbels.

"See this, Joseph? My official dinnerware, this is. Look at that," he says, wiping thick brown sauce from the rim of the plate with his thumb. "Right there's the national eagle in gold hovering over two marshal's batons, see? Look at the gilding on that."

"You showed me last time, Hermann," grumbles Goebbels. But the Reichsmarschall presses on.

"Mussolini's son-in-law, Count Cinzano, presented me a full service when I was in Rome."

"*Ciano*," Emmy cuts in, shaking her head.

Music plays, wine flows. The chattering and chirruping of light conversation rolls on into the afternoon accompanied by a symphony of tinkling glasses. Beatrice has sent Bertrand to their room to rest and following their morning hike and the copious lunch, she now decides to retire herself. Other guests follow suit, drifting from the scene into the forest, the gardens, the house.

Göring retreats into his own private sanctuary of the library. Emmy knows that this is where he does his most profound thinking. Servants and adjutants will not disturb him here. Only Kropp is permitted entry to the holy of holies. The emperor is quite alone once again in his library. Ruby claret sloshes in the goblet pinched between his fingers while two 'jewels' dissolve, course through his veins and slowly, lovingly intoxicate him in a warm embrace. With a shrug, the shroud slips from his shoulders and onto the cherrywood floor. The most surprising thing for those who see him like this is that his gut is solid and immoveable. Lampooners and caricaturists would have his public believe that he is flabby and ungainly, but he has a certain grace that belies his 270lb bulk. Two large, brown saucer nipples peer in opposite directions across the room, a few random black hairs sprouting from each like antennas twitching in the breeze. He takes a deep breath. Setting the goblet down, his left-hand plunges into a large brass vessel stuffed with semi-precious stones that dance between his fingers as his wrist slowly swirls. His right hand fumbles in his crotch as he gazes above to the naked Spring Nymph staring down achingly at him, one hand resting suggestively on her thigh. Once sated, he draws the large crimson sheet across his lap, under which the *Marschallstab* shrinks into the shade following active service, a sulking, wet and fleshy bulbous stub. He reaches for his laurel wreath and returns to his claret.

It is an hour later and Göring's chief adjutant and handsome blue-eyed boy, Bernd von Brauchitsch, has sought out Beatrice's room. He is tapping on the door with increasing emphasis. Beatrice is forcefully woken in a fug and hurries to the door, her throat dry following several glasses of champagne at lunch. Opening the door slowly, Göring's dashing adjutant explains that the Reichsmarschall would very much like to speak with her privately. Fifteen minutes later he is accompanying Beatrice out of the house, across the gardens and into the depths of the forest. For the meeting, the Reichsmarschall has chosen somewhere discreet, explains Brauchitsch, so they make their way through quiet woodland towards a mausoleum on the edge of Lake Wuckersee which bears the remains of Göring's first wife Carin. It is an ominous setting. Arriving at the site, they pass a series of large memorial stones, each one at least six feet high and forming a ring around the tomb. Beatrice can only wonder how Emmy must feel making home in a place so indelibly infused with the memory of the former Frau Göring. The Reichsmarschall is waiting for her, facing away and gazing out over the lake with his hands clasped behind his back holding a wooden cane. No longer Emperor Göring, he is now the *Reichsjägermeister*, complete with suede breeches and black leather waistcoat. Beatrice recognizes it as the outfit he wore for the article in *Time* magazine, complete with his famous hunting knife. Upon hearing them approach, he turns, smiling.

"Ah! Drink it in, Beatrice. May I call you Beatrice?" It's not a question. Drawing an enormous breath and sliding his hands over his paunch. "The most important thing to know about Carinhall is that it is my haven. It nourishes my many facets, you might say. One moment, balm for my soul; the next a bacchanalian circus where we revel throughout the night, the children of Dionysus," he adds with a saucy wink. Then, more seriously, "I read somewhere that the German forest and the German soul are inextricably linked. Do you believe that? I do. I believe that the forest really knows me. She can read me and responds to my every mood." He casts her a dubious look. "Do you think I'm mad? Perhaps. You're French," he says dismissively, "you wouldn't understand. But we Germans speak of *Waldeinsamkeit*, a sort of – 'forest-aloneness'. It refers to that deep sense of peaceful isolation that we feel only in the woods." Göring begins to move his cane in slow deliberate contemplative swirls on the grass.

*That's my boy. Keep this up. Time for the bit about the sensitive soul of the artist.*

"I know what they call me, *Fat Hermann*. And worse. But those are merely personas. Perhaps you will see beyond this…" – a beat for dramatic intensity – "*character* they depict, and see that I'm actually a sensitive soul – an artist really."

If Hermann Göring is capable of believing anything, he believes this. And with absolute conviction. He has a fedora and cape to prove it.

*Aristide Bruant as depicted by Lautrec, Emmy. Got the red scarf, too.*

He can parrot anything the experts have written in the Inventory. He knows his Carracci from his Caravaggio and so long as he can rub that in Goebbels' nose, it's enough for him.

Now Beatrice is the latest recipient of this well-rehearsed routine. The Reichsmarschall has metamorphosed from self-styled Paladin of the Third Reich into Hermann Göring, Aesthete. He's laid the groundwork with his well-worn flim-flam about the mystic qualities of the German forest and now he's poised to launch into a verse or two from von Eichendorff that he likes to trot out for lunch guests, while standing under the bower of an old oak tree.

*Von Eichendorff for lunch; Goethe for dinner, I always say.*

Before he can begin the recitation, Beatrice is caught on a flight of her own fancy.

"I can empathize, Reichsmarschall. I know something of *Wald-in-sam-keit*, is it? I love the woods. I ride most mornings in the Bois de Boulogne. My horse is saddled and ready for me almost every day by 8 o'clock."

As Beatrice speaks, Göring examines her profile more closely now, deciding that her slightly upturned nose is an indication of bearing and grace.

*Be a good fuck, this one.*

"However, October is my favourite month," she's saying now. "I adore seeing the morning sun through marmalade leaves."

Never one to let a pretty lady monopolize the conversation, Göring cuts in loudly.

"These woods appeal to the military tactician in me. Did you know that during the Battle of Teutoburg, the forces of Arminius used the trees here as camouflage against the Romans? It's all there in Tacitus."

Not quite sure where the conversation is meandering, Beatrice feigns interest by raising her eyebrows and mouthing surprise.

"If I'm honest my dear, I was being a little tactical myself in bringing you here. There's something terribly important I'd like to discuss concerning your art collection, Beatrice."

"My collection?" she says wide-eyed, as if this is the first she's ever heard about the family's nationally renowned collection.

"Perhaps you've had the opportunity to see the works I'm collecting here at Carinhall? I like to think of it as my legacy to the nation.

Something I can bequeath the people when I…" he lets the sentence drift over the lake as he turns theatrically and stares at the mausoleum.

*Might even manage a tear.*

She's seen the collection. It's largely gauche and incoherently curated.

"Well, since we entered France," he continues, "I've tried hard to make the most of the opportunities to develop it." He now faces her intently. "There are a number of pieces you have that I am interested in acquiring."

Here it comes. What Leon warned her about.

"You have a watercolour by Mallet. Then there's the Renoir: a portrait of a little girl with a ribbon in her hair. It's sentimental chocolate box stuff, not what we National Socialists approve of, but it is of interest to an associate of mine."

Beatrice gathers enough self-assuredness to respond with steely civility.

"Oh no sir, that's quite out of the question. The Renoir has huge sentimental value."

Göring the Aesthete exits stage left. Enter the boor.

"Rubbish. Sugary fluff that's all. Kid's not even that pretty."

"It's a portrait of my mother," says Beatrice, bridling. "She was eight. It was commissioned by my grandfather."

"Mumsie's all grown up now, isn't she? Come on, think of a number between one and five thousand."

Beatrice grows indignant. "I'm sorry, Reichsmarschall. It's not a question of price."

He leans in towards her slowly.

"I'm sure you're right. Perhaps it's more a question of motivation. So now I'm wondering how we might be able to motivate *you*, Madame Beatrice Steiner of the 16th arrondissement, Paris?"

There follows an image that will endure in Beatrice's mind as she lies awake over the next few nights: the Reichsmarschall is smiling at her. Or is he bearing his teeth?

* * *

"Now, who wants to be a satyr for me? C'mon, don't be shy. Hands up."

The scene is the sumptuous *Jagdhalle*. Evening has descended and the houseguests are now bathed, rested and dressed in their finery. At 7pm four waiters sweep into the room with silver trays bearing yet more potation. They converge to hover over concoctions in tumblers, flutes, snifters and goblets, while Göring, surprisingly fleet of foot, hops over to the gramophone, whips off one of Emmy's 33s and tosses it aside. He replaces it with a new record that he waves at his guests with a cheeky smile. He slips the vinyl from a flimsy paper sleeve and thirty seconds later he's swaying his hips from side to side as *Let's Misbehave* crackles across the room at full blast. Magda claps and Goebbels sways on the balls of his feet. It is now the turn of the Monsignor to raise an eyebrow. As the music continues, it slowly dawns on the party that the tremulous voice on the record is none other than the Reichsmarschall's. Göring shouts above the music.

"What do you think? Studied a bit of piano last year with an American prisoner of war. Died of tuberculosis – *but* – not before I recorded a few jazz favourites. Wait till you hear 'I Surrender Dear'!"

The Bulgarian monarch grumbles something about un-Aryan music but Göring is oblivious. He grabs Emmy around the waist and the two begin embracing, then dancing, then pirouetting and giggling their way around the room. At one point Emmy trips on the rug and the pair collapse in fits of laughter and proceed to tickle each other mercilessly on the floor. The guests chuckle along half-heartedly and then, realizing that they are surplus to requirements, slowly drift into the trophy room where they fall under the watchful observation of a bevy of Renaissance beauties and mounted trophy heads all staring down at them, like one set of prey to another.

A short while later an octogenarian gentleman in a pin-striped suit appears in the trophy room and bids the guests accompany him to the Great Hall. No one is quite sure who he is or whence he materialized

30

but they oblige his request, if only to chase the tray of cocktails which follows the mystery man. It soon becomes clear that, though no one has caught his name yet, he is an academic on loan from the Universität der Künste in Berlin. He is joined by an intense looking middle-aged lady in a beige suit who is bearing a greyish blue book. The group is ushered on through the Great Hall past innumerable canvases haphazardly arranged on the walls in columns four or five high in some places. They stop under an oil painting approximately a metre in width, and the woman in the beige suit whispers '147' to the academic.

A cough. A nudge of the spectacles. A glance down at the sacred Inventory, and we're off.

"This is the latest addition to the Reichsmarschall's collection," gushes the academic. "An oil on a wood panel entitled *The Golden Age*, by Lucas Cranach the Elder. Here is an Elysian paradise: men and women gambol naked around a fruit tree in a typical pagan ritual. Others bathe in the waters from the spring while some of them –"

"Some of them look like they're about to get a bloody good seeing to! That's just like the Greeks – at it like rabbits," roars Göring from the other side of the room.

The academic continues with his prepared remarks. As rehearsed, he begins speculating about whether Cranach's work suggests a tension between the harmony of Man's natural state and the chaos of the so-called civilized world. As he does so a voice booms from the shadows. It is that of General Antonescu.

"Are you saying that we'd be better off cavorting stark naked through a garden than worrying about affairs of state? What about now, in times of war? What's the order of the day, man, fighting or fucking?"

As the general continues his spittle-flecked tirade, Göring gives a sulky nod to an officer with a severe crew cut and the academic is conducted swiftly from the room and, for all anyone knows, bundled into a *Kübelwagen* bound for the Eastern Front.

The guests linger in the Great Hall admiring Göring's burgeoning collection. Beatrice drifts aimlessly. Since her meeting at the mausoleum she has been left feeling suffocated by her surroundings. She longs for Leon and for Paris. Meanwhile, Joseph and Magda Goebbels stand in reverence gazing up at Heinrich Knirr's portrait of the Führer. The Papal Nuncio roams back and forth along a quadriptych of saints by Friedrich Pacher. For once Göring is content simply to stand holding his wife's hand and quietly observe his guests. He watches Beatrice the most. While Antonescu succumbs to the effects of his third daquiri, Göring is intoxicated by something quite different. His imagination stirs at the heady notion that tonight the great and good are in his thrall.

Leni Riefenstahl is the only one staring at a 30 x 40 cm gap on the wall.

"I'd say you have a light-fingered pantry maid, Hermann," she teases. The others drift slowly over to where she is standing. Magda Goebbels speaks up.

"What's all this then, Hermann? You haven't lost one, have you?"

"I'm saving that for something special," he says enigmatically.

Mutterings of speculation follow about what the mystery canvas might be.

"Let's just say that she's a friend of a friend," he says, his eyes glinting at Beatrice. Her blood runs cold as recognition dawns.

"Come on, Hermann! Tell," cries Goebbels, the wrong side of a bottle of kirsch.

"I'm keeping that space warm for a watercolour by Jean-Baptiste Mallet called *La toilette de la fiancée.*"

"And when will you possess her?" asks Riefenstahl.

"In time. For now, I'm seeing to it that her owner is sufficiently motivated."

Beatrice is experiencing an altogether different kind of *Waldeinsamkeit*, and one worthy of the Brothers Grimm: an innocent woman; her sleeping son. Trapped together in a vast house in the middle of an immense forest. *Here be dragons.*

# The Rape of Lucretia

Collection: The Grote family, Germany
Artist:       Cranach, Lucas the Elder
Medium: Oil on Wood
Title:        *Lucretia*
Measurements: 39 x 26 cm.

*Note*:   Lucretia's story is originally recorded in
Livy's *Ab Urbe Condita*, in which she is raped by
Sextus Tarquinius, son of the Roman king Tarquinius
Superbus. Here, Lucretia is shown in the act of
plunging a dagger into her chest, a representation of
her suicide which was seen historically as a defense
of personal honour and chastity which have been
violated. The story of Lucretia contributed to a moral

outcry that led to the overthrow of the monarchy in Rome. The Rape of Lucretia is a story that has been told and re-told in art and literature by the likes of Titian, Rembrandt and Shakespeare. Its popularity is surely explained by its value as a timeless allegory about the abuse of power, the subjugation of human beings and Man's capacity for brutality. Lucretia's story was a subject to which Cranach returned again and again, with over forty different paintings recorded.

One of nine recorded in the pages of this inventory. See B.L. for details.

* * *

"What win I if I gain the thing I seek?
A dream, a breath, a froth of fleeting joy.
Who buys a minute's mirth to wail a week?
Or sells eternity to get a toy?"

*The Rape of Lucrece* by William Shakespeare

With a nod, Robert Jackson looks at Göring and, as is customary, taps on the headphones: channel 5.

"We will now take up the subject of art," he begins. "I call your attention to Document 141-PS, a decree on the confiscation of Jewish cultural property."

Göring's left eyebrow raises as if to say 'What of it?'

"In the document, reference is made to art objects that were sold at auction."

"If they were sold at auction then this was at the behest of one of my art associates," says Göring, bored.

"You had agents operating in France as well as Germany?"

"I don't want to say agents. You make it sound grubby. I made use of experienced, knowledgeable professionals. They had private circles, knew people socially. I received offers from all over the place. You know how these people operate."

"Actually, I have no idea how these people operate. I was hoping you might be able to enlighten me."

He leans in and smiles. "With pleasure."

"Where was the money for the art kept?"

"The *Kunstfond*."

"Which was…?"

"Which was an art fund I had instituted for the purchase of cultural objects."

"Where did the money come from that went into that fund?"

"Private contributions."

"Meaning?"

"Donations which I received."

"From?"

"Everyone. Anyone. Everywhere."

"Might this include reluctant donors?"

"Reluctant? What do you mean by this?" he says archly.

"By this I mean those who had no choice but to donate. Those who donated as a means of saving their homes, their possessions. Perhaps even their lives."

"The reasons for their benevolence are unknown to me – and frankly, unimportant."

"To which bank were the donations made?"

"I would have to have the documents here for that."

"In fact, despite numerous interrogations you have never been able to point out where that fund is, have you?"

"Alas!" he shrugs his shoulders in mock exasperation. "You would only have to question my secretary. She kept account of all the funds."

Feverish thumbing through notes ensues, before Jackson resumes.

"Lotte Linberg, yes? Unfortunately, we have not been unable to trace her."

"Pity."

"In fact, since being interviewed by the American military, she seems to have disappeared without trace."

"Does she really? Oh dear, dear."

"Furthermore, it is alleged that she disappeared with a book. An inventory. A document containing a detailed list of the particulars of every piece of art that came into your possession, including its provenance."

"She was a frightfully efficient woman. Disappeared without trace, you say? Alas."

Feeling the blood rise, Jackson pursues a different line.

"Do you know a Mr Lohse?"

"Yes."

"He had to do with confiscated Jewish art treasures, did he not?"

"Mr Lohse had nothing to do with that."

"Exhibit Number USA-783, is a letter from Mr Lohse. Perhaps this refreshes your recollection of events: 'On Tuesday, 2/4/1941, I was ordered for the first time to report to the Reichsmarschall at the Jeu de Paume. The Reichsmarschall gave over photographs of those objects of art that he wanted to acquire for himself. Then, with me as his guide, he inspected the exhibited art treasures and made a selection of those works of art which were to go to the Führer, and those which were to be placed in his own collection. He directed that the art objects were to be loaded on a special train immediately and taken to Germany. The special train consisted mainly of the most important parts of the collections of Rothschild, Seligmann and half a dozen others.'"

"Yes," says Göring with a loud, distorted bark into the microphone.

"Yes what?"

"Yes to all of the above. I have already stated before that at Jeu de Paume I selected art treasures which were exhibited there. As for the transporting of art, the only thing which I can remember is that I was asked that a train was put at their disposal to ship the art treasures."

"And the train wa-"

"Er, excuse me. No *ordinary* train. This was the Sonderzug! My own *armoured* train that was put at their disposal."

Jackson was saving this, but since Göring has opened the door, Jackson wedges his foot firmly in it and, leafing through a dozen sheets of paper, barges through.

"Quite so. This would be the same train that, as well as transporting art for you from all over Europe, was equipped with a photographer's darkroom."

"I enjoy photography."

"And a six-bed clinic with operating theatre."

"In war, Mr Jackson, one must always be prepared."

"A barbershop?"

"No."

"No?"

"It was more part-*coiffeur*, part-beautician salon. There can never be a good excuse for inelegance, even on the Front!" This evokes a ripple of laughter from the gallery. Göring is delighted, Jackson is not.

"Two flat cars carried your fleet of American, French, and German automobiles."

"As well as my six-wheel-drive Mercedes W31 *Geländewagen* convertible, yes."

"That seems an awful lot of cars."

"One never knows when one may need to make a swift getaway."

"Then there were two freight cars with rapid-fire anti-aircraft cannons."

"What can I say? I put on a good show," he adds with a wink to the other defendants.

"I put it to you that in the eyes of the world you have taken art treasures which for centuries belonged to other countries and brought them to your home in great quantities, which was *not* a laudable activity. I also put it to you that you lived to excess while Europe endured the hardships inflicted by war."

"Of all the charges which have been revealed against me, the so-called looting of art treasures has caused me the most anguish."

"Isn't it true that you profiteered from war, seizing the property of private individuals, non-combatants, for your own private pleasure?"

"Can you really be so naïve Mr Jackson? Everybody loots a little bit."

"Indeed?" It is Jackson's turn to raise an eyebrow.

"You know of van Eyck's *Adoration of the Mystic Lamb*? An altarpiece of twelve panels depicting religious scenes. A masterpiece, to be sure. It was installed in the Saint Bavo Cathedral in Ghent. Then, in the middle of the 16th Century, the Protestants and Catholics were going at it hammer and tong – aren't they always? The Protestants stormed the cathedral with the intention of stealing the altarpiece but the clever old Catholics had already ferreted it away to who knows where. Then there was the time when the very same piece was censored by the mayor of Ghent after the Pope objected to Adam and Eve's genitals bobbling about on the altar. It doesn't end there. During the Napoleonic Wars, the central panels were swiped for the glory of the French monarch, only to be returned in 1814. Even the bloody clergy were up to no good! In 1816, the bishop himself stole some of the panels, and they ended up with Kaiser Frederick III. So, if you please, Mr Jackson, don't talk to me about looting as if I'm the only person to have ever coveted beautiful works of art. Furthermore, none of my so-called looting was illegal. More often than not, I *paid* for the items in my collection – frequently being fleeced by unscrupulous dealers, by the way – or they were donated to me through official channels. If it is a crime to have a weakness for being surrounded by beautiful things, then guilty am I!" he says, thrusting out his upturned wrists theatrically, outstretched and awaiting shackles. "Always the intention was to contribute these treasures, paintings, sculptures, altarpieces, jewels, et cetera, to a state museum for the greater glory of German culture. Looking at it from that standpoint I really can't see that it was ethically wrong. It was not done in the spirit of looting. I didn't want them for myself. They would have gone to the museums of Germany for posterity."

"But you testified recently that none of these objects have ever been turned over to the government. Is that correct?"

"Yes. Well, no. That is, I mean I did. I *am* the government, so in point of fact – according to the *Constitution* – if they were in my possession then, strictly speaking, they were held by the government.

"How convenient."

"It's not a question of convenience, Mr Jackson. My collection has been lovingly curated for the German people.

"But, once again – *in point of fact* – none of these objects has ever been given to the German people."

"Well, how could they be? The gallery was never built."

# Christ and the Adulteress

Artist:          ?
Medium: Oil on canvas
Title: ?
Measurements: 100 x 89.9 cm

Amsterdam,
March, 1944

Within this room, craftsmanship and artistic subterfuge is unfolding. At its heart stands an easel that has borne the weight of a thousand creations; its aged wood witness to countless compositions. Here, upon a cluttered table rests a wooden palette, its surface is a kaleidoscope of dried pigments. There, beneath the artist's slippered feet, the floor is a mosaic of paint stains, a tapestry of colours, each blotch holding a secret that seeps into the foundations. Behind the easel, stands The Dutchman. Small, wiry and grey haired, he makes barely discernable touches to the painting, channelling the spirit of an Old Master, summoning him onto the canvas.

"You sure they'll fall for it?" says his associate known only as München.

"I've got a twelve-bedroom house in Nice paid for by the first one, haven't I?" replies The Dutchman dryly. "They'll fall for it," he nods.

"*The Supper at Emmaus,*" says München with a grin. He remembers it well.

"Besides, I've got someone on the inside."

Restlessly, München begins to wander around the studio. He is taking in the detritus scattered over the enormous table in its centre, inspecting the room for any tell-tale clues about the artistic alchemy taking place. A motley collection of brushes bear marks of innumerable creations on their handles. There are flat ones, round ones, and filbert; there are sable ones, hog hair and even badger ones – just like the man himself once used. A sagging bookshelf exhibits volumes on the history of art and technique. In a secluded corner stands a pizza oven. Both incongruous and indispensable, it regularly bakes a concoction of lapis lazuli and white lead; sometimes indigo and cinnabar, all at 120°C. The special ingredients however are phenol formaldehyde and lilac oil. It is only with these most precious components that The Dutchman can achieve the craquelure and patina of a three-hundred-year-old master work.

"Nice spot here," says München, staring out for miles over the flat, golden fields.

"I've got Abe Bredius to thank for it," replies The Dutchman, setting down his brush and walking slowly to the bookcase. He slides out a magazine which he tosses across the room to München.

"Page 47," he says, returning to his labours. München begins reading aloud.

"'It is a wonderful moment in the life of a lover of art when he finds himself suddenly confronted with a hitherto unknown painting by a great master, untouched, on the original canvas, and without any restoration, just as it left the painter's studio.'"

München now brings the magazine closer, peering at the accompanying photograph and screwing up his face.

"The funny thing is...it er..."

"Doesn't look like a Vermeer?" suggests The Dutchman.

"No offense."

"None taken. That's completely the point. It's precisely because it bears so little resemblance to his other work that the experts were prepared to believe it. The trick is making a Vermeer that's not too…well, Vermeer, if you see what I mean. Greed fills in the gaps. Greed is the ganache on a chocolate truffle cake, München. People always want to sink their finger in and have a taste. I make sure that there's just enough of a taste of Vermeer to want to take a bite. Actually, this stuff owes more to Caravaggio than Vermeer. For years, the experts always said that Vermeer must have spent time developing his craft in Italy. So it wasn't a great leap to conjure a Vermeer that was in the style of Caravaggio's *Supper at Emmaus* in the Pinacoteca di Brera."

"And that's where Bredius comes in, I imagine."

"Exactly. I needed an endorsement. I made contact through a friend and let some vague gossip reach him about a discovery: old house, family treasures, blah, blah. Once he wrote that article for the Burlington, well, the rest is…"

"…is a twelve bedroom house in Nice," interjects München.

"Quite. That's when the fun began. Because now there's one that's been certified a 100% honest, genuine, fake Vermeer, then you can keep churning out more of the same. No one is looking at the real stuff for authentication anymore, they're assessing the fakes according to the, er, original fake. See, the beauty of Vermeer is that there's so little known about him. He only ever produced about thirty paintings. So, once again, it's a chocolate truffle cake. The experts have been desperately waiting, thinking that somewhere out there are all these undiscovered Vermeers just waiting to be unearthed."

Having now orbited The Dutchman's world, München is back where he started, standing before the easel. There's only one thing left to ask.

"May I?"

While some artists are prickly about sharing their work before completion, The Dutchman feels no such modesty.

"*Christ and the Woman Taken in Adultery* by Johannes Vermeer," he says proudly. "Circa 1657," he adds, smirking.

"And you *really* think they'll believe it?" he asks, peering in.

"Well," slapping a hand on München's shoulder, "I'm not the one walking into the lion's den. So the real question is, do *you* think they'll believe it?"

"You're sure that this person on the inside can smooth the way?"

"She can."

* * *

Paris,

March, 1944

Like the rest of the 8th arrondissement, the Musée du Jeu de Paume is picture postcard Paris in vivid, autochrome colour. On one side is the vast expanse of the manicured Tuileries Gardens, while on the other is Place de la Concord. It is a wet Spring morning, and these tourist traps look less than their usual photogenic selves. A lingering fog hangs in the air and the flower beds of the Tuileries are sodden, clodden and bare, while the Place de la Concorde hums with the honks, hoots and toots from assorted vehicles jostling for position as they make their way amid the blue haze of acrid exhaust fumes. All of this unfolds beyond the well-tended box hedge that surrounds the Jeu de Paume, and feels a world away from this haven of fine art.

Here the *lingua franca* is euphemism, lest anyone should compromise themselves about the important but top-secret work undertaken within these hallowed halls. Today, the working week begins with another Procession of Eligible Works for Reichsmarschall Herman Göring, followed by a light buffet washed down with whatever Cru Classé Médoc the staff have managed to source at forty-eight hours' notice.

Where once the Jeu de Paume echoed with the *poc poc* of tennis balls under Napolean's gaze, today a hushed reverence has descended. It is broken only by the quiet exchanges that take place between a small but reliable, dedicated and – *bien sur* – discreet team of experts, restorers and movers. This is the cultural holy of holies. Here, numerous works of art are collected, collated and catalogued. The Führer has cultivated a maleficent manifesto on cultural heritage that will set the tone for his thousand-year Reich: degenerate art is out; an infestation eroding the purity and beauty of the Aryan race. Perpetrators of the hideous canker must be exorcised. His esteemed champion, Reichsmarschall Hermann Göring has espied an opportunity.

*If foreign markets choose to pay into the coffers of the Party for the excrescence of talentless degenerates, then more fool them!*

The Jeu de Paume is transformed into a glorified warehouse where Göring gorges himself on the booty plundered from those who have, thanks to the National Socialists, reached the end of their line. This is no carefully curated gallery for the discerning connoisseur. At times the sheer volume of artworks passing through the grandiose entrance taxes the capabilities of the team of experts within. At one time or another it has housed the entire contents of several Rothschild Collections, much to Göring's delight.

*5009 pieces, you say? Don't stop there, boys, keep it coming. I want it inventoried and crated by Monday.*

Standing on the steps of the museum this morning is an oddly mismatched triumvirate. On the left a tall, slim, debonair rake in his early thirties named Bruno Lohse is smoking a cigarette. His face is framed by a receding hairline meticulously combed. His impeccably tailored dark blue suit gives him an air of elegance; the silk pocket square adds raffish charm. Lohse is Deputy Director of the *Einsatzstab Rosenberg*, and Göring's personal finder and fixer. Though an art dealer, he is now a veritable Mephistopheles to the Reichsmarschall's Faust, tasked with lining the walls and pockets of the Reichsmarschall with an art collection to rival that of the Führer himself. Lohse has a *weiße*

*Karte* to amass and acquire works of art by whatever means he sees fit. He has also been tasked with feeding the Reichsmarschall's appetite for intellectual titbits about the artworks in his collection, so that he can sound all the more urbane at functions.

Next to him is a smaller man whose hands are thrust into his pockets. His face is thin and angular, while his piercing blue eyes exude a disconcerting intensity. Pursed lips complete the stern and resolute expression. Unlike Lohse, Dr Alfred Rosenberg wears the uniform of a high-ranking Nazi official, complete with swastika armband and various decorative badges of rank and service. Rosenberg bears the lofty – if incomprehensible – title of Commissioner of the Führer for the Supervision of the Entire Intellectual and Ideological Training and Education of the NSDAP. No one is quite sure about the hows, whys and wherefores of his doctorate, but it would be a brave man who asks the good doctor the circumstances of its bestowal; he's got one and that's that, no questions asked. Antisemite *extraordinaire*, he is the proud purveyor of whatever ideology chimes with Hitler's impulses. To wit, *Der Stumpf*, The Swamp comprises three hundred pages of Rosenberg's musings on how homosexuality is hindering the Nordic race. Meanwhile, *Zionism, the Enemy of the State* and *The Plague in Russia: Bolshevism, its heads, henchmen, and victims* have both helped put the knuckle duster into Nazism. Rosenberg answers directly to Göring.

*Current orders as follows, Rosie: confiscate all Jewish-owned cultural treasures. Shouldn't be too difficult, it's all officially ownerless by order of the Führer – get me?*

The third member of the trio pales in comparison to the other two imposing figures. Slim and elegant in a simple, bookish fashion, her natural shyness continues to charm Göring even after all this time, particularly when he teases her mercilessly about the pink circles that appear on her cheeks whenever he makes one of his saucy jokes. Lotte Linberg – "Linnie" for short – is neatly dressed in a beige Anastasie Couture suit and wears her shoulder length brown hair in a French twist, secured by a handcrafted two-prong horn hairpin with old cut rhinestones in a rose gold platted mounting. Her role is that of Private Secretary to the Reichsmarschall and Registrar of the Inventory. That is, the *Inventory* which includes copious details of the entire Hermann Göring Art Collection. As Keeper of The Most Important Book, presently clutched to her chest, for over seven years she has known all its secrets, imbuing her with an encyclopedic grasp of the minutiae of Göring's affairs. She is one of only three people, including Göring himself, entrusted with the particulars of his financial accounts. Outwardly, she is a woman more interested in serving the Reichsmarschall diligently than with adorning herself in glamour. Unlike many of her peers who desperately cling to the wreckage of their youth, she has not allowed the lure of Paris high society to distract her from her work.

Lohse takes a final, lingering drag on his Sturm and flicks the stub onto the gravel.

"I trust that we can expect an exemplary showing for the Procession?" says Rosenberg.

"Some real gems. Everything from Francesco Albani to Januarius Zick. There's a magnificent Caravaggio, Three Clouet. I've sourced a Cranach the Younger and a couple of 'school of'. Lotte?"

"Spanzotti, Spranger…Steenwyck." It's all committed to memory, she has no need for the Inventory. "There's a Tintoretto…a Tischbein. A Worst, a Wouwerman and and two Wyck. 276 paintings in total as well as 14 tapestries and a small selection of Japanese porcelain."

Rosenberg receives a light tap on the elbow from one of his aides.

"They're arriving now, sir."

Soon the gleaming five-ton chassis of Göring's Blue Goose swings into the driveway and the Reichsmarschall emerges. Today, he has eschewed his usual white double-breasted tunic and gone is his military regalia. No medals bedeck his breast and there is no elaborate epaulette, gold piping or collar tab in sight. This is Göring the connoisseur, patron of the arts. Maecenas of the Third Reich. He's

47

dressed for the occasion in a tan double-breasted Chesterfield overcoat and a jauntily tilted sable fedora. To complete the look, he swings a cane at his side; now a walking aid, now a military baton, now a pointer.

*Such exquisite brush strokes, don't you think Lohse? Tap, tap.*

Rosenberg becomes aware of a peculiar noise, something akin to toy marbles. He glances at Lohse and Linberg, neither of whom has noticed – or at least reacted. It's a jingling. There's a tinkling coming from the Reichsmarschall's coat. Göring's right-hand has slid deep down into the pocket of his Chesterfield and he is fidgeting furiously with a generous handful of precious stones nestled in the dark fabric. Rosenberg casts a sideways glance and sees the Reichsmarschall's hand feverishly fingering the jewels with a beam of satisfaction on his face. The prudish Rosenberg averts his eyes, slightly disgusted by the image of the fleshy hand fumbling under the cloth like a randy schoolboy.

Before the Procession of Eligible Works begins, there's important administration for the Reichsmarschall's attention. Linnie is on hand, omniscient, sagacious and silent. Her role is that of clerk, taking the minutes of their discussion unless one of the men clicks their finger at her in time-honoured tradition, signaling that what follows is off the record. Today, business is positively booming for the committee. The munificence of Europe knows no bounds and the Reichsmarschall's coffers have swelled with the generosity of citizens who have parted with works of art that have, regrettably, not been able to accompany them on their hasty journeys to undisclosed locations and with no forwarding address supplied.

Today there are two large wooden tables set up in the centre of a former dining room, transforming it into a temporary *Oberkommando* for all matters relating to The Acquisition & Management of Impounded and Confiscated Cultural Objects. On one table is a collection of dossiers, on the other is an assortment of savoury pastries, smoked hams and thick blocks of assorted Alsatian cheeses on wooden platters, served with grapes and figs. Standing to attention alongside the *Büfett* are two magnums of Bordeaux. Göring settles into an antique mahogany chair with emerald brocade.

"Where are we with the Belgian? Has the bastard seen reason?" grumbles Göring.

"I'm afraid, sir that…"

"I do not bloody well believe it!" he snaps. "Linberg!"

Linnie's low-heeled brown Oxfords clip-clop on the parquet floor as she hastens to serve.

"Get this down, Linnie: 'My representatives have appraised me of the ongoing discussions regarding your collection of paintings, stop. To my grave displeasure, they have informed me that you have withdrawn from your earlier position, despite my generous terms, stop. Should you not be able to reach a favourable inclination regarding the matter then – italics here, Linnie – it would be necessary for matters to proceed to their normal conclusion, without my being able to do anything to impede their course, stop. With German greetings, etcetera, etcetera.' Let's see if that doesn't give him a kick up the arse." Brief pause to fill a plate with food. "Now, the Braque stuff?"

"Yes, sir. As directed, I have dealt with Monsieur Braque personally about the Cranach of a young girl and I have insinuated that, should he part with the portrait, then the rest of the collection may be restituted back to Bordeaux all the more quickly."

"Is he a Jew?" he asks, clicking his finger at Linnie, who sets down her fountain pen and notepad.

"The *Reichssippenamt* people are making inquiries as we speak, sir. Meanwhile, the paintings remain in the bank's safekeeping."

"He'd better be a Jew, Rosenberg. See to it, will you?"

Perplexed, Rosenberg looks at Lohse; Lohse looks at Linberg. Göring looks at a generous wedge of *Tomme Fermier* and sinks his teeth into it.

"Uffabizzis?" asks the Reichsmarschall, poking two *vol au vent* into his mouth.

"In other business, we have received a letter from Mr Donald Wilkinson of the Quai d'Orléans. This was the gentleman whose wife was in an internment camp. You had taken a liking to the portrait of Juliana von Stolberg in his drawing room. Well by a curious coincidence, his wife's imminent release from the camp has coincided with the arrival of said portrait at our very door. A donation from the owner." A click of the fingers and there, before the Reichsmarschall is Juliana von Stolberg, mother of William of Orange, resplendent in an azure robe. This is met with a bored nod from Göring.

"Touching," he murmurs, more enamoured of the puff pastry selection assembled on his lap.

With that, the business of the day is completed and the men can proceed to the main event, the Procession of Eligible Works. As Göring stands, golden flakes of pastry fall like snowflakes from his lap, his boots crushing the greasy fragments into the antique rug underfoot. Lohse leads the way and after a short walk down the corridor, pauses at a set of double doors and with an exaggerated flourish, hurls them open.

"Sir, may we present the latest and very best of the ownerless Jewish collections that we have been safeguarding for your delectation."

Within seconds, Göring beams and suddenly the stubborn knot that has sat in Lohse's stomach all morning unties itself.

"Oh bravo," gushes Göring, rubbing his hands together and beaming. "Bless my soul, it's a beauty today!"

As he enters the special room he can barely contain his delight. His right hand plunges into his coat pocket once more and wriggles furiously amongst the precious stones. Floor to ceiling is lined with great works of art on each wall. In some places six frames are hung one above the other, in higgledy-piggledy fashion. Random sizes, assorted frames; 17th Century jostles for position with 19th Century. The air is thick with the scent of aged wood and linseed oil. On one wall, a masterpiece by Édouard Manet stands with unabashed confidence, juxtaposed with a tender pastoral scene by Pissarro.

Across from them, a 14th Century tapestry depicting chivalrous knights in dazzling armor engaged in valiant battles is contrasted with the tumultuous beauty of one of Turner's maritime storms; one can almost hear the clinking of steel swords and the roar of tempestuous waves mingling in the same air.

For the next hour, Göring gushes with the hyperbole of the dilettante. Rosenberg nods enthusiastically, Lohse flatters and Linnie scribbles. In arbitrary disorder, mediocre paintings are seized upon, added to the inventory and whisked away to await Göring's Special Train, while Old Masters are completely ignored and, in one case, given an unceremonious kick by the Reichsmarschall's leather boot. Göring selects an Altdofer landscape of the Danube near Regensburg for no other reason than he thinks he may have holidayed there once. A Lorrain landscape with Apollo and Mercury is snatched up on first glance. Göring decides that it will hang behind the *bergère* in the library because its blues match the damask perfectly. When Lohse senses that Göring's interest is waning, he whispers to an assistant and within seconds, two men in brown coveralls carry in a frame covered in grey cloth and set it down on an easel.

"What's all this, Lohse?" asks Göring in mock surprise, now well-used to Lohse's special treats that always round off the Procession of Eligible Works.

"Something rather wonderful, Reichsmarschall. It was brought to us by a dealer from Amsterdam."

"Dutchman?"

"German. A Party man from Munich. Name of Miedl."

"Miedl? I partly know the man," says Göring. "Miedl. What goodies have you got for us? Haven't seen you since those nine Rubens last year."

"You have an excellent memory, Reichsmarschall, excellent."

"Well, my dear wife is partial to a Rubens, so…"

"A woman of discernment, sir. True discernment."

"Don't tell me you've been fleecing our Hebrew friends again have you? You know, Miedl, you really are the limit." Göring lets out a guffaw but Miedl doesn't react.

"You unwell?" he asks suspiciously.

Suddenly, with Miedl's arrival the mood has changed and Göring is wary.

"You're perspiring, man. For God's sake somebody give him a handkerchief." It falls to Linnie to dig an embroidered kerchief from her clutch bag. Miedl dabs it across his forehead and around the folds of fat squeezing over his sodden shirt collar.

Göring is now on his feet and looking guardedly at Miedl.

"You're not skimming are you?"

Everyone in the room is now aware that Göring the Great White has emerged from the depths, he is staring at Miedl with one black eyeball. "Not creaming a little off the top, eh?" He circles Miedl slowly. Then Rosenberg and Lohse. He smacks a hand on Miedl's shoulder, and appears to relax.

"Long as you keep the train on the tracks," says Göring.

"I'm not sure that I…"

"Give us a moment, Linnie – and shut the door."

Linberg closes the *Inventory*, collects her handbag and departs. Göring is now tapping his cane rhythmically on the floor and addressing the three men.

"So what if the Führer deems that some fat old *bubbe* is no longer fit to sit in her armchair gazing at a Kandinsky? Who are we to reason why? Flog it! Oil the great wheels of commerce for the good of the Reich. And if by some small twist of fate an insignificant Heckel lithograph should catch your eye, well what of it? How can it be theft if the Führer himself has decreed that such work should be annihilated? What harm can it do if a dedicated servant of the state should feather the meagre nest of his dotage with the proceeds from a modest commercial venture here and there. Hmm? Am I wrong, boys? What say you? Speak up."

But they don't. He does.

He has moved so close to Miedl now that the banker can smell alcohol on his breath.

"But you try and shaft Uncle Hermann, and by Christ you better know that I'll shaft you twice as hard. Just remember, those trains run like clockwork and it makes no difference to the Reich if we squeeze one more greedy little pig on board. Mind you," he chuckles, "it's a long way East - and you're not exactly kosher meat, boys."

The blood has drained from Miedl's face. As quickly as it emerged, the Great White Shark has retreated into the depths and cordiality remerges. Göring walks to the door and opens it for Linnie, giving her a conspiratorial wink as she brushes past him.

She hands the Inventory to Lohse, whose duty it is to present the particulars of the latest hand-picked item for special consideration.

"The usual, Mr Lohse, if you please. Facts with fancy. Bit of history, bit of iconography."

Lohse turns to the latest page of the inventory and runs his thumb down the ivory sheaf, reading.

Artist:     Johannes Vermeer, 17th Century

Medium: Oil on Canvas

Title: *Christ and the Woman Taken in Adultery.*

Measurements: 100 x 89.9 cm

"Here, Vermeer combines technical virtuosity with masterful storytelling, offering viewers a window into the complexities of human nature, morality, and redemption. At the heart of this narrative tableau stands Christ, a luminous beacon of divine compassion. His countenance radiates a soft, celestial light, casting a warm, embracing aura around Him. I believe that in these details we find the roots of Vermeer's later domestic scenes." Lohse suddenly loses his thread, distracted by Miedl who is fidgeting with his tie and sweating more than ever. "Er, soft, celestial light…"

"You've done that bit," growls Göring.

"Um, to Christ's left stands the adulteress, a figure wrought with palpable vulnerability. Her downcast eyes are shadowed by a curtain of tangled auburn hair. Throughout, the artist's palette is a harmonious blend of warm, earthy tones. Ochres and burnt siennas dominate, conveying a sense of timelessness and grounding the viewer in the ancient world of the Bible. It's so very typical of Vermeer's Italian period, just like the *Supper at Emmaus*."

Göring is now peering closely at the painting.

"How much have we negotiated?" he murmurs.

"*Well…*" Lohse gives a nod towards Miedl.

"Fuck off, Miedl," barks Göring, and the dealer from Munich does so.

In the distance a telephone rings.

"Well?" Göring resumes.

"We've negotiated an exchange. The Vermeer for 137 paintings. A chance to offload degenerate art. We think it's fair."

"Fair! I don't give a fuck about fair."

"Well, that is to say, *advantageous* – to us, sir," he hastens to add. "We've always suspected that Vermeer spent time studying in Italy and the religious paintings which have emerged over the last couple of years appear to confirm this."

"Wait till Goebbels sees this! I've got just the spot behind my desk at Carinhall."

The mood of self-congratulation is broken by a knock at the door. An officer enters and hands a note to Rosenberg who reads it.

"Not now," he tells the officer, who withdraws.

"Hmm? Matter?" asks Göring.

"It appears that Madame Beatrice Steiner has been trying to make contact through an intermediary again, sir."

Göring looks blankly.

"There was also a message waiting when we arrived at the Quai d'Orleans actually."

"Probably found some motivation at last. Let her sweat a bit and she'll drop the price," then with an elbow nudge to Lohse, "an' her panties, I'll wager." All boys together, they share the laugh whether they want to or not.

It has been a productive morning. Lohse and Rosenberg are relieved to have delivered a pleasing selection for the Reichsmarschall. Linnie has copious notes to file before this evening's return to Germany. Göring feels in the mood for a drop more Bordeaux with some Munster.

In the distance a telephone rings. And rings. And rings.

Outside, the veil of fog has lifted to reveal a crisp blue sky. It's a fine day, and München is standing on the stone steps lighting another cigarette, his third in a row. As he digs in his pocket for the lighter, he realizes that he's still got the secretary's embroidered kerchief. *Linnie.* His mind is racing. He has quite the story to tell The Dutchman on his return. All about the swanky car with the flag that picked him up; the food (he never did catch the name of that cheese); the Reichsmarschall himself (fatter than he remembered), and the rest.

"The rest," he smiles, "is a twelve-bedroom house in Nice," he says aloud.

Three hours later, Göring is sitting in an armchair in the Imperial Suite at the Ritz, overlooking the *Place Vendome* and holding a hand-written letter which arrived this afternoon, marked urgent for his attention. It begins 'Dear Reichsmarschall Göring, Regretfully...' and that's all he reads before he tears it neatly into four strips. He can guess what follows.

*Regretfully...Sentimental value...couldn't possibly part...*

He reaches for the phone that is sitting on an ormolu table, and demands to be connected with the senior officer on duty at *Rue Lauriston.*

*It's 16th arrondissement, they won't have far to go.*

Within a minute he has put inexorable wheels in motion that will secure the paintings for him once and for all. Moments later, with a flick of the wrist her letter is caught in the warm embrace of the fire and Göring turns to more pressing matters.

# A Conference of Lawyers

Inventory of the Art Collection
of
Reichsmarschall Hermann Göring

Collection: David David-Weill — Neuilly s/Seine,
France
Artist:      Gabriel de Saint Aubin
Medium: Works on Paper, reworked with pencil and
ink by the artist.
Title: *A Conference of Lawyers*
Measurements: 17.6 cm x 12 cm

Note:  One of a total of 2687 items from the David-
Weill Collection that have been seized by the
Einsatzstab Rosenberg.
In a towering library hall, lawyers sit in robes of their
office, flanked by disproportionately large leather-

bound tomes. The emphasis on books and legal texts in the etching symbolizes the adherence to the rule of law and that, whatever the crime, legal principles must prevail. The scene is sombre, dark. Some of the men sit at a table, illuminated by candle-light. The figures are largely indistinguishable; we could be any European nation. However, the central figure in the etching, likely a senior lawyer, holds a prominent position, directing the discussion and making a key point. This figure likely symbolizes the guiding principles of law or the authority of the legal system. Many of the lawyers are huddled together, apparently conversing of weighty matters. The cloud-like formation at the top with figures reminds us that justice is a higher power and that legal decisions should be informed by divine or moral law. On the cloud, and dominating the scene, float the allegorical personifications of justice, truth and eloquence. They oversee the proceedings, dwarfing the lawyers below them, their size suggestive of the import of the judicial process.

B.L.

* * *

The panel before Justice Robert Jackson lights up, the red bulb blinking furiously.

Someone behind him says something about a change in translators and he gives a nod to his associates who gather round.

Göring watches them from behind his black polaroid glasses, both hands outstretched, gripping the edges of the witness box.

*Looking a bit peaky there Robert?*

Are there heavy bags under the prosecutor's eyes? Perhaps it's the lights. His forehead is shiny with perspiration.

*Long night Robert?*

Is Göring imagining it or has Jackson deliberately avoided his gaze so far this morning? The Reichsmarschall can't help a self-satisfied smile.

*'Oh the shark has pearly teeth, dear*
*And it shows them pearly white.'*

The red light goes out, a hush descends and Jackson is waving a pair of headphones at him.

"You are perhaps aware that you are the only living man who can expound to us the true purposes of the Nazi Party and the inner workings of its leadership?"

"I am perfectly aware of that," Göring says haughtily. "After Germany's collapse in 1918, Jewry became powerful in all spheres of life. There was an uninterrupted attack on everything from many Jews. Magazines dragged through the mud everything that was holy to us. Distortion was practiced in the field of art and befouled the idea of the brave German soldier. Everywhere Jewry was in the fight against National Socialism by making us appear contemptible."

*'Befouled,' – nice touch, poetic.*

"I'd like to read a letter that you wrote to Reinhard Heydrich, the main architect of the Holocaust," says Jackson. "'I hereby charge you to make all organizational preparations for bringing about the accomplishment of the desired final solution of the Jewish question.' Am I correct so far?"

"No, that is in no way correctly translated," says Göring leaning into the microphone so forcefully that each consonant puffs and cracks loudly in the headsets of the listeners. "Much has been made of my use of the phrase 'the final solution'. The decisive word has been mistranslated. '*total* solution,' is what I said, not 'a final solution.'"

Jackson wonders at the Reichsmarschall's pettifogging. Does quibbling semantics alter the face of the holocaust?

"And did you write this letter?" he asks.

"Is it on my official headed paper with my name typed at the bottom?"

"It is."

"With my signature?"

"In your hand."

"Then I think it is safe to assume that I wrote the letter, don't you?"

Göring feels smug. He sounds petulant.

"On the day after the riots known as *Kristallnacht* you opened a meeting thus: 'Gentlemen, I have had enough of these demonstrations. They do not harm the Jews. If today a Jewish shop is destroyed, the insurance company will pay the Jew for the damages. If, in the future, demonstrations occur then I ask that they be so directed that we do not cut our own throats.' Did you make these remarks?"

"Absolutely I made those remarks," he snorts.

"And later you established that 101 synagogues were destroyed by fire and 76 synagogues demolished during the riots?"

"Yes."

*When's lunch?*

"Then Dr. Goebbels interposed –"

*Trust the cripple to open his trap. Emmy always said that Goebbels and I bickered like an old married couple.*

"And you have a discussion about the transport system, have you not?"

"No. That is, Dr Goebbels had a discussion. He was quite capable of having whole conversations with himself. That was Goebbels for you."

"Dr. Goebbels raised the question of Jews traveling in railway trains?"

"Oh yes," Göring sighs, rolling his eyes at the memory.

"He said, 'The Reich Ministry of Transport must issue a decree ordering that there shall be separate compartments for Jews.'"

Göring closes his eyes in exasperation as Jackson quotes verbatim Goebbels' views about the Jewish question and its implications for public transport.

"'They can only be given separate compartments after all Germans have secured seats.'"

Göring blinks, adding quickly, "I was getting exceedingly irritated because Goebbels always came up with irksome, irrelevant minutiae when important laws were at hand." Unease begins to dawn on him. He's remembered something that happened at that meeting.

"Let us skip to the part of the meeting where Goebbels brings up the subject of the German forests."

*Shit. Here we go.*

He knows what Jackson is setting him up for. Göring tries to explain.

"Goebbels asked for a decree which would prevent Jews from going to German holiday resorts. I replied that it would be better to put a certain part of the forest at the disposal of the Jews. It was then that I, er, made a remark which, ah, perhaps in context..."

"Let us have that remark," Jackson cuts in. The lawyer appears to be awaiting a drum roll that never arrives. "Then *you* said, 'We will give the Jews part of the forest and see that animals which are damnably like the Jews – the elk has a hooked nose – go into the Jewish enclosure with them. Is that what you said?"

Göring squeezes his fists in his lap.

*You know fucking well it is. You've got the minutes.*

61

"Yes, I said it," then adds quickly, "b-but it should be considered in the context of the whole atmosphere of the meeting. Goebbels kept going on and on and on."

Dozens of pencils scrape, slide and scrawl across foolscap, notelets and pads as assorted members of the press record for posterity the gem their readers can enjoy over breakfast. All anyone will remember of the morning's proceedings is that the Reichsmarschall believes that – quote – 'various animals are like the Jews – like the elk with its hooked nose.'

It's not that Göring cares about the fate of European Jewry or even about the court of public opinion, but he knows that the remark makes him sound peevish, undignified and boorish when he has spent weeks trying to cultivate an air of erudition and statesmanship for the world. He hates himself because it's grist to the mill of his detractors.

*And I served it to them on a silver salver, bent double, trousers down.*

"Let us turn to other matters," says Jackson, now relaxed, enjoying himself. "Since the time you were taken into custody, you have had regular psychiatric evaluations. Is that correct?"

Göring bristles. "That is *not* correct. Please can the transcript record that these are conversations. I have *conversations*. If an evaluation takes place, it is because I allow it." The word 'it' cracks like a whip in the headphones.

"I will now read your words that were recorded by Dr Leon Goldensohn: 'Even if one has no compunction about exterminating a race, common sense dictates that in our civilization that this is barbaric and would be subject to so much criticism from abroad and within that it would be condemned as the greatest criminal act in history.'"

Göring is listening intently, aware that the air in the courtroom is heavy, portentous.

"'Understand that I am not a moralist,' you said. 'Although I have my chivalric code. If I really felt that the killing of Jews meant anything, such as it meant winning the war, then I would not be too bothered by it.'"

Göring can sense the unease that descends on the courtroom and begins infecting the other defendants, a contagion squirming along the benches. He's one of them whether they like it or not. *Ein Volk. Ein Reich. Ein Führer.*

"You went on, 'I have a conscience and I feel that killing women and children simply because they happen to be victims of Goebbels's hysterical propaganda is not the way of a gentleman.'"

*See! Here I am, a gentleman. I am not a barbarian.*

Göring nods.

"You said, 'I don't believe that I will go to heaven or hell when I die. I don't believe in the Bible or in a lot of things which religious people think. I revere women and I think it unsportsmanlike to kill women and children.'"

*Quite right.*

The red light flashes.

The Sir Geoffrey Lawrence looks up.

"Was that 'unsportsmanlike'?" he asks, "I couldn't…"

"That's the adjective he used, sir," clarifies Jackson. Then, leaning in for emphasis, "'unsportsmanlike.'"

There is a red light is flashing again. Or perhaps it's only in Göring's mind.

*Unsportsmanlike.*

He remembers a painting of a girl with a ribbon in her hair.

*Beatrice.*

# The Consuming Fire

Inventory of the Art Collection
of
Reichsmarschall Hermann Göring

Owner: Mme. Aschberg – Paris, France
Collection: Victor Aschberger, 1637
Artist: Stefano della Bella
Medium: Works on Paper
Title: *Scena quinta d'inferno*, from *Le nozze degli Dei*
Measurements: 208 x 292 mm

Note: An etching on paper by Stefano Della Bella
from 1637. The scene is based on the work of
Alfonso Parigi, a Florentine architect and set
designer and depicts one of the sets that Parigi
designed for a ballet sequence for the opera *Nozze*

*degli dei*. Della Bella's etching formed part of the programme for the production.

The *Ballo dell' Inferno* – the Dance of Hell – was the fifth scene in the opera. It bears witness to the torment of the infernal realm: flames lick at the edges while all manner of demonic beasts leap amid the chaos. It is noteworthy for the number of centaurs – at least twelve – which traditionally typify the duality of human nature and represent our struggle to regulate our primal impulses. They are a reminder of our potential for violence and unrestraint. In Parigi's vision of Hell, the very worst of Mankind is unleashed amid the flames.
B.L.

\* \* \*

January, 1945

The Pelikan fountain pen of SS-Obersturmführer Robert Mulka records the details clearly and succinctly in the logbook in blue ink: Convoy 69 arrived at Auschwitz II-Birkenau from Drancy with 1501 deportees aboard, of whom 1311 were liquidated upon arrival. Of the 190 remaining, 80 were female. All were assigned labour. Since that time, 392 more lines of Mulka's logbook have been completed. Despite its precision and amplitude, what the record does not mention is that ninety-seven days have elapsed since Mme. Béatrice Steiner last rode her beloved mare through the Bois de Boulogne. Béatrice began to mark the days herself, but lost count after day thirty-eight. Or thirty-nine. She blames this on the increasing *brouillard* that has slowly enveloped her mind since the officers arrived from *Rue Lauriston* on that Thursday in March. Or April. Shorn of hair and feeble of mind, Béatrice no longer resembles a wealthy society hostess who once mingled with the best of European society.

The line inches forward as hundreds of pairs of feet shuffle along, never quite leaving contact with the hard, frosted earth underfoot. Béatrice hears it before she sees it; a distinctive whinny that captures her attention. Ten metres ahead to the right of the line stands a beautiful mare, perhaps six years old. The doctor, *Der Todesengel* – The Angel of Death – sits atop, holding the leather reins lightly. His eyes rove from one grey specimen to the next as the line lumbers past. Occasionally, he smiles at one and nods. Presently, the specimen is removed from the queue by his assistant, Hans König, who has learnt to read the doctor's expression and follow his line of sight.

Béatrice is touched by the mare's beauty – so incongruous – and is instinctively drawn to it. For so many nights she has willed herself to sleep by imagining cantering through the Bois de Boulogne on an autumnal day. At first, her recollections were vivid; the soft leather saddle, the jangle of the stirrups. If she tried hard enough, she could even conjure the smell of the stables and the horses within. But that was in the early days at Drancy and long before she arrived here.

The line meanders on. Béatrice is now five metres away and captivated. She suddenly leaves the procession, veering off to the right making directly for the horse, held in its thrall. The bald woman behind her lifts her head and raises the skin-and-bone hand to tug at Béatrice's coarse jacket, but she's out of reach. Béatrice is enveloped in her *brouillard* once more. It's Anastasie, she knows it. 'I'm here,' she whispers. Blinking her rheumy eyes, she frowns; the fine chestnut hair has not been groomed this morning. Beneath the sleek coat she can see the firm, well-defined muscles and the smooth curvature of its withers. The mane is matted in places with flecks of dried mud. Béatrice wavers and raises her hand, partly to steady herself on the frosty earth, but mostly to touch Anastasie's mane once more. The beast whinnies and shakes its head. Béatrice shuffles on, drawn to its muzzle now. The moist flesh is dotted with fine hairs, and quivering slightly in the dewy morning air. Béatrice's bruised fingers reach out and tickle the hairs on its flank. She manages a weak smile.

As soon as *Der Todesengel* notices the specimen at his feet, he whistles to the nearest guard who marches over, takes one look at the offending inmate and drives the butt of his rifle into her cheekbone with full force. The bone shatters on impact, cracking the floor of the eye socket as Béatrice collapses onto the ground. *Der Todesengel* peers down, pivoting his boot in the stirrup to see the damage to the specimen slumped beneath him. Notwithstanding the fact that the left side of her face has caved in, Béatrice is conscious and therefore, according to protocol, able to rejoin the line. The bald woman who stood behind her is beckoned over together with another lady. They half carry, half drag Béatrice back to the line which trundles inexorably on. Whether it's the disorientation brought about by her injury, or the ever-advancing *brouillard*, she is now enveloped in a reality all her own.

"I was thrown," she tells the women. "Anastasie threw me. She must have been startled. Thank goodness you were here, ladies." Then, touching her face lightly she adds vaguely, "My eye…"

She's trying to blink but wondering why her eye is not responding; her face is numb. Lifting her upright, the women can see the extent of the damage. Béatrice's left cheek has been replaced by a bloodied hole displaying a small shard of bone. She continues mumbling incoherently. She teeters slightly and the women help her stay upright. She thanks them for their kindness but tells them not to worry, she will telephone the cabinet of Dr Bernhardt on her return to De Monceau Street. She tries to manage a polite smile in gratitude, but only the right side of her face responds, the left is thick with sticky red-black liquid. She continues muttering on but her words are drowned out by the putter of a Red Cross van which approaches from behind, coughing black fumes into the cold January morning air.

The van passes the women and continues onwards, following the line and trundling down towards the large red brick building with the chimney. Despite outward appearances, its contents have not been approved by the International Committee of the Red Cross. Perhaps the most prominent feature on the greenish-yellow tins stacked in the rear is the skull and crossbones on the label. Each canister of Zyklon B contains five hundred grams of pellets soaked in liquid hydrocyanic acid, a cyanide-based pesticide that is 'For use against vermin', according to the canister. The van draws up outside the building and two SS guards alight, slamming the doors simultaneously. They go about their business with the air of well-practiced but indifferent professionals.

By now, Béatrice has reached the building. She is disorientated, her nose is bloodied and she is acutely aware of the throbbing pain in what is left of her cheek. She is oblivious to the peculiar smell in the air from the chimneys that burn twenty-four hours a day. The ash flakes fall thickly and she is consumed by past remembrances, unaware of the sobbing around her and the air of agitation from the other women in the line. She looks down at her grubby blue and white striped clothing, smoothing it down.

"I'm not properly dressed," she mutters.

Turning around, she sees the queue of perturbed women and begins to make her way backwards, brushing past the throng, intent on heading towards her boudoir. A hand seizes her collar and yanks her back as she is swept along in the crush of bodies. A flake of ash settles on her forearm. She sees it, and remembers a fireplace and a magnificent house in a forest as she is dragged into the darkness.

In the anteroom a guard yells something about delousing and the women begin undressing. Béatrice unfastens only two buttons and with a casual tug, her clothes slip easily from her shrunken frame. In an attempt at modesty, she draws her arm across her breasts which hang like paper bags. Her left eye is purple and swollen shut. She tips her head back slowly and remembers crossing the threshold into an enormous hall lined with Old Masters. Now, as then, smoke from the chimney is in the air. There are more guests this time, she thinks, wondering why the hall is so very crowded. The throng presses forward into the chamber. She stands on tiptoes, straining to see her host. 'He's here,' she whispers, and she smiles now as the door slams shut behind her.

A signal is given from somewhere above. The chamber is ready; small levers open the chutes. The two SS guards, now in masks, remove the lids from the tins of Zyklon B and slowly pour the granules into the openings. Their job done, the guards now have twenty minutes to wait. Customarily, they remove their masks and pause for a cigarette.

"C'mon then," says one, wiping a dewdrop from his nose.

"What?" says the other, eyeing him.

"Your turn."

"You had one of mine yesterday."

The other guard screws up his face then nods, and reluctantly slides his hand into his pocket. As they light the cigarettes, they instinctively wander away from the building so as not to have their moment of calm disturbed by the noise and pounding inside. They each take a long drag and watch the tendrils of smoke climb into the air.

Within, Henryk Tauber waits with his team of Sonderkommando, Jewish prisoners who work in the gas chambers and crematoria. They perform their roles with dispassionate efficiency. According to SS-Obersturmführer Robert Mulka's logbook, the four crematoria can process 4,736 cadavers in twenty-four hours. After twenty minutes followed by sufficient airing of the building, the Sonderkommando are permitted to enter. Tauber knows to stand to one side when opening the door, so that he is not surprised by any bodies that may spill out. This morning he swings the door back to find four corpses wedged in position, knotted together like a ball of yarn. He gestures to a co-worker for the crook, and with a few well-placed tugs, the contorted remains untangle and spindly limbs wave and kick as the bodies fall clear of the doorway and collapse onto the stone floor.

The Sonderkommando clear the chamber of its contents. On more than one occasion Tauber slips and slides on the liquid faeces spattered on the tiles. He knows that time is of the essence, because the longer the corpses remain in the chamber, the colder and harder each one will become, especially given the seasonal weather. As he sets to work dragging, lifting and hauling, from the corner of his eye he becomes aware that Gradowski has stopped work and is kneeling over one of the bodies and muttering quietly. Tauber's immediate reaction is anger; Gradowski should know better, they're on a tight schedule. Perhaps he's removing a pair of glasses or a set of dentures or perhaps a gold tooth. Tauber walks towards him and realizes that Gradowski has donned his tallit and is saying kaddish over the body of a woman in her fifties with a caved-in face. Tauber stops himself, not intruding on this moment of intimacy. As he walks back to the door of the chamber, he holds the image of the woman in his mind: a caved in face and – is he imagining it, or is she smiling?

After just under two hours, the chamber is clear. It then takes the team a further fourteen minutes to wash the room clear of postmortem fluid on the floor and walls. Only when the SS guards are satisfied will the men be permitted to commence the next stage. There is a brief opportunity to step outside, away from the fetid smell to gasp at something approaching normal air. Tauber leans against the wall of the entrance; Gradowski retches. There's always one.

The crematoria are formidable, each one contains fifteen ovens. Each oven has two iron stretchers for loading. By now, Tauber has spent the last few hours permanently hunched. He stands and arches his back, letting out a low groan. He waits for the rest of the team to assemble so that they can begin. It is at this moment that he notices the woman lying at his feet. Though the most striking feature is her caved-in face, once more it is the faint trace of a half-smile that haunts him. Gradowski nudges his arm and the team go about their wordless routine. Tauber points at the iron stretcher, and the corpse of a woman of about thirty is dragged onto it and positioned face upwards. Tauber then takes a step towards the smiling woman and straddles her. He bends over to take her hands in his. In doing so, his thumbs stroke gently at her palms which are now warmed by the heat from the ovens. Her left eye is swollen shut but her right is half open in a glassy stare. As carefully as he can, he raises her arms and gently lays her on top of the other corpse, face up with her head between the feet. The SS call this 'top 'n' tailing'. It increases productivity by 12 per cent.

The stretcher is ready for loading. One man opens the door of the oven and immediately a fiery breath fills the room and the team are aglow in a rich orange light. Another man wheels rollers underneath the stretcher while a final team member lifts the handles. Suddenly, a guard shouts from across the room.

"*Zulege!*"

The team wait for the 'bonus', a last-minute addition to the pyre for maximum efficiency. Hurriedly, a prisoner waddles across the room dragging the body of a small girl who must be no more than ten. Sliding her over the tiles, he swings the torso onto the two pale, bruised waifs and then tosses the legs up onto the pile. With a nod from the guard, the team heave forward, rolling the stretcher into the oven. The last thing that Henryk Tauber sees of the smiling woman are the soles of her blackened feet as she slides towards oblivion.

\* \* \*

April, 1945

'When the morning dawned, the angels urged him to hurry, saying, "Escape to the mountains, lest you be destroyed." Then the Lord rained brimstone and fire on Sodom and Gomorrah from out of the heavens.'
*Book of Genesis, Chapter 19*

71

The temperature inside is now several hundred degrees Celsius. It begins with smoke and soot. Discoloration follows, then charring and blistering. Her body, once vivid and lifelike, now withers. The bare skin, soft and delicate is consumed by the relentless heat. The figure appears to writhe in agony under the tightening embrace of the fire, her fine hair trickling down, melting into the ivory of the silken sheet that lies at the base of her spine. As smoke curls its ghostly fingers around the body, the colors begin to shift, their vibrancy devolving into a spectral mirage. Now, the edges of the canvas curl upward like wilted petals and the varnish that once protected her cracks and sizzles, revealing the raw, exposed layers beneath. The oakwood frame contorts and the wood warps. The mournful transformation of Besnard's girl is now almost complete. In its final moments, the last traces of the beautiful figure flicker like a dying ember. She disappears from view, an unwitting victim of one man's cupidity.

"Besnard was a traitor," Göring grumbles bitterly. The Reichsmarschall is slumped into the rear leather seat of a Luftwaffe blue Mercedes-Benz 540K W24 saloon. His arms are folded morosely, and he is staring out of the windscreen down the driveway at Carinhall – ablaze – and where five trucks are loaded with crates of precious cargo. "Besnard spent three years in England under the tutelage of Reynolds and Gainsborough," he continues. "Won the *Prix de Rome* with his *Death of Timophanes*. Then for some bloody reason he broke away completely from tradition and began to emulate the style of the degenerates. As I say, a traitor to his art. Nevertheless," he adds glancing back wistfully towards his beloved lodge, "she was not without merit. That coquettish pose. I'll miss her." His face is illuminated by the orange glow of the flames as he remembers the *Nude woman with coiffed hair.*

*Leave a few breadcrumbs for them to find. Throw them off the scent.*

He imagines his train hurtling towards the mines of Altausee.

*'Looks like he burned the lot, sir.' Might work.*

Brauchitsch is watching his crestfallen master carefully in the rear-view mirror.

"Perhaps it may help to remember sir, that she is a necessary casualty of war. Remember what you told Frau Göring, 'Sacrifice a few dirty Impressionist works, save a wealth of Old Masters.'"

"Hmph," Göring shrugs sullenly. "Those Bolshevik bastards will be here in under a week. Their grubby little hands fingering whatever they can scavenge. God in heaven, when I imagine this place being lauded as some disgusting victory trophy on a newsreel in Moscow. Why, it makes my fucking blood boil! It's more than I can bear."

There's a tap at Brauchitsch's window and he opens the front passenger door.

"We're ready, sir," a paratrooper tells him.

"It's time, sir," says Brauchitsch solemnly, turning to face the Reichsmarschall.

Within a few moments, they are marching together along a small path through the woods, navigating their way over fallen branches towards a meadow beyond. They can feel the heat of the flames on their backs and hear the cracking and splitting of wood as Carinhall, Göring's beloved lodge, is consumed by fire. Emerging on the far side of the wood, the scene is one of peaceful serenity. It is dusk and the shouts of the paratroopers and the heat of the blaze seem far away. The grassy clearing slopes downwards, and slowly falls away until the forest begins again in the distance. This was where his legendary hunts began. To the left, a marquee with refreshments for the guests; to the right, the horses were readied with the dogs; the hunt masters, kennel staff, and whipper-ins all busying themselves. This evening only three gamekeepers remain. Two of them are holding an enormous bison. This one is majestic, an embodiment of raw power. Its unshorn coat is a rich tapestry of earthy browns that hangs in heavy, weather-worn curtains. Its head is adorned with curved horns that curl upwards in an imposing arc. The broad, muscular body is supported on trunk-like legs. It stands in wait, held by the gamekeepers. With each breath, plumes of steam escape from its flared nostrils, hanging momentarily in the cold, evening air. Göring stands for a moment staring at it. The third gamekeeper readies a Mannlicher-Schönauer bolt-action rifle. Göring snatches it out of his hands and points it at an angle slightly behind the front 'elbow' of the nearest bison and fires two blasts into it. The beast shudders and drops to the ground, its eyes rolling up and back into its head. Göring knows a double shot is best; the thickness of the skull means that a bullet will not necessarily penetrate the bone, while the stoutness of the neck makes locating the spinal cord difficult. With a double shot behind the elbow there's quick penetration into the heart and a merciful kill. Göring turns and thrusts the rifle back into the arms of the startled gamekeeper. Without a word, he turns and strides into the forest and back towards the waiting Mercedes. Brauchitsch looks at the three men, each one has been a loyal servant at Carinhall for longer than they care to remember. He nods, mutters 'Gentlemen' and then follows his master back into the darkness of the forest.

Slamming the car door, Göring folds his arms and scowls.

*It was the honourable last act of the Reichsjägermeister. I kill my own. I will not leave them behind for those bastards.*

Göring can feel the heat on his cheek even through the window in the rear of the car as the blaze encroaches. He reaches for the handle and gives it two rotations. With a wobble, the window lowers and suddenly the car is filled with the smell of burning wood and a heat that almost singes his nostrils. With a loud crack, another of the rafters falls to the floor, releasing embers like fireworks into the air.

*The library, gone. My very own Nero Decree.*

"For God's sake, Brauchitsch let's go. I can't bear it any longer."

The car pulls away down the driveway and into an uncertain future. Behind it, an eerie crimson glow flickers against the night sky as Carinhall's once-stately hallways become ablaze with a macabre dance of fire and shadow. Flames lash out hungrily, consuming the aged wood, thatch, and stone that have stood as a testament to avarice. The sound of crackling timber and the acrid scent of burning history fill the air. The thatched roofs erupt into fiery waterfalls, sending sparks skyward. The stone archways, meticulously crafted to the Reichsmarschall's own design, crumble under the relentless onslaught of heat and smoke. Within, every timber beam groans in agony as the inferno claims it, room by room. The surrounding Schorfheide forest watches silently, its ancient trees bearing witness to the final reckoning of Carinhall. Once a monument to sybaritic excess, it is now funeral pyre for a past that has no place in the future.

The Mercedes speeds on into the night. On Göring's lap sits a last memento. It is the second most important book in his realm (the first is in the hands of a most trusted devotee who has, for the last decade, watched as the ink dried on his iniquities). His fat fingers grip his prized guest book, fashioned in solid silver binding with Bavarian embossed relief. It was a wedding gift from the Prussian State Consul. Within its covers is a host of illustrious names that have basked in the Reichsmarschall's largesse down the years. There's the Führer, of course, Mussolini and Franco. Arno Brecker and Richard Strauss have pride of place. King Gustav V of Sweden dined there once. Charles Lindbergh visited, as well as the King of Siam, Herbert Hoover, too. The daytime hunt followed by the evening revels; sumptuous feasts served to the strains of Wagner – halcyon days! The entry for 14th October 1937 records in blue ink a visit from the Duke and Duchess of Windsor. Another name, long forgotten, sits in small but delicate script: Mme Béatrice Steiner, De Monceau Street, Paris.

* * *

Following destruction of the bodies, the burnt remains are gathered from the furnace by the Sonderkommando. Typically, the ashes of an adult at Auschwitz weigh just over 500 grams – the same weight as a canister of Zyklon B. Fragments of pelvic bones, skulls and kneecaps have not completely cremated in the ovens and will need to be pulverized before being dumped in one of the pits or in the Sola River;

'fish food,' say the SS men. It's unpleasant work for Tauber, but at least the dead have stopped staring at him.

# Fox Hunting: the Death

Inventory of the Art Collection
of
Reichsmarschall Hermann Göring

Collection: BN [Belgien und Nordfrankreich]
Artist:     G. Moreland 1769–1804
Medium: Works on Paper, Colour Lithograph
Title: *Fox Hunting, the death*.
Size: 56cm x 66cm

Note:   A highly sought after lithograph by the
perennially popular English artist, George Moreland.
Entitled *Fox Hunting: the Death*, it is hard to think of
a more typical scene depicting the country life of the
British establishment. Here, the hunter has become
the hunted. We are presented with the climactic
moment in which trained hounds have finally caught

the cunning and elusive fox. On the right two huntsmen, depicted in traditional red hunting coats, arrive at the scene. One opens a gate while the other vaults a fence. In the background two cottagers peer out of the window of a meagre, thatched dwelling. The cottage, and the simple rural life it represents, stand in stark contrast to the violent activity taking place. The inclusion of this setting by Morland, who often commented on rural life, adds a layer of complexity to the scene, possibly hinting at the disruption caused by the hunt to pastoral life.
B.L.

\* \* \*

The sun dips over the Bavarian Alps, casting long shadows across the Obersalzberg and *Landhaus* Göring. Once a picturesque summer retreat for the Reichsmarschall, it can no longer defy the tumultuous winds of change blowing through Germany. Ominous undercurrents course through its corridors as its inhabitants contemplate an uncertain future.

Göring sits in his study gazing out as the Untersberg Mountains are slowly enveloped by the darkness.

*'Time, the fickle friend that is always and never on your side.' Who said that?*

He reaches for the comfort of his stones, plunging his hand deep into the pool of emeralds and sapphires mingling with opals and topaz. He gropes his way to the bottom of the bowl, slowly quelled. He is also mollified by the copious amount of pills he has swallowed as the afternoon has given way to evening. As intoxication takes hold, he slumps lower into his chair, transfixed by the oily swirls of the twenty-year-old scotch in the crystal glass lolling pendulously in his hand.

He slowly becomes aware of a voice. It is that of von Brauchitsch, who is standing before him speaking urgently.

"Sir, Koller's been trying to get word here for over twenty-four hours. The communication lines have taken a battering."

Göring sits staring at von Brauchitsch with wide eyes and quivering jowls. He stuffs a fat finger down his collar and unfastens two buttons on his shirt.

"Hitler's vacillating," Brauchitsch continues. "Koller says that one moment he's saying all is lost and the next he's ranting for planes to be put in the air to defend Berlin.'

It is only now that Brauchitsch notices the whisky, sees his pills and understands Göring's detachment.

"According to Koller, Hitler was screaming down the phone at him to scramble aircraft, get airborne and resist the attack to the northeast of the city. Before Koller could say anything he'd rung off. By ten thirty he called again and he was threatening to send Koller's wife and neighbours on the next train to Theresienstadt – all because troops hadn't been sent to join a non-existent counter offensive. Then later, Koller spoke with General Christian to say that the Führer had suffered a complete mental collapse. Well, that's when he decided to reach you in the hope that…perhaps…" he lets the phrase fall. Göring picks it up.

"…Perhaps I could salvage something from the wreckage?" he says wearily.

"There's another thing, sir. Apparently Hitler said 'There's no more fighting to be done. I'll leave the rest up to Göring. He can negotiate for peace.' Well that was that. Koller has been trying to get word here. I received word via a dispatch rider and, well, that's when I knew I had to come directly up here to the house. It's chaos out there, sir."

And with that, the moment that The Reichsmarschall never thought would arrive is here.

"How do we even know Hitler's still alive?'

"But surely sir, if he was dead then you would have been one of the first to know."

'You're forgetting that thug Bormann. Who's to say that bastard hasn't ordered radio silence, sworn the inner circle to secrecy and is setting himself up as rightful heir? Bormann's waiting for his chance to liquidate me, you just see if he's not."

"Unthinkable, sir. How can you entertain such thoughts?"

"Because it's exactly what I'd do."

Göring strides to his desk and swipes up a mother of pearl box. Flipping the lid back he picks up a pill between finger and thumb and drops it onto his tongue. He then glugs a large dose of whisky into his glass and washes everything down with a loud gulp.

"Christ almighty. I was there with him in Munich, Brauchitsch. We built this nation together. He wanted me there at his side to carry it forward."

He rushes to the oak door, swings it open and yells for Kropp. Göring's valet arrives and there follows an exchange of hushed voices. Brauchitsch strains to hear but then Kropp turns and paces down the hallway.

"On your feet, Brauchitsch. I'll not shirk destiny."

A short while later Kropp returns carrying an envelope. He hands it to the Reichsmarschall and then disappears. In this most innocuous of wrappings lies Hitler's decree of 29th June 1941. Göring lifts out the paper and opens it.

Should I have my freedom of action curtailed or be somehow removed, Reichsmarschall Hermann Göring is to be my deputy or my successor in all my offices of State, Party and Army.

Brauchitsch chimes in.

"If you want to be absolutely sure you could send a message to the Führer – eyes only – and double check the protocol, sir."

Göring nods vigorously.

"You get this down Brauchitsch: 'My Führer. Since you are determined to remain at your post in the bunker–'"

"Forgive me, sir, but 'bunker' suggests a hiding place. Do we want to imply that the Supreme Leader has scuttled into hiding?"

"Good point. What about '...remain at your post in the *fortress*?'"

"'The Reich Fortress!'" gushes Brauchitsch.

"Too much. "'Fortress Berlin'."

"Perfect."

"Er...blah, blah, blah 'Fortress Berlin – comma – do you agree that I, as your deputy, in accordance with your letter –'"

"'Decree'?"

"Better, 'Decree of June whatsit, 1941, assume immediately the total leadership of the Reich with complete freedom of action at home and abroad, stop.' That last bit should stick it to Bormann, no equivocation there." A hitch of the belt, a puff of the chest and Göring's getting into his stride.

"Er...new paragraph I think," says Göring "'If by' – when? Eight?"

"Dinner."

"Nine."

Brauchitsch screws up his nose. "Brandy."

"Ten it is. '...by ten p.m. no answer is forthcoming, I shall assume that you have been'....er....need to be delicate here."

"'Been incapacitated'?" offers Brauchitsch.

"He *is* the Führer," counters Göring.

"But flesh and blood, sir."

"Yes, but you know how he gets. I don't want to be the one to remind him of his mortality. What about 'indisposed'? Christ, no. That sounds like he's got the trots."

A heavy sigh and Göring looks out of the window for inspiration. Brauchitsch's mind frantically works through a mental index of appropriate euphemisms that will result in Göring securing his future and not a bullet in the head for both of them. A clap of the hands and he has it.

"'...been deprived of *your freedom of action*.'"

"Brilliant! Inspired. Show me what we have so far." Göring scans over the few lines, his jowls twitching as he scans the text.

"'I will then consider the terms of your... decree... to have come into force and act accordingly.'"

"'For the good of the people?'" Brauchitsch is hitting his stride.

"Oh, lovely. 'For the good of the people'. Oh, 'and the Fatherland.'" Göring adds, not to be outdone by his subordinate. As he reaches the final paragraph he is now swept up in the sense of occasion.

"'You must realize what I feel for you in these most difficult hours of my life, and I am quite unable to find words to express it. God bless you –'" He spins towards Brauchitsch. "Too much?"

"Oh no, sir. Gravity of the moment and all that. Spot on, I'd say."

"'God bless you and grant that...er...angels....' er....Christ, help me here, I'm losing it," he pleads, clicking his fingers for inspiration.

"Angels? Might not be wise to hint at death, sir. What about a reference to you being reunited?"

"Good, good. '– and grant that you may come here after all as soon as possible, stop. Your loyal' – no – 'your *most* loyal Hermann Göring, stop.' Lemme see, lemme see."

Over the course of the next hour, *Landhaus* Göring bristles with anticipation. Typically, the highly confidential information about Göring's ascendency is irresistible gossip and rips through the household like the *foehn* wind: Brauchitsch is dispatched to find the nearest functioning radio, but between the study and the front door he's exchanged a knowing wink and a few words to Kropp, the valet. Kropp scampers to the kitchen where Frieda Zychski is never too busy that she can't skip a few stirs of a steaming broth to lend an ear. Handing the ladle to her assistant, she dashes up the stairs – two at a time – to where her husband Josef is stoking the fire. Thereafter, Josef sees a pal who tells his son, who knows a girl, who couldn't possibly say anything, but does so on the promise of two tickets to the picture house. Frau Emmy Göring is therefore the last to know about her husband's accession to the title of most powerful man in Germany.

Nevertheless, while the occasion brings a sense of nervous expectation to Göring, for Emmy it's the news that she has dreaded ever since her husband told her about the decree almost four years ago. Playing the dutiful wife, she brushes her fringe from her face, smiles and embraces him warmly with congratulation. She tells him that she loves him.

"So what's wrong then?"

"I'm sorry Hermann, I can't help it. It's a poisoned chalice. Everything you've built is in tatters and the Americans will likely be driving up here within days which means that they'll have you in fetters within a week."

"You worry too much."

"You drink too much."

"Tomorrow, I will arrange to meet General Eisenhower. Hitler has tasked me with negotiating the peace and someone's got to salvage something from the jaws of defeat."

"And Eisenhower has agreed to this?"

"Well, not as such – but how can he not?! Man's a tactician, he'll listen to logic," and with a 'Hey presto!' gesture, he's pouring out another generous whisky and popping another 'jewel' for good measure. He can feel Emmy's eyes boring into him.

"Leg's been playing up, darling. Cold weather." Wink. He turns towards the window.

"Come and stand with me." He slips his arm around her waist lovingly. "Do you know something, my love? I think the clouds have lifted. We can see the stars."

He takes her unresponsive hand in his.

* * *

Over seven hundred kilometres away, deep beneath the red marbled halls of the Reichs Chancellery, the Führerbunker stands in eerie silence, a subterranean bulwark against the weight of impending doom. The grey concrete walls pulse with suffocating disquiet and the distant rumble of artillery fire fifty feet above. In every chamber, from the grandeur of the command room to the modest quarters of secretaries and aides, a strained hush hangs in the air. The flickering glow of dim bulbs plays tricks with the shadows, accentuating the distorted reality unfolding around them. Secretaries, once busy transcribing the edicts of power, now huddle together in muted conversations that speak of impending terror. In the command room maps lie still, sprawled on tables. They are adorned with small red pins that depict the relentless advance of the Red Army, as if bearing witness to the disintegration of the dream of a Thousand-Year Reich. Hitler's pugnacious personal secretary, Martin Bormann, moves through the labyrinthine passages, the clattering of his footsteps reverberating like a morose drumbeat.

Gertrude 'Traudl' Junge is sitting at her *Continental* portable typewriter staring forlornly at the keys. The moment she has been dreading has arrived: her 'T' has died, finally broken from its spindly arm. Normally, she would swap it with the one on the *Remington* in the radio room, but that machine lost its 'A' last Friday, so she's reluctant to deprive it of another character. She hears Bormann approaching and customarily busies herself with nothing whatsoever in an attempt to avoid interaction with the man that the ladies in the bunker call 'the Pig'. Bormann appears in the door frame clutching a telegram and points towards the door into the Führer's office.

"Anyone?" he asks brusquely.

She manages a 'No' before returning to sliding metal dividers back and forth. Bormann marches towards the door and straight into the office.

Over the last few months, working only ten feet away from Hitler's office, Junge has inadvertently become something of an amateur expert in psychoacoustics, reading the timbre, pitch and amplitude of conversation within. She sits perfectly still, closes her eyes and listens. The conversation begins as a series of dull murmurs. Bormann is doing most of the talking: his voice is low and modulated, like a running motor. Occasionally she can hear the Führer interrupt, a terse question stabbing into the air in a higher pitch. Bormann responds in the same low murmur. As one minute becomes two, it's clear that Bormann has ratcheted his master up tighter than a tin monkey, and now lets go of the key. Hitler's angry, barking a word here and there. Then Bormann again: low, measured. Hitler speaks again in short bursts of five or six words at a time. Junge knows he must be issuing final orders because with each burst there's a metallic tapping, the sound of the front left table leg rapping on the floor as he drives home each point with a stab of his finger on the desk. The door opens.

"Junge," growls Bormann, "urgent message."

He's leaning over her and smells every inch the overworked bureaucrat; two days too long in the same stuffy room wearing the same strangulating uniform.

"Get this to *Landhaus* Göring without delay," he orders, his fingers splayed over a telegram written in his own hand.

"I've no 'T'," she explains apologetically.

"Tea?"

"'T'. On my typewriter, sir."

"Get it done, Junge. Now."

So she types:

'Decree of June 29, 1941 is rescinded by my special ins ruction. My freedom of ac ion undispu ed. I forbid any move by you in the direc ion indica ed. Adolf Hi ler.'

Emmy and Göring have lingered at the dining table. With supply lines severely hampered, dinner is modest – mostly: pork steaks with boiled potatoes and broccoli accompanied by a vintage Burgundy, an 1895 Corton that Göring's been saving. Though there is much to be discussed, the meal is bereft of conversation, with neither of them quite knowing where to begin. Emmy is doing a fine job of being stoic and playing the ever-supportive spouse. She's terrified about what will become of their six-year-old daughter. Göring meanwhile has important negotiations with the Americans to deliberate. He is giving serious consideration to meeting Eisenhower with an olive branch in one hand and a 1788 *Clos de Griffier* in the other.

*Does Eisenhower even drink?* Clos de Griffier*'s not your standard table fare and it breaks my heart to gift it to a philistine who won't appreciate it, Emmy.*

These and other considerations have passed between them like condiments. Husband and wife are on different trajectories. He'd like nothing more than to kick off their house slippers and play footsie before the fire, but time is precious and tomorrow will see significant changes, so Emmy is politely told to retire. He has an important meeting to conduct.

Ten minutes later, he's in his study with a 'jewel' in one hand and a warming glass of *Clos de Griffier* in the other (all things considered, Eisenhower just doesn't seem like a cognac man). Linnie has been summoned and as soon as she arrives he beckons her to an armchair by the fire.

"You've heard?"

She has.

"Dear, sweet Linnie," he says touching her face. She begins sobbing but immediately chastises herself for doing so.

"Going to make this simple for you, Linnie. One job, just the one. The accounts will likely be seized by the Americans, albeit until I can thrash out a deal about my position in the new, post-war government. I'm saying don't worry. Now, your job. Ready?"

She is.

"The collection. It's my legacy for the German people, you know that don't you?"

She does.

"I've always said that haven't I? Well, it's also my insurance, too. For my girls. The bulk of it is on the way to Altausee, but you have the key – as it were – the Inventory, right? You must get that book to friends. There's a church."

As the light of the fire casts orange shadows over their faces, he tells her of a beautiful church with stunning red onion domes and beautiful stained-glass windows. It floats on mist that hangs over a lake. Find it. Take the Inventory there.

"You'll be quite safe. Once I've established my footing, I'll send word. Meantime, you need to get that book as far away from me as you can. It's dangerous."

"Dangerous?"

"It could haunt me. It's filled with ghosts, you see, Linnie."

There's a curt knock at the door and Brauchitsch makes his way into the study. It takes him a moment for his eyes to adjust to the darkness.

"It seems that we have a spot of trouble, sir," ever the master of understatement.

Göring holds Linnie's hand in his. A moment later she's gone.

In the entrance hall two SS men stand stiffly. They introduce themselves as Officers Bredow and Frank, but Göring immediately dubs them Chinless and Gormless. Chinless steps forward. He's never seen the Reichsmarschall this close and never in silk house slippers and dressing gown.

"Sir," he begins, looking straight above Göring's head and apparently addressing the coat rack. "Orders direct from Berlin. Radiogram from Secretary Bormann, sir."

*There it is. Bormann.*

"We have been instructed to place you under honourable custody, sir," his voice faltering.

Göring flinches. Emmy has arrived at his side and is tying her dressing gown as she floats down the stairs.

"Hermann?"

"Nothing to concern yourself with, my dear," he says breezily, not taking his eyes off his quarry. "I seem to be developing a hearing problem in my old age, young man," he adds, now turning to pick up an ivory shoehorn from the coat rack. He's brandishing it like a mace, slapping it into the palm of his left hand. "Because I could have sworn that you said that you were going to take me into custody. Me. *Leader of the Reich* – as decreed by the Führer himself."

Chinless turns to Gormless for support. Gormless appears to have a little more spark about him.

"Thatsrightsah. Remain confined to quarters until further orders. No contact but extend all the usual comforts. Sah."

What begins in normal volume is, by the time Göring has finished the sentence, screamed at full pitch into the face of Gormless.

"You wearing a jockstrap, sonny? Because you must have a beautiful set of balls on you to speak to me like that!"

Emmy seizes her husband by the arms, playing the voice of reason. She nods to Brauchitsch, who slowly unpeels Göring's fingers from around the shoehorn as the Reichsmarschall bears down on Gormless. Kropp has the presence of mind to dash into the study and fetch the Reichsmarschall's small mother of pearl box. In a flurry of Emmy's blandishments about a terrible mistake, everything being sorted out and damn these faulty communications, Göring is, to the surprise and relief of Chinless and Gormless, ushered to his private room upstairs, popping pills as he goes.

A quarter of an hour later, by candlelight and with terrific urgency, the Reichsmarschall is scrawling a letter to Karl Dönitz, now Commander-in-Chief of the Wehrmacht, Minister of War and President of the Reich. Despondently, he searches for the words that might spare his life and give him hope. He seems to find inspiration in the bottom of his bottle of *Clos de Griffier*.

Are you, Admiral, familiar with the intrigues, dangerous to the security of the state, which Reich Leader Bormann has carried out to eliminate me? All steps taken against me rose out of the request sent by me in all loyalty to the Fuhrer asking whether he wished that his orders concerning his succession should come into force. I think it important for the interest of our people that I should approach Eisenhower as one marshal to another. Moreover, both Great Britain and America have proved through their press and their radio that their attitude toward me is more favourable than towards other political leaders in Germany. I think that at this most difficult hour all should collaborate and that nothing should be neglected which might assure the future of Germany.

Yours,
...in an act of desperation, he almost adds.

# Figure with Janus Head

Inventory of the Art Collection
of
Reichsmarschall Hermann Göring

Collection: Hugo Daniel and Elisabeth Andriesse
Collection, Brussels, Belgium
Artist: Lodewijk van Schoor
Medium: Decorative Arts – Tapestry
Title:        *The winter, scene with a figure with
Janus head*
Measurements: 350 x 365 cm

Note: A Flemish tapestry by van Schoor, in exquisite
condition given its age and size. Certainly late 17th
Century when the artist was at the height of his
powers. Entitled *The winter, scene with a figure with
Janus head*. An unusual variety

of Janiform art. The two-faced god Janus represented the beginning and end of conflicts in classical civilizations. The doors of his temples were open during war and closed during times of peace. An enduring subject in art as a symbol of change and transition, he faces into both the past and the future; frequently worshipped at times of new beginnings.
B.L.

* * *

Pill. Swig. Tilt. Gulp. Repeat.

Göring swallows three 'jewels' in total. He tugs at his collar.

"Christ, Brauchitsch, it's hot in here, isn't it? Open a window, will you?"

Brauchitsch strides towards the study window and levers it open, letting in the Alpine air and the distant sounds of spring. All things considered, the Reichsmarschall is in a cautiously optimistic mood: Hitler is dead. Martin Bormann is missing, presumed dead, and Admiral Dönitz has formerly surrendered to the allied forces. All of which mean that Göring is no longer under honourable custody.

*Time the fickle…something something. Who said that? Damn pills.*

"It's an auspicious day today, Brauchitsch, did you know that? 1824. Beethoven's 9th – his best work to my ear – premiered in Vienna."

"I'm not much of a music lover, I'm afraid, sir," mutters Brauchitsch.

"That's not all. 1919. A draft of the Treaty of Versailles was published for the first time. Know what that is?" It's a rhetorical question. Every soldier – every German – knows what it is. Göring fiddles with the small glass bottle containing his 'jewels'. His eyes stare absently at the bronze of Diana on his desk but his mind is in the past. "That," he continues, "was the day Germany was castrated. The day that everything changed. For us. For Hitler, of course." He shrugs. "And here we are."

"Today is also an auspicious day, sir," ventures Brauchitsch somewhat hopefully.

Goering turns towards him dubiously.

"Think so do you? It's certainly a step into the unknown. What do you think they'll do, tar and feather me? Drag me through the streets, hung, drawn and quartered?"

"You're a German war hero, sir. I'm sure they'll treat you with the dignity and respect that you deserve," offers Brauchitsch. Goering snorts with derision.

*Don't try to placate me, I'm not an infant.*

"They need a prize, don't they?" Göring snaps. Then, more calmy, "That said, it's true that the foreign press have always been kinder to me than the rest of them. Hitler was quite mad in their eyes. Even by '37. Himmler was a sadist. As for Goebbels," he scoffs at the very thought, "a puny cripple and a pervert, to boot. No, you could say I did rather well in the eyes of the foreign press, all things considered. A sort of Falstaff, you might say. I'll take that any day over an anti-semite."

Brauchitsch notices a subtle shift in Göring's demeanour that he puts down to his paracodeine 'jewels' taking effect.

He's no longer loafing morosely around the room. The pill bottle now replaced in the drawer, his hands are rubbing together keenly. Göring nods gently to himself and then rests his behind on the desk, considering new possibilities.

"Might do the trick. Let's just reflect for a moment on what we've discussed. Just to be sure." He folds his arms together decisively. Brauchitsch feels compelled to do the same in a meagre show of complicity in their plan.

"Now, if you can convince them that I have value as a negotiator," says Göring, "then there lies my hope. My future." He turns slightly, reaches behind him and fumbles through a sheaf of papers on the desk. "Stack." He holds a sheet at arm's length, struggling to acclimatise to the abbreviated American military ranks. He reads, "'Brig. Gen.', says here. 'Brig. Gen. Ass' – assistant, obviously – 'Div.' What's 'Div' again?"

"Division, sir, " replies Brauchitsch.

"'Assistant Division Commander'," continues Göring, "'Robert I. Stack'." More fumbling through papers. "I for Ignatius, apparently." His arms drop slightly and a jowl twitches. "Ignatius. That name have a whiff of Jew about it to you, does it Brauchitsch?" asks Göring suspiciously.

"Er no, I don't think so," replies Brauchitsch honestly, but with about 60/40 certainty. *Not great odds given the stakes. Better check.*

"Check will you, Brauchitsch? Makes it a bloody sight more difficult if I'm to do business with a Jew. Need to give myself a fighting chance." He dwells for a moment. "Look what happened to Himmler. Tried to negotiate with the wrong types and they put him on the list of war criminals. Christ only knows where he is now, poor bastard."

Göring is worried not only for himself, but for the welfare of his wife and child. He feels queasy at the very thought. At night, when the demons come, in his torment it's Edda and Emmy that he sees. Then he always imagines those six little corpses. The limp, white bodies under the blankets. He shudders at the thought of the desperation that drove Josef and Magda Goebbels to commit infanticide. They say that Helga even had bruising around her mouth from struggling against the cyanide pill that her mother forced between her thin lips.

*Her own parents.*

"I won't put Edda and Emmy through that, Brauchitsch, I won't." He blinks the demons away and takes a breath.

*P'raps I need another pill?*

"As long as my girls are with me, I can protect them." More slow contemplation. "Things are also less likely to turn ugly with a wife and a six-year-old accompanying me. They're not barbarians are they, not the Yanks. The Bolshies are a different matter." Dark clouds form again and Göring slumps into a leather chair. He drums his fingers on the desk and looks squarely at Brauchitsch. "Now, you tell it back to me, Bernd, just to be sure."

Clearing his throat and shifting his weight from one foot to the other, Brauchitsch begins reciting the scene that they have spent the last three hours agonizing over.

"I go to the division command post…"

"Which one?" demands Göring, like a schoolmaster drilling times tables.

"36th Division of the 7th U.S. Army." Göring nods him on, "And I ask to see the Assistant Division Commander General Stack. I give –"

"*Brigadier* General. Get the rank right, Brauchitsch. Have some respect for heaven's sake. It's all in the details. That's what Himmler forgot. Poor bastard." He flaps his hand, urging his adjutant on.

"*Brigadier* General Robert Stack."

"Right, don't worry about the Ignatius, I don't think he uses it." Another flap of the hand.

" – Stack… and I say I have a letter to give him for the attention of General Eisenhower." Brauchitsch casts a glance across the desk, searching for a glimmer of approval. None is forthcoming from the impassive Reichsmarschall staring at him, so he continues. "When I'm asked about the contents of the letter, I'm to say that it bears the surrender of –"

"No, Brauchitsch, no. We're trying to avoid using 'surrender' at this point in time, remember? It may be semantics but there's a poker game going on. We agreed on 'intent to cooperate', yes? Remember?"

"Sorry…bears the *intent to cooperate* of Commander-in-Chief of the Luftwaffe, Hermann G –"

"*Reichsmarschall. Reichsmarschall.* Dammit man." An impatient flap of the hand.

"Reichsmarschall Hermann Göring, who wishes to inform General Eisenhower of his intention to fully support the allied forces in negotiating peace in Europe." Done. Finished. Sigh of relief.

Göring nods and turns his attention out of the window, following the distant sounds, out beyond the garden and towards the final remnants of snow on the peaks.

*Seasons change. Time melts like snow. 1919. A nation castrated.*

He suddenly yearns to hear Edda's voice echoing somewhere in the house, but the only sound is that of Brauchitsch tidying the papers on the desk.

Göring's mind switches to the immediate future. "That should do it. Might do it," then after a pause, "Christ, I hope it does the job." But Göring doesn't like the odds.

*What if it doesn't?*

*Six little corpses.*

* * *

With a hearty growl from the engine, the sleek Mercedes 200 readies itself for the final sweeping climb up to Schloss Fischorn at Zell-am-See. A right towards the gatehouse but there's no need to stop – no need for formalities for this VIP guest. A wide left turn and the car lurches to a halt with the satisfying sound of gravel crunching under the weight of the car. And Göring. *Der Eisener* – the Iron Man – swings open the door, pivots his considerable mass to the left and grips the sides of the car firmly as he hauls his body out of the driver's seat with a sigh. A moment to steady himself after the exertion and, hands on hips, he breathes in the country air of the Salzach Valley.

*So far so good. I've already done better than poor Himmler. Behave yourself Hermann, you're not out of the woods yet.*

He breathes in the refreshing, crisp air and squints in the sun, admiring the 19th Century architecture. The white stonework glints in the early afternoon sun. Edda squeals and he hears Emmy pacify her. Suddenly remembering his wife, patiently sitting in the front passenger seat, he waves nonchalantly to a somebody anybody nobody of the domestic staff who, catching on, scampers over and releases Frau Göring from the car.

"This is a bit more like it, eh, Emmy?" whispers Göring, mollified at being received into such opulent surroundings. Emmy straightens her dress and makes a few discreet alterations to her hair which has suffered somewhat from Göring's impassioned antics behind the wheel as well as from Edda's frequent pawing throughout the journey.

By this time, the small convoy – *entourage* as Göring might have it in this gay mood – have parked, walked over and are stood expectantly around the Reichsmarschall. It's clear that nobody knows quite what to do next, so Emmy, ever the hostess, gushes rather self-consciously and recites a line she recalls from a Hollywood film.

"Why, it's simply sublime!" she squeals.

Brigadier General Robert I. Stack of 36th Division picks up the repartee.

"Great place, great place." Observing Göring and his wife, it seems that sniffing the Salzbach air is *de rigueur*, so Stack follows suit.

As the company cross the castle's threshold, there is a shared fit of blinking as their eyes adjust to the darkness of the cool interior. Göring is now in his element breathing in an aroma he knows well. It's the smell of furniture polish on oak mingling with the dampness of the stone walls and the mustiness of antique rugs, enormous tapestries lining the walls and leather-bound first editions in a library somewhere in the distance. The scent is more than pleasant to Göring – it's intoxicating. It's the scent of wealth and privilege; it's his beloved Carinhall all over again. With that thought, Göring experiences a pang of melancholy for the old life he's left behind.

His eyes drink in a canvas depicting an Elysian scene and he's reminded of a wood panel that hung on a wall at Carinhall.

*A Wouvermans, wasn't it? No. Jan von Kessel. From the Goudstikker collection.*

His eyes rove from one antique to another, recalling once more the halcyon days when he would shop for must-haves in the *Jeu de Paume*.

"Oh yes, this will do nicely, Brigadier General, very nicely indeed." Göring's about to embark on a monologue he learnt about the life and works of Cranach the Elder, when he suddenly checks himself and remembers where he is. This is not the audience for that.

*Ignatius old bean, let me tell you a story all about looted priceless art at rock bottom prices.*

Göring needs to stay sharp, but he's struggling to adapt to these straitened times.

*Over here an interesting new acquisition, Ignatius: The Sacrifice of Hermann the Humble. School of Eisenhower.*

Emerging from the gloom is a sight that's balm for Göring's troubled mind. Faithful, dependable Kropp stands before him. His back slightly arched, his tummy thrust forward, straining ever so slightly at the buttons of his ivory jacket. Kropp is kitted in familiar attire: white shirt, black tie, pressed black trousers. His shoes have a sheen that reflects the additional effort Kropp has gone to for the occasion. He smiles nervously. He needn't worry, the ebullient Göring strides forward and grabs his arm between his hands. He shakes the limp hand vigorously. A beaming smile, a chuckle.

"Kropp, you old devil! Ha! Wonderful, wonderful." Göring jerks Kropp's hand like a water pump. "Been treating you well, I see," says Göring with a nod at Kropp's stomach and knowing wink. He flicks his head towards Stack. "Yanks been fattening you up, eh? Good man." Then Göring suddenly stiffens.

*Why did I say 'Yanks'? Is that derogatory?*

Stack takes charge.

"Well, we thought you and your wife would appreciate a little help since you're in unfamiliar surroundings," he says warmly.

"Most kind, most kind," mumbles Göring. There follows an awkward pause which Emmy is suddenly anxious to fill.

"Why, it's simply sublime!" she says. Again. This time clapping her palms together. Stack looks slightly askance.

"Er, you're on the second floor. Kropp knows where. He has a small room next to your own and is familiar with er, what's what. You should find the accommodation very comfortable."

There is a momentary pause. No one has yet made it plain to Göring what his status is exactly.

*PoW? Please God no.*

Stack feels obliged to clarify the situation.

"I have spoken with the, er, that is, General Eisenhower." Göring, ever the poker player, betrays no emotion.

"He tells me that you both are here as my guests and that you have complete freedom of movement," explains the Brigadier General. "I hope that makes things a little clearer. My understanding is that the general would like to meet you soon, marshall to marshall, if you follow me. More details on that to follow."

Göring beams. His mind takes flight with fanciful notions.

*Marshall to marshall no less!*

"Well, I'll let you get settled in," says Stack with a clap of the hands. "Kropp and the other staff can manage your luggage. I'll see you on the terrace later for drinks before dinner. Say, seven o'clock?"

Göring can hardly contain his glee. "Pah, well, wonderful. Drinks at seven then! Kropp should have time to press my uniform, hmm Kropp?" he says, casting an expectant eye towards his manservant. A curt nod and Kropp emits a half-whispered "Yessir".

With that, an almost noiseless dance begins, with Kropp making his way into the bright sunlight outside to the car while Göring and Emmy are escorted upstairs by a seemingly mute butler who communicates only through a series of nods coupled with mechanical movements of the hands and arms. Other staff, mainly servicemen and women in army uniform, skuttle to and fro across the hallway.

As they ascend the grandeur of the staircase, the wood groans with each step. Göring is once again admiring the canvases that line the walls, darkened with age. Emmy is in a more contemplative mood, her eyes cast down towards the faded carpet and gleaming stair-rods. At one point she squeezes Edda's hand so tightly that the little girl emits a yelp of discomfort. While Hermann seems to be warming to his new circumstances, Emmy is not entirely convinced. 'This cannot last,' she tells herself. 'We're not the victors, Hermann. As usual, you find comfort in the trappings of wealth. You've drunk too much privilege already today so for Christ's sake sober up.'

With a slight rattle, the mute butler jiggles a brass doorknob and leans in to reveal the Görings' quarters. The room is grand. Four rectangular windows line one wall and look out across the Salzach Valley and the blue waters of the Zeller See. Like the rest of the castle, the furniture is heavy and dark, and its solidity seems to reassure Göring still further as he paces around, running his hand over the desk and across the front of the armoire. In the absence of any luggage to busy herself with, Emmy fidgets with a tassel on her dress and then walks over to the gilt-framed mirror to reapply her rouge. Göring senses that she is ill at ease. He walks over and looks at her in the mirror. He leans in, his hands resting gently on her shoulders. He whispers.

"We're fine, see? Didn't I say? I *told* you. These people are not barbarians, they're not the Bolshies. The Americans want a quiet life and a swift and amicable end to all of this. I'm useful to them. A figurehead. With contacts." He ambles to the window, looking across the lawn to the pine trees and beyond. Beyond the Zeller See and into the distance. "I can see a real opportunity here. You heard Stack, didn't you? 'Complete freedom of movement', that's what he said. You heard him. He said that Eisenhower has given us complete freedom."

" – of movement," adds Emmy.

" – of movement yes, but it's the principle. He's the head of the American armed forces, yes? The government speaks through him." Excited, Göring nimbly steps back over to Emmy who still fusses at herself in the mirror, doing everything and nothing. This time he turns her towards him and looks directly into her eyes. He whispers to her with all the excitement of a child planning an excursion into the scullery for a midnight feast. "I'm one of the few left who can actually help rebuild this country again. I'm a distinguished military officer who has served my country since my teens and I want to continue to serve. Now, if I have the Americans onside – and the signs are good aren't they? Hmm?" He raises his brows, prompting her to agree. "Well then, there's no question that they'll bring the Brits on board, too. The British are civilized people. Adolf always said the same, didn't he? He never wanted war with Britain. A man of my calibre, experience, my artistic tastes. I may even speak in the Houses of Parliament about the future bonds between our two great nations. Help negotiate the peace. Navigate a course to rebuild Germany. The French? Bit more tricky, always were. They'll need some convincing. But you know the French; long as there's something in it for them, they'll come on board. I might need to make a few donations from my collection to various galleries, show some largesse, patron of the arts, we'll see." He's lost in thought, making a mental inventory of some of the larger items from his collection that he might bequeath to a grateful French nation. *The Rodin!* Emmy drags him back to reality.

"And the Russians?" She leaves the question hanging as she fidgets with a pendulous earring. He's caught off guard.

"Well, those bastards would like to watch me hang until my tongue turns purple and I shit myself," he fumes. He immediately sees the look of horror this image has provoked in Emmy, and is quick to pacify her. "My darling, I'm so very sorry. Believe me, it won't come to that. Take a look around you. Look at this place and tell me seriously that we're prisoners! We're sticking with the Americans. There is our salvation. There is our hope. Guests of Eisenhower." He casts his eyes down and runs a hand over his left breast where his medals of office once hung. "You know, Emmy, I might even be asked to be part of the post-war government, one day."

\* \* \*

"Bloody hell! Everybody down, they're firing! Somebody tell the Bolshies it's all over!" Göring bursts out laughing, delighted at his quick witticism that has followed the rapid firing of three champagne corks. While Emmy stifles a sharp intake of breath at her husband's attempt at humour, the American officers on the terrace seem untroubled and laugh along with Uncle Hermann. She's relieved, if bewildered, and makes her way to fetch a drink.

It's shortly after eight o'clock. Göring has perched himself precariously on the balustrade at the edge of the terrace that overlooks the modest grounds of Schloss Fischorn. He's in a dove grey uniform by master Viennese tailor, Tiller. In this light, the uniform looks almost powder blue in colour. The tunic bulges around the middle and strains at his breasts; the light colour accentuates the ever-widening rings of sweat that are clearly discernable under each arm. Göring sports one of his many visor caps; this one in the same cool grey, exhibiting a laurel wreath and an eagle stitched in gold. Similarly, the collar and shoulders of his jacket are covered in gold braid piping. He sweats under the warmth of the evening sun as well as the tightness of his uniform. It's been a little while since he wore it. Only an hour before, he was wiggling his behind from side to side in an attempt to squeeze into his breeches. The sight had reminded Kopp of a childhood summer watching his Aunt Janne exasperatedly trying to get the hang of his hula-hoop.

*The Yanks have shrunk these fucking trousers, Kropp. You be sure to hand wash 'em yourself next time.*

Now, in one hand lolls a champagne flute which the Reichsmarschall gaily swishes from side to side like a stein of beer. He is regaling a small party of American officers with tales of derring-do from his days as a World War One fighter ace. He's decided not to speak of this war, the Reich, the Führer and the rest. Best not to until he's got the measure of things. Despite this, he's aware that the officers – they're bloody young for officer class soldiers, thinks Göring – want the juicy details: 'Was Hitler as small as they say?', 'He looked much taller in Triumph of the Will, right?'

101

Here is Göring the raconteur. His English is just up to the task of spinning a yarn. One moment he's leaning in, dropping his voice and setting a scene of intensity; the next, punctuating what's preceded with a ribald remark that triggers an eruption of guffaws and a light patter of applause from the officers. Here is Göring *mein host*. The wily Reichsmarschall knows what he's doing.

*We're red-blooded males together, boys. I'm jus' like one of you, see?*

He's in full flow and emboldened by the chilled champagne.

"Is there anymore of this, perhaps…?" he wonders, forlornly proffering an empty flute in the direction of a junior officer. Emmy has long since given up watching. She is making polite conversation with General Dahlquist, both of them exchanging pleasantries over cream sodas.

Meanwhile, Göring is patting the forearm of Paul Kubala, the American major assigned as his translator. Göring cosies up, hugger mugger.

"See these, Paul?" He is tapping at one of two embroidered patches on the collar of his uniform. The major leans in, taking a good look at the patch as well as the pale-white fold of cleanly shaven fat that curls over the collar. "Tha's my own design, see? Guess what it is. Bet you can't, hmm?" Without missing a beat, Göring goes on. "My marshall's baton! Ha!" A slap of the thigh, he's delighted with himself. "Designed 'em myself. Designed my baton, too. Beautiful piece of work. Exquisite. Trouble is Paul, they've taken it from me. Can you imagine?" He's crestfallen. His shoulders give a discernable slump.

"You know, Paul, you might perhaps see your way clear to helping me to retrieve my baton, hmm? Purely of sentimental value, see. Would that be beyond your capabilities, helping an old army officer? Lord knows what they think I'm going to do with the baton." He can't help himself, and with a twinkle in his eye he nudges Kubala and says, "Know what they call it, my baton? The boys in the Luftwaffe, they call it the Reichsmarschall's whack stick. Pah!" Another slap of the thigh and Göring's shoulder's shake with mirth.

Kubala smiles awkwardly while a few of the officers, slightly the worse for wear, laugh along with Uncle Hermann who, encouraged by this, promptly puts his right elbow to his crotch, swings his forearm up and makes a fist with his palm.

"Whack stick. Pah! Ha ha."

Brigadier General Stack stands some ten feet from tonight's Hermann Göring Show. He's in prime position for tonight's performance. Stack is momentarily distracted by a flash in the corner of his right eye and he turns to see the gentlemen of the press lapping up the scene unfolding before them. Two or three more flashbulbs let off their distinctive *poc-hiss* sound. The newshounds have caught the scent of opportunity in the air and call out to the participants of tonight's show.

"P'raps we might get a few pictures for our readers? One of you with the major, Mr Göring?" suggests a voice from behind a Speed Graphic camera.

A steely glare and a mock chastising wag of a fat finger, "That's *Reichsmarschall* Göring, young man!" grins *The Fat One*.

Happy to oblige, the assembled officers change position and take up seats on the terrace, the air filled with the noise of metal patio furniture being dragged into position. One officer has the presence of mind to disappear briefly inside the drawing room and then returns with an armchair for the guest of honour. It's not quite adequate to accommodate Göring's meaty rump.

"I wonder if someone might fetch me a cushion?" The Reichsmarschall doesn't need one but, never one to miss an opportunity, feels that there's a more significant point to be made here in front of the crowd. "Ah, *danke shön*," he whispers sweetly. Ensconced in the comfort of the well-sprung chair, he rests his elbows on its arms and settles in for a few questions from some of the more senior officers and newsmen.

*Are you sitting comfortably, children? Then I'll begin.*

103

Major Kubala sits beside Göring, ready to translate as required. The armchair is cosy, if somewhat prosaic for a 19th Century German schloss. It's upholstered in a tired beige tapestry with garden flowers climbing across its high back. It's an armchair for a Norman Rockwell character to knit in, not one in which Hitler's paladin should be holding court. The scene is incongruous. What will readers of the Houston Chronicle make of it all over breakfast in forty-eight hours? Here sits Reichsmarschall Hermann Göring in grandma's chair, thighs apart, stomach bulging and ample bosom clearly visible beneath his sweat-stained tunic. From time to time, the gold eagle brooch on his right breast glints in the light. It's immaculate in its detail, the drooping tail of the bird leading the eye down to the distinctive swastika clutched in its talons. A balmy evening, a swastika, some champagne, flashbulbs and a cheerful chintzy chair.

Stack stands rather pleased with the way in which the evening is progressing. Hands on hips, he's no longer Brigadier General but impresario Phineas T. Barnum overseeing the three ringed circus unfolding before him. He thinks it prudent to remove the empty champagne flute from Göring's foot before the photographs begin again, and does so. Though it seems hard to believe, the event is an opportunity for senior American officers to interrogate the Reichsmarschall in front of members of the press. It's a means of underlining the fact that the 36th Division – or the 'Texas outfit' as the Houston Chronicle has it – have captured Hitler's number two. Who can blame them for wanting to rub it in the noses of the other allied forces?

More soberly, it is hoped that the "interrogation" (such as it is) might garner some insights from the Reichsmarschall that may prove useful for the allies. Some of Göring's responses are surprisingly candid.

"What's he up to?" asks General Dahlquist, leaning conspiratorially towards Brigadier General Stack. The two men stand shoulder-to-shoulder, their arms crossed.

"'Mazing what a few glasses of champagne will elicit, isn't it?" says Stack with a wry smile.

"Can't figure if he's trying to tell the truth and get ahead of the prosecution or curry favour. He's a slippery one," mutters Dahlquist.

Above the hubbub a voice under a peak cap begins.

"Lt. Gen. Hoyt S. Vandenberg, Ninth Air Force. Would you contrast the air forces of the Allies for us, please?"

"Well," responds Göring, slowly bringing his fingertips together and snuggling into the chair. "The Russians are no good, except on undefended targets." There's furious scribbling of pencils on notepads and more than one or two surprised glances exchanged. He continues. "You need only three or four Luftwaffe airplanes to drive off a 20-plane Russian attack. The Americans are superior technically. As for the personnel, the English, German, and American are equal as fighters in the air, in my opinion." A broad smile.

Alexander M. Patch, commanding general of Seventh Army catches Göring's attention with a gesture akin to bidding in an auction.

"Did the Luftwaffe have priority in the distribution of manpower?"

Göring is delighted with the question; it provides the opportunity to reinforce his own importance.

"Yes, the Luftwaffe had first priority and thus had the cream of Germany, the U-boats were second, and the panzers third. Even at the end, the best of German youth went into the Luftwaffe."

The evening draws on in this manner. General "Tooey" Spaatz, commander of US Strategic Air Forces in Europe, wants to know when Göring knew the Luftwaffe had lost control of the skies; wants to understand if Germany could have been defeated by airpower alone; wants to hear all about strategic affairs. Göring's responses are honed, well-considered and refreshingly frank.

*Now where did I put my champagne? I wonder, could someone just…? Ah, danke schön.*

\* \* \*

General Dwight G. Eisenhower can feel the blood rising as he sits at his desk. It's a kind of thumping in his ears. His physician said this wasn't good for him and, God knows, his wife Mamie has berated him about it when he gets what she calls 'the red mist'. Today, no amount of chamomile is going to abate the impending storm on the horizon. This morning, Eisenhower has considerably more to digest than his frugal bowl of muesli. His fingers are gripping the Houston Chronicle so tightly that the ink is smudging.

"Music fan, Stack?"

"Sorry Sir?" says the Brigadier General. He's nonplussed. It's been a long flight and he's barely caught his breath in the whirlwind from plane to car to office of the Supreme Commander of the Allied Expeditionary Force in Europe. He's only met him twice.

"Like music, do you?" asks Eisenhower.

"Well, I, er, I like music plenty, sir."

"'Bout Gene Autry? Gene Autry fan are you, Stack?"

"Well…"

"Because I'm sitting here reading about how a senior ranking officer of the American military," a forefinger jabs at Stack, "quote 'tapped his foot' - tapped his god-damn foot whilst - quote – "Deep in the Heart of Texas' was played on the accordion of Fat Nazi No.2.'" Eisenhower momentarily sets down the paper. "The fucking accordion?!" Wiping a palm across a drop of stray spittle on his chin, he resumes. "The Houston Chronicle is even good enough to inform it's however-many-thousand-readers that an American officer obligingly – quote – 'played the 1941 Gene Autry hit on behalf of the Reichsmarschall because he was unable to get the instrument over his stomach.'" Eisenhower now emits a sort of choke, his eyes skyward. He goes on reading. "The former head of the German airforce was happy to join in by clapping his hands in accompaniment to a wide range of German and American musical favourites.' End quote."

With that, Eisenhower tosses the newspaper sideways, sending it spiraling to the other side of the room.

"I mean you can see the problem I have here, can you not, Stack? One minute we've captured one of the engineers of the Holocaust and the next I'm seeing pictures of him in what looks like my sister-in-law's fucking armchair, playing hits from the singing cowboy. I mean you can see why this might be a problem?"

"If I may, sir, the interrogation did elicit useful information about the enemy that is likely to help with future prosecutions. Göring was sufficiently relaxed that he dropped his guard and spoke with greater candour than he might have otherwise."

"Dropped his guard!? With scenes like they're describing here, I'm surprised he didn't drop his god-damn pants! Sounds like it was a helluva party, Stack."

Before Stack can offer further defense, Eisenhower raises his palm at him and takes a much-needed breath.

"Look, I understand the importance of this man. I also understand what we want from him. And what we need. What I need you to realize is that for right now, he's the biggest prize we've got. Hitler and Goebbels are dead; Himmler is God knows where. Same with Bormann. Speer? Well, his name just doesn't carry the same gravitas as Göring's does." Stack nods. Eisenhower continues, this time more calmly. "We need something tangible to show the parents of the boys who won't make it home, Stack. Sure, the end of the war, that'll be something. But what about when the dust settles? When the ticker tape's been swept from the streets, people are going to want to see justice served. And that means someone's got to pay. And that means Göring, front and centre. Imagine you're a farmer in Wyoming, you don't give a shit about maps, charts, troop maneuvers and logistics. You want someone to show you a bad guy getting served justice. Sure, it's tokenistic but that's how it plays."

Lecture over, Eisenhower stands and walks towards where the scattered pages of the Houston Chronicle lay. He stoops to pick them up, then turns and walks over to Stack. He looks the Brigadier General in the eyes, searching for comprehension.

"Sir," mutters Stack, chastened.

"Henceforth, Reichsmarschall Hermann Göring is to be treated as precisely what he is: an ordinary prisoner of war. On 21st May we're transferring him to 'Ashcan'."

# Pity the sorrows of a poor old man!

Inventory of the Art Collection
of
Reichsmarschall Hermann Göring

Collection: David Weill – Neuilly sur Seine, France
Artist: Théodore Géricault (French, 1791–1824)
Medium: Lithograph
Title: "*Pity the sorrows of a poor old Man! Whose trembling limbs have borne him to your door.*"
Measurements: 31.5 cm x 37.5 cm

Note: A lithograph that Théodore Géricault* produced in 1821 following several months spent in England. The artist was particularly struck by urban poverty and made a series of drawings collectively known as his English Series, largely depicting the lives of the impoverished. The title comes from a poem (likely by Rev. Thomas Ross):

'Pity the sorrows of a poor old man!
Whose trembling limbs have borne him to your door,
Whose days are dwindled to the shortest span,
Oh, give relief, and Heaven will bless your store.'
*NB: The poem's sentiment is perhaps a little too
Bolshevik for National Socialists tastes but the
lithograph itself is not without merit.*

* Géricault is perhaps best known for 1818's *The
Raft of the Medusa.*
B.L.

* * *

His head is pounding. It's keeping time with the drone of the engines. The rattle of the metal interior is unbearable. Every surface seems to vibrate and hum, shaking and juddering as the Douglas C-47 careers through the air. They had originally arranged a Piper L4 but, alas, the Reichsmarschall's weight rendered it unable to take to the skies.

*Oh, for the days of my beloved Albatross D-III.*

This journey is pure hell for a man who recalls the glory days of the reconnaissance flights over the Western Front in his sesquiplane almost thirty years ago. He remembers those sorties as noiseless, though of course they were anything but. He is still enchanted when he calls to mind the feeling of the wind rushing into his face with such ferocity that his breath was literally taken away; great gusts of air would dry his throat, flap at his cheeks. His recollection of the feeble plywood fuselage and the paltry wood, wire, and fabric construction is pure fantasy, eschewing any trace of the very real peril that cost the lives of his comrades on a daily basis.

*The glory of the skies! And now this piece of shit.*

Northwest out of Austria, over Germany and towards Luxembourg. Below him lies the remnants of his beloved homeland. A landscape he helped to shape from the ashes of World War One and the dishonour of the Treaty of Versailles. Ashes to ashes. Thank God he can't see out of the windows of the plane and down to the earth below. He can only imagine the devastation of the medieval towns and cities lying beneath his feet, burned and broken. Dignity lost, splendour beyond reach.

He stares morosely at twelve red suitcases stacked opposite him and strapped in place with thick US Army khaki webbing. They contain some of his most prized possessions; each case is just under a metre in width, scarlet in colour and bears the Göring escutcheon; a small embossed golden shield depicting an uplifted arm sheathed in armour, its fist grasping a steel ring. This golden symbol of strength and prowess now seems to mock him from behind the constraints. Splendour beyond reach. He is reassured to have these items with him but also dismayed as to what the Americans might do with them.

*Who's to say that they won't be plundered by Yanks wanting their piece of war booty. Some of these belongings could garner a pretty price abroad given their provenance – and my name.*

What price for his tunics, neatly pressed, folded and packed by Kropp? Or for his creams, salves and unguents that have all formed part of his daily ablutions and skincare routine for the last decade? Little pieces of history. Some will scorn at the contents of those cases. How journalists will sneer at his Kaloderma Kosmetik range by F Wolff & Son, Karlsruhe. Hermann the Vain. Little more than a fat war criminal who preened in the mirror while the nation burned. A prissy Nero.

A crackle from the intercom followed by a nonchalant "Ready for landing", and Göring is hauled from his reverie and back into the maelstrom of rattling metal, the whine of rotor blades and the incessant vibration of the fuselage as it makes its descent. He's momentarily reminded of the opening scene of Riefenstahl's *Triumph of the Will*, with its beautiful images of Hitler's plane soaring over Nuremberg, above the curving rooftops and steeples before descending through the clouds, hastening Germany's saviour down towards his people.

As the plane lands at Sandweiler Airport in Luxembourg, Göring is jerked so violently that he tries to grab onto something to steady himself, pawing at the inadequate pull-down metal seat beneath him for support. He starts fumbling at the belt to free himself, but this catches the eye of a member of the crew who calls out to him.

"Gotta wait until we come to a stop, sir. Short runway here, only a thousand meters," says the voice from somewhere in the gloom.

Göring strains to see through a small window opposite him. It's grey in Luxembourg and clearly colder and wetter than the weather was this morning in Austria.

*It's a portent.*

"About my escort?" shouts Göring, straining to hear himself above the hammering of the engines. "Is there a car or something? Wasn't my man Kropp going to…" the remark trails off in the damp air. A creeping dread gnaws at Göring's mind.

*General Stack had said 'marshall to marshall'? Might General Eisenhower be on his way?*

As the air crew busy themselves in a flurry of activity, he lets out a cry as the plane judders to a halt. The door suddenly disappears from the side of the plane, and he sees only misty grey outside.

*I've died. I've died without realizing it and this is heaven. St Peter is waiting in judgement.*

But he's not a religious man. He winces as the steps are lowered, the metal squeaking into position. A black man's face pops into view through the aperture where the door was.

*Definitely not heaven.*

"C'mon, sir," shouts the face above the noise, "gonna need to hustle. Transport plane circling overhead needs to land. This way," he yells, beckoning.

Göring's soon on his feet, but he's unable to stand fully upright in the interior of the plane. He lumbers towards the door and any vestige of dignity is extinguished as he lurches towards the opening. The movement of the plane, the cramp in his left foot and the darkness of the interior mean that he stumbles over the lip of the door, slams both shins against the dun metal of the steps and lets out a howl of agony. Instinctively, his hands thrust forward to break the fall, only to embed the heels of both palms into the wet gravel on the ground below. He slumps, his white tunic instantly turning black from the small puddles on the floor. Before him, Göring sees a pair of highly polished black brogues that he would know anywhere. His trusty valet bends down and fusses over his master, helping him to his feet, brushing down his white woollen greatcoat which is smeared with grime. Kropp is furiously dabbing patches of wet filth with his own sleeve.

"Oh God, Kropp," mutters the Reichsmarschall in his ear, "something is very wrong. No American escort, no officer to accompany me. Tell me old friend, have you seen General Eisenhower?" he pleads.

* * *

Of all the things that Colonel William Wilson Quinn, of the Seventh Army is expecting to see that Sunday morning, the prickly scrotal sack of the second most powerful man in the Reich is not one of them. Göring's wrinkled, dangling bag is not a sight that Quinn is going to forget in a hurry. He coolly receives Göring into an anonymous white-bricked anteroom at the airport. It's austere, functional. Impersonal. The most interesting detail in the room is an ornate wrought iron radiator, painted white in slap-dash fashion. In one corner is a curtained medical screen on wheels. The flooring consists of small grimy terracotta tiles. There is a wooden chair to the side but, upon inspection, Göring knows that it would suffice for only one buttock. The room is freezing. Quinn stands bolt upright. To Göring he is every inch the American serviceman: square-jawed, tanned, with heavy eyebrows and a large, angular forehead and slicked-back hair. He smells strongly of cologne that is potent enough to repel the advances of the most ardent would-be paramour. Quinn stands at ease, military style.

"Puddem there," he nods to the small train of lackeys who follow Göring into the room, each one carrying two of the large red suitcases. The men do as they're ordered, stacking the cases in the corner of the room. They retreat, the last one closing the door behind him, and suddenly it's just Quinn and Göring face to face. The Reichsmarschall is clutching a small attaché case that Kropp has given him. He shouldn't be. Prisoners are not permitted to bear personal items. Quinn frowns and nods at the case.

"Whassat?"

"I beg your pardon?" asks Göring.

"What is that?" he repeats, pointing at the case.

"Ah, my most personal items. Just a few…fancies, you might say. My accoutrements," explains Göring. He's perspiring from the stresses and strains of his arrival. He looks vaguely like an obese Dalmatian dog in his white greatcoat blotched all over with grey watery stains. Quinn's face offers not the tiniest hint of interest or empathy.

"*Akyewtreaments* is it?" says Quinn in mock ignorance, playing along. "Les see it," followed by another nod of the head.

For a moment, Göring doesn't move. He is weighing up his options, sizing up the opposition. Deciding to play the long game, he slowly sets the case down in front of him for Quinn to come and retrieve.

*I'm the senior military officer in this room, sonny boy, so I won't actually hand it to you.*

There follows a small but not insignificant battle of wills. Does Quinn order Göring to put it on the table, establishing the captor-prisoner status? Or does he walk over and pick up the case, being the bigger man? Without a word he points at the case and then points to the table, as one might with a pet dog. A Dalmatian perhaps. Göring could follow the order. He *could*. But right now he is the most senior man in the entire German military, and that's got to be worth a little more respect than this, he reasons. Tugging slightly at the fabric of his trousers, he gently plants his rump on the wooden chair and folds his arms.

*Check.*

Quinn takes a slight breath and allows Göring to see the crack of a smirk on his face. He's going for laconic. It's an expression that he remembers from an Alan Ladd Western he saw. Quinn slowly, exaggeratedly steps over and picks up the case. Then, in a move that Göring hadn't anticipated, he flicks open the latch and flips the case upside down, letting the contents cascade onto the floor, the table, over Göring's lap, everywhere.

*Check mate.*

Watching his valuables clatter to the ground, Göring realizes his folly. His most prized possessions treated with such disdain. He cannot help himself, and swipes his marshal's baton from the floor, lightly brushing it down.

"Ah, ah, ah, Mr Göring," berates Quinn, his forefinger gesturing for the Reichsmarschall to hand it over.

*"Mister" Göring?!*

Quinn snatches the baton from him and places it on the desk, out of Göring's reach.

"Genuine?"

"Of course it's genuine!" he scoffs. "It was specially hand-crafted for me in 1940. A present by the Führer himself on receipt of the title Field Marshal General of the Air Force." Göring can't resist, so adds, "The shaft is white elephant ivory, though there's also platinum incorporated into the banding on the end caps. See? It's jewel-encrusted with diamonds." He pauses for a moment, savouring the chance to brag. "Can you guess how many? 640 of them. It cost just short of 23,000 DM then. Now, who can say? Double perhaps – given the, er, provenance associated with it."

*I wonder how long it would take you to earn the equivalent of 23,000 DM, Colonel?*

"Now," says Quinn in a slow drawl, "let's see what else we've got here, Mr Göring. This Celtic?" he asks, holding up a dagger about ten inches in length. He unsheathes the blade and lets it glint in the light of the bulb suspended overhead.

"Sámi, I think. Scandinavian, certainly," replies Göring. "The geometric design and the braided patterning on the hilt and pommel are quite typical of the Sami people, I seem to recall."

"And this?" demands Quinn, holding out the hilt of the knife, "what does this say?"

Göring has no need to read the inscription for he knows it well.

"It says 'From Eric to Hermann'. That would be Count Eric von Rosen of Sweden. My former brother-in-law."

Göring is caught off-guard as the mood suddenly changes. Quinn seems bored now by Göring's baubles, trinkets and paraphernalia. He gathers together the contents of the case with a haste that, to the Reichsmarschall, is indicative of the man's utter lack of appreciation for art and militaria.

*Philistine.*

His arm extends, sweeping the assortment back into the case in one fell swoop. Clapping his hands together, Quinn is ready for business.

"Well, Mr Göring, you'll shortly be moved to Ashcan, but before you d –"

"I'm sorry," interrupts Göring, "Ashcan?" He's perplexed. He's now playing the part of the compliant but bemused elder statesman. "What is this, please, this Ashcan?"

"Central Continental Prisoner of War Enclosure No. 32. Code-named Ashcan. Formerly the Palace Hotel, Mondorf-les-Bains," replies Quinn.

*Palace, no less? Then there is a glimmer of hope.*

"S'what the boys call it. Ashcan. You'll be moving there after processing."

*Processing? So clinical.*

"It's our job to see to the removal of contrabands. Weapons. Also jewellery, cash. Basically, everything that's not toiletries or necessary clothing. Oh, and we need to check for poison."

"Poison?" Mock surprise from the Reichsmarschall.

"Hitler used it. And Braun. Goebbels and his wife, too. We know some of you were supplied with hydrocyanic acid. I've seen modified cartridge cases for the purpose myself. There was a small supply coming out of Sachsenhausen concentration camp under the guidance of Dr Kramer – an inmate, would you believe? A PoW manufacturing suicide devices for the Nazis. Now that's what I call irony. We need to make sure you're clean," Quinn explains.

"Well, you have my word as an officer –" but before he can finish, Quinn has paced over to the door, opened it and, half leaning out, yells "Lieutenant Braddock" into the corridor, but which sounds to Göring more like "Nent Brayk".

A well-built, taciturn black soldier with a crew cut strides into the room. He stands to attention, his boots thundering on the tiled floor. Quinn gently swings the door shut again and resumes his position opposite Göring.

"Braddock here will conduct a body search Mr Göring. Now, ah, military rules dictate that Lt. Braddock needs to be very thorough."

Quinn is rather enjoying himself. He knows what's coming next. He intends to savour the indignity that Göring is about to suffer as Braddock prods, pokes and prizes at Hitler's second in command. Quinn imagines a time six months hence, sitting in the chair of Jim Slocombe's barber shop, telling Jimmy about the time that he spent an hour in the company of Fat Hermann. Göring sits absolutely motionless. His hands are clasped together and placed firmly in his lap. He frowns morosely, his eyebrows like black hoods over his eyes.

"So," continues Quinn, "I'm gonna take a back seat and let Braddock take over. Don't worry Mr Göring, you're in very good hands. We're gonna need you on your feet now." With that, he takes a tooth-pick from his pocket and begins patiently probing his teeth one by one.

*Not fucking likely.*

"I demand to see General Eisenhower. As I was promised," declares Göring very loudly and defiantly. "Nobody, repeat nobody, is to touch me. Not you and certainly," he casts a glare of abject disgust towards Braddock, "not *him*."

The lieutenant is undeterred and makes towards the Reichsmarschall.

"Get your filthy fucking paws off me!" he snarls at Braddock.

The next sound in the room is the massive dull thud of Braddock's clenched right fist slamming, full force, into Göring's gut. It's a tougher hide than Braddock was expecting, but still bends the Reichsmarschall over and sends a sharp stabbing through his stomach and up into his lungs. As Göring hauls his shoulders in a desperate gasp for air, Braddock's clenched left fist isn't far behind and sends Göring onto the floor. Sheer spite sends the heel of Braddock's right boot slamming down onto Göring's left hand which is splayed on the floor. The crunch of bone which accompanies this makes Quinn wince and Göring piss himself. He screams and assumes the foetal position, as best a man of his size can. Braddock stares down at the huge bulk, satisfied that this is what's called compliant.

Over the course of the next ten minutes, Göring is subjected to the most excruciating humilities and ignominies. Within seconds of Braddock hauling him upright, he's unbuckling Göring's belt and unthreading it. The Reichsmarschall stands there, now obliged to clutch his trousers to stop them from slipping. As he grasps the fabric, he's reminded of an evening ten months ago when he was with Hitler in the Reich Chancellery.

*It was an evening in late July, yes, the 23rd. We sat together in the lamplight of the Führer's office. I enjoyed a brandy, Adolf an elderflower water.*

Hitler had survived an attempt on his life by the von Stauffenberg plotters. He ordered the killing of the conspirators of course, but also a show trial of their families. *Yes, that's it. The families.*

*Adolf was showing me the photographs of the family members standing trial for their complicity in the nefarious plot. Roland Friesler, the Hanging Judge - a bastard of the first order, that one. There was Friesler, screaming at the defendants; them standing there in oversized prison uniforms that were so big they had to clutch the trousers to keep them from pooling around their ankles. An expert lesson in humiliation. Like this. Victor's justice.*

Göring is ordered to strip, the pretext being that he might be concealing hydrocyanic acid about his person. He slips off his silk undergarments with his one good hand. Glass vials just over 3cm in length and less than a centimetre in diameter can be easily secreted, Quinn explains as Braddock's hands probe his flesh. It requires all the self-control that Göring can muster not to seize Braddock by the lapels and slap him hard about the face. He is ordered to bend over, his hands resting on his knees. Naked and cold, he stares straight ahead at the paint peeling from the walls.

*How this? I commanded the Luftwaffe, played host to Mussolini and Lindburgh. A man with judgement over life and death and I'm having my ball sack poked by a nigger. And worse.*

The coldness of the room means that every orifice is tight; puckered and dry. Braddock must apply an extra blob of paraffin gel to his fingers so he can insert them more fully through Göring's sphincter.

The moment that finally provokes the Reichsmarschall is when Braddock stands facing him, nose to nose and running his hands over, under and around Göring's armpits and flaccid pectorals. The Reichsmarschall can smell the lieutenant's coffee breath and sweat. Braddock hands feel under a wave of fat, hoisting the belly of the beast and then sliding his fingers in to feel for a small vial or miniature canister secreted in the ample fold. As his fingers probe, Braddock looks Göring squarely in the eyes. Göring contemplates that no one has been this close to him other than Emmy and Edda. In an act of

119

petty defiance, he gives a sharp cough straight into Braddock's eyes. Before he can savour the moment, Braddock counters with a wet cough that hurls a gobbet of green phlegm into Göring's face. He tries to blink but in doing so seems to make the viscid sputum congeal even more between the eyelids. His hands are all over his face trying to wipe away the thick, wet hate that is now dribbling down to his lips.

*Get it out! Get it off!*

He sputters in disbelief and turns, glaring at Quinn, waiting for him to respond, berate Braddock, help the Reichsmarschall. Quinn's reaction is minimalist in the extreme: he merely blinks twice and raises a quizzical eyebrow. He reinserts the toothpick and resumes poking at a stubborn remnant of oatmeal.

Following the body search, one more procedure awaits. Braddock strides over to the corner and slides the medical screen aside, its wheels rattling back and forth as he does so. A physician's beam scale stands ready to read the Reichsmarschall's weight. Göring manages to summon his dignity once more and, taking a breath and arching his back so that he is now at full height, he mounts the scales like an actor taking to the stage. Quinn moves into place behind his left shoulder, peering at the scale. He reads aloud.

"281lbs."

"280," corrects Göring icily. Then, in a flash the old Göring's back, "Don't fret, Colonel, I'm sure we can do better than that. The boys served me delicious lamb cutlets for lunch yesterday washed down with champagne. With hospitality like that, I'll be 281 again before you know it."

"Oh, I'm afraid not, Mr Göring," counters Quinn. "You're to be on a strict diet at Ashcan. Oatmeal and bread for breakfast. Then it's soup, fish and salad for lunch and bean stew for dinner. But speaking of champagne, the men of the 101st Airborne Division enjoyed the bottles in your cellar at Berchtesgarten, I hear. Very generous of you."

*I didn't know that. I'll spare a thought for my favourite Jews; Jeroboam, Rehoboam and Methuselah.*

He sighs.

*All gone. Washed down the gullets of guzzling Yanks. Bastards.*

Then, from somewhere deep within, Göring is reminded of a poem.

'Heaven sends misfortunes – why should we repine?

'Tis Heaven has brought me to the state you see:

And your condition may be soon like mine,' he recites, looking into Quinn's eyes.

"Poetry?" asks the Colonel.

"From a lithograph I own." A blink. "Owned. The title was from a poem. *Pity the sorrows of a poor old Man! Whose trembling limbs have borne him to your door.* By the Reverend Thomas Ross. A man of God," he snorts, wavering slightly in the quietness of the room; naked, staring down at his paunch and the judgement on the scales.

"What now?" he sighs to no one in particular.

*'Marshall to marshall' they told me.*

*Ashes to Ashcan.*

*Dust to dust.*

* * *

If it weren't for Hitler, Mondorf-les-Bains would have remained the rather unremarkable town that it had always been. Sleepy and conventionally pretty, rather than picturesque, the ancient spa settlement is wedged between Luxembourg's borders with France and Germany amid unoffensive countryside. It's the kind of place that motorists putter through, perhaps slowing to remark on the impressive Town Hall or neatly tended park. Having mumbled a few platitudes, they speed up, move on and drive out. It once boasted a fine hotel, the Palace, opened in 1926. But not today. Today the Palace Hotel is subdued behind a stockade of a fifteen foot high electrified barbed wire fence, machine gun posts, floodlights and guard towers. It is under the charge of US Army Colonel Burton C. Andrus, who is at pains to stress that despite all evidence to the contrary, this is *not* a prison. This is an internment centre. Burton is proud of the installation and equally proud that any evidence of luxury, pampering and comfort

121

have been removed, packed, stowed, stored, stacked and locked away. No longer festooned with the fripperies of the gay Thirties, the Palace is under new management and known simply as 'Ashcan', run by the 391st Anti-Aircraft Battalion. Welcome to Camp Ashcan.

Without, the white stucco edifice hints at the halcyon days of yore, when this four-story retreat pulsed with the energy of the well-to-do who came to take the waters. The well-tended lawn, neat flower beds and gently winding path recall better times and cling to the hope that once again they will be well-manicured by attentive groundkeepers. Should such men return from the war. Within, chandeliers, soft furnishings, porcelain, walnut furniture and upholstery are entirely absent. Rather than echoing to the strains of Mozart, played on its grand piano, the Palace now rattles to the cacophony of American servicemen going about their duties and the clatter of tin dinner plates in the restaurant-turned-mess. The hotel is naked and skeletal and that's how Burton likes it. Queen sized beds with mattresses that envelop the discerning guest have been replaced with army-issue cot beds. Once opulent suites now contain flimsy deal tables.

"They've got to be able to collapse easily in case one of the inmates decides to try to hang himself by standing on the table," explained Andrus to a visiting dignitary once. "These ones will crumple right under the weight of anyone heavier than my grandson." A pitiful tin bucket stands sentinel by the door in most of the rooms, and the delicate floral wallpaper is now at odds with the refurbishments that scream at the occupant 'Eat. Sleep. Shit. But that's your lot.'

The figure standing before Andrus this morning is not quite what he was expecting. Moody, hunched and somewhat dejected, the man does not have the bearing of the fearsome paladin of the Reich. Andrus had been expecting Göring the raconteur, all charm and ebullience. Or perhaps Göring the comrade-in-arms, feigning chumminess, toadying up to his new host. Perhaps he expected to encounter Göring the huntsman; a threatening presence, capable of striking with expert precision. Whatever his preconceived ideas, the fat man slouching before him is neither charismatic, good-humoured, threatening or statesman like. It suits him perfectly. If Andrus has been spoiling for a fight, Göring looks as though he's already had the stuffing knocked out of him. Nevertheless, Andrus is a spiteful man and he won't let anything mar the enjoyment of delivering this particularly bitter blow to his newest resident.

"Thank you for coming to see me," says Andrus, not acknowledging the Reichsmarschall, not looking up from his desk. The irony is intentional and surprises Göring, who thought Americans incapable of comprehending irony, let alone conceiving it.

"Did I have a choice? I wish I'd known, I was writing some important correspondence," he says weakly.

"I wanted to inform you of an important development," replies Andrus blandly.

He slides a manilla envelope across the desk towards Göring. For a moment his hand remains splayed on the packet. He looks up for the first time, directly into the eyes of his quarry, removes his hand and then sits back and folds his arms, watching Göring's next move. The Reichsmarschall glances down at the envelope. It's portentous, he knows it. He reaches down, swipes it up and tears open the top, sliding his hand within. It's photographic paper.

*Wasn't expecting that.*

Showing no reaction, he slowly draws the image out of its sleeve and stares at it in dread.

"I received that this morning," explains Andrus coolly. "Died yesterday. The British got sloppy," he hastens to add.

But Göring isn't listening. He's staring at the photograph of Heinrich Himmler. Taken in this way, he looks peculiar, as though he's standing upright but with his eyes closed. The tips of the fingers on Himmler's right hand are clasped in his left. It's an odd position and, with the blanket folded around his middle, the cadaver reminds Göring of an elderly woman sitting in a bath chair by Lake Wannsee.

"I called you here to say two things," explains Andrus, "and neither one is my condolences, by the way. Firstly, I think your friend took the coward's way out. Secondly, I want you to understand that you won't have the opportunity to wriggle through the same door. You *will* face justice, sir. You're going to be put on trial for war crimes and I'll see to it personally that you make it to the courthouse."

Göring is still looking at the photograph. Of all things, he's now thinking about Himmler at Carinhall.

*That time before the war when he came for a hunting weekend at the start the autumn season. Never did get the hang of that rifle. Stupid bastard.*

He finally looks up.

"How did he die?"

"Badly," replies Andrus. "The British had him captive. Apparently, it was during a body search. Himmler wouldn't open his mouth properly and when the officer in charge finally made him do so, he noticed the glint of something under his tongue. He tried to fetch it out but couldn't. All Himmler had to do was chew down on the glass and that was that. The officer shoved two fingers down his throat to make him vomit but it was too late. By the time the Brits knew what was happening it was all over and your Himmler, er, 'fell asleep in Jesus', as you might say."

"Actually, I wouldn't say that at all," replies Göring, sliding the photograph back in the envelope and tossing it lightly onto the desk.

"Think he's gone the other way, eh?" asks Andrus, pointing downwards.

"It's of no consequence to me, I'm not a religious man, Colonel. I believe that it's little more than an emotional crutch for a weak mind." He dwells for a moment, then adds, "Although, they do say that the devil plays all the best tunes, so on reflection I think I might prefer eternal damnation. Besides…" he is about to add something but instead leaves the remark hanging in the air, unspoken. He stares at Andrus for a moment.

*You smug little prick. Himmler outsmarted your lot. And if he can…*

It is six hours later. Lunch has been served. Soup. Fish. Salad, as promised. The exercise routine now finished, the afternoon draws to a close and evening approaches apace. The soldier stands back from a window in a former suite somewhere within Ashcan. He's chosen a wing of the hotel that, for now, remains redundant. He won't be disturbed. He leans against a wall, wearing his army trousers and stripped to his white vest. He's smoking, occasionally flicking ash into a stand topped with an onyx ashtray; all that remains of the former grandeur of the suite. The only light in the room comes from the glow of his cigarette. His focus is fixed on something beyond the window and out across the courtyard into a room directly opposite. He had no intention of coming here to watch each day, had no knowledge that it was even possible until fate intervened. Two days ago, he was bringing boxes of toilet rolls up here for storage and, in a casual glance out of the window, noticed the figure opposite him, unshielded by any curtains (removed, lest he should hang himself no doubt). The soldier realised that where he now stands affords him a perfect view into the quarters of Reichsmarschall Hermann Göring. Whenever he likes he can stand away from the window, retreat into darkness, lean against this wall and simply watch.

On the first day, it was a strange fascination. Him. Here. One of the engineers of Europe's misery. How might he spend his time? What does he read? How does he sleep? Shit? By the third day, he was intrigued by Göring's little rituals. Like the ones he is performing right now. The Reichsmarschall has been permitted a small number of toiletries and he seems to find solace in them. On the third day, while Göring was exercising, the soldier entered his room – the holy of holies – and took a closer look at the products. It was never his intention to touch them, smell them. However, as the minutes went past – three, four, five – he was inexplicably drawn to know each item more intimately, and by extension, know their owner. Before leaving, he dabbed the smallest drop of Kaloderma Gelee onto the back of his hand, massaging it into the skin. Walking back to his own room, he could faintly smell the honey.

"We have shared an intimacy, the Reichsmarschall and I. I have shared his privileged world," he told himself.

Now, the soldier stands once again, cigarette in one hand, ersatz coffee in the other, looking out and watching. The ritual begins. Göring stands facing the window. If the soldier didn't know better, he'd swear that the Reichsmarschall knows he's here. It's like he's performing to him, like those girls in the windows of Montmartre that the guys told him about. Göring wears a dressing gown with a wild flower motif. It felt like parachute silk when the soldier tried it on. Too big of course. Sweet peas, knapweed, clover, gorse and spurge. He remembers their vivid colours all over the garment. As he watches, Göring's hand drops to the region of his belly button and momentarily fiddles at the sash which falls undone. With a shrug of the shoulders, the gown sinks to the floor, leaving Göring perfectly naked before the window. He turns now and from the small table picks up his tub of Kaloderma cleansing cream in its distinctive ivory and lime box. He unscrews the lid and dips two fingers into the ointment, taking an ample dollop, which he daps in small drops over each leg, each arm. Beginning with his left leg raised on the bed, Göring slowly massages the cream into the skin. His body gyrates slightly with the rhythmic movement as he works in the salve. He spends thirty, forty seconds working his thigh, then calf, then ankle, repeating the process with the other leg. The pale white flesh glistens, his varicose veins changing shape as his fingers smooth them back and forth. Then to the arms. He arches his back and stretches out his left arm. He runs his right hand up and down the opposite arm in small circular movements, occasionally dipping his head slightly to smell the cream on his skin. Repeating the same in reverse, he then waggles his arms slightly, drying them in the air. F. Wollf and Son, Karlsruhe. That's what the box said. Perhaps the soldier could go there one day? He could enter the shop and, like a member of Göring's staff must have done – perhaps even

Frau Göring herself – he could walk to the counter and ask for Kaloderma cream, just like the one the Reichsmarschall has. The 150ml pot.

Göring replaces the tub into its box and now reaches for his *haut puder* – powder that guarantees the wearer 'genuine Viennese charm'. Momentarily, Göring turns away and bends down, disappearing from view. He stands again, clutching a powder puff onto which he gives two liberal shakes of the talcum. The soldier takes a long drag on the cigarette and smiles to himself at Göring's artfulness.

"Bet that's contraband. How did you get that in there, you sneaky bastard?"

The Reichsmarschall now dabs the puff lightly over his chest and stomach, up to his armpits and then round to his back. Dropping into a fleeting half-squat, he taps the puff in his crotch then straightens himself. Next comes the small yellow tube of Kaloderma Gelee, his preferred hand care cream. Göring massages it gently all over his hands, fingers, wrists. The soldier tries to call to mind the scent but cannot. He vows that next time he watches he'll have a small amount of the cream of his very own that he can apply at the same time. Together. But that will first involve another trip into the holy of holies.

Finally, Göring tidies the small boxes on the table, before taking up a bottle of Caron's *Pour Un Homme* which, according to an advert the soldier recalls, promises a harmony of lavender and vanilla with a musky amber and cedar wood base. He unscrews the black bottle top and pours two splashes into his palm. He slaps his hand on each cheek, then slides it down and around his neck, finally wiping it over a buttock. Replacing the lid and setting the bottle down, the ritual is over. Göring bends down, once again disappearing to replace the puff in its hidey-hole. Emerging again, he slides each arm into the dressing gown and then ties the sash. He drags the table over to the bed, sits, picks up his pencil and begins writing.

The soldier has butterflies in his stomach. He stubs out the cigarette and leaves.

* * *

Notwithstanding the humiliations that Göring believes he has endured over the last five days, he has rallied.

*Pull yourself together, man. Adolf's gone. Goebbels too. Now Himmler. You're the last of the top brass. You can do better than this. Ignite that Göring fire in your belly.*

He has decided that he needs a timely act of self-preservation and, as if by divine intervention, one has presented itself in a most unusual form.

He first noticed the young man this morning, standing at the threshold. Tall, slim and good looking in an unconventional way. With his wavy black hair and prominently arched eyebrows, it was his narrow eyes that spoke to Göring. Something in their glint suggested that he might be just the man for the job. He stood diffidently in the doorway. As soon as Göring saw him, he swung his legs off the bed and, resting his hands on his thighs, slowly tottered to his feet.

"Lieutenant? It is lieutenant, isn't it? Only, in this light and from this distance I can't quite make out the insignia." Fat Hermann decided to play the part of the kindly but slow uncle, the advancing years taking their toll on his eyes – and – 'Oh, this cold air! Cough, cough.'

"It's Wheelis. Lt. Jack G, sir."

*'Sir.' That's promising.*

Within fifteen minutes, Göring had Wheelis fetching him a mug of ersatz coffee. It was the most disgusting thing he'd tasted since the First World War.

"How kind," he said in breathy gratitude, smiling sweetly. "Mmm, delicious!"

Within thirty minutes Wheelis agreed to retrieve two items for the Reichsmarschall from the storeroom where his cases are kept under lock and key. The first was his hair net, the second a small red cardboard box, five inches in length and embossed with the Göring crest in gold.

It's now 1700hrs on the same day and Lt. Wheelis has returned to Göring's room-cell to find him sitting at the small table writing a letter to Emmy and sketching a picture of a swan on a river for little Edda. As Wheelis enters, Göring sets down the pencil and stands. Wheelis reaches into his coat pocket and draws out a small piece of webbing that Göring does not immediately recognise.

"Ah, my hair net! Thank you Wheelis, thank you. I'm sure it seems rather petty and vain that I ask this of you, hmm? Perhaps. But you know, in my confinement I find that it's the little things that matter. I am not permitted to take pleasure in the company of my darling wife, or my daughter – alas, what torture these days are when I may not feel her soft blonde hair on my cheek. But this!" he says, tossing the hair net onto the bed and now turning his attention to the red box that Wheelis holds before him. He straightens himself and takes a deep breath as Wheelis hands the box over. For a moment, Göring turns away, deliberately hiding the contents but making sure to open it with as much noise as he can, just enough tapping, sliding and rustling to pique the attention of the impressionable young army officer meeting a living legend.

"Look, boy. Look," he says in an excited whisper, now turning around and beckoning Wheelis towards him. "By Professor Herbert Zeitner, my personal goldsmith in Berlin," he says proudly, tapping a solid-gold three-inch collar pin. "Hold it," he urges Wheelis. "Please, hold it." The Lieutenant does so. "Is it not exquisite?"

Wheelis is spellbound. He studies the pin sitting in his palms. Its centre point depicts the head of a golden stag, its antlers encompassing a swastika surrounded by a sunburst. The swastika is comprised of nine rectangular blue sapphires. Riveted below the stag's head is a banner bearing the initials 'D' and 'J'.

"That would be for *Deutsche Jäger*, my beloved hunting organization," Göring explains. The gold crossbar bears eight rectangular emeralds running down either side.

"It's magnificent," gushes Wheelis.

"You have seen it before, perhaps? I wore it in a very famous photograph that was on the cover of your *Time* magazine!"

Göring places a paternal hand on the lieutenant's shoulder.

"Do you know what this pin depicts, boy?" Wheelis shakes his head while Göring gently takes the collar pin and holds it up to the light trickling through the window in the early evening. There is a gentle luminescence outside that Göring has not noticed until now, seeing motes float around and about the pin as he holds it in front of the young man's face like a shimmering talisman.

"The motif goes back to the 8th Century and the legend of Saint Hubertus. He was a widower who had never recovered from the death of his beautiful wife. She died giving birth to their son, Floribert. He was practically inconsolable and the only solace he could find was hunting. Not unlike myself. I lost my first wife, you see. Did you know that?" His eyes move slowly from the pin to Wheelis who is entranced by two merging legends.

"One Good Friday morning, while the faithful gave worship, Hubertus was out hunting. He was in pursuit of a most magnificent stag when suddenly, the beast stopped and turned towards him. There, between its antlers glowed a crucifix. A voice seemed to call to him from out of the forest, saying 'Hubertus, unless thou turnest to the Lord, and leadest an holy life, thou shalt quickly go down into hell.' Well Hubertus fell to his knees and asked the Lord, 'What would you have me do, Lord?'" Göring's voice now mingling fear with veneration. Slowly twirling the gold pin in the light, he continues softly. "The Lord bade Hubertus to seek out Bishop Lambert of Maastricht. He did so and thereafter embarked upon a life of great service and piety." Göring slowly brings the pin down to rest once again in Wheelis' palm.

*Don't stop now, he's taking the bait.*

"From that auspicious day forth, the young Hubertus and Lambert were held together by a most special bond, the one putting his trust in the other."

Göring paces to the window, his words floating on air like motes in the sunlight. Wheelis is looking at the pin. The stag, the sunburst. The swastika. His eyes drink in the sapphires, nine of them. Emeralds, too. Eight. Göring now finishes his tale.

"Hubertus eventually became Bishop of Liège in 708. This is where my family connection comes in. As bishop, he laid down the first principles for ethical hunting and wildlife management. I myself have personally seen to it that as *Reichsjägermeister*, Hubertus' principles remain enshrined across my homeland."

He chuckles.

"Mind you, my goldsmith added his own cheeky embellishment to the legend – d'you see? Where Hubertus saw the Christian crucifix, Zeitner has substituted it with our symbol, the Hakenkreuz – the swastika."

Göring now seizes the moment and leans in a little, just enough so that Wheelis smells a subtle trace of lavender. *Pour Un Homme.*

"You know, boy," he murmurs, "there are so many unscrupulous types here who would dearly love to rob me of the pittance I have left in this world. I wonder," pause for dramatic effect, "do you think you might help an old soldier?"

*Hook.*

"You're the only one I can trust to look after this precious item. And perhaps a few other meagre oddments? Hmm, boy?" he looks expectantly into the lieutenant's eyes.

*Line.*

"And should I –" biting his lip for added gravitas, "should some harm befall me, well then at least I'll know that these trinkets can give my Hubertus and his lovely family" – *that's a nice touch* – "some small

131

pleasure in the future." A gentle bow of the head and a self-conscious, humble smile.

*Sinker.*

# A Bear. Tamed?

Inventory of the Art Collection
of
Reichsmarschall Hermann Göring

Owner: Jacques Goudstikker — Amsterdam,
Netherlands
Collection: J. Goudstikker, Amsterdam
Artist:     Friedrich Pacher (painter) & Hans
Klocker (sculptor)
Medium: Painting, oil on panel & sculpture
Title: *Hail Andrew. Hail Corbinian. Hail Florian. Hail
Magdalena.*
Measurements: 221 x 78 cm (painting); 3.5metres
(including sculpture)

Note:     A Korbinian late Gothic winged altar
dating circa 1480 from the late Gothic church of St.
Korbinian in Unterassling, Tyrol. The paintings are

by the painter Friedrich Pacher, while the statue is one of the earliest autograph works by the sculptor Hans Klocker. In its centre, a sculpture of St Korbinian* in oak by Hans Klocker. The 3.5metre high ensemble remained on the altar until 1660, when a baroque altarpiece was installed in its stead, and this earlier one was moved to elsewhere within the church. (The assembly originally had double-sided wings which disappeared in the 19th Century. More recently, in the late Twenties the predella, containing scenes from the life of the saint, was stolen. Since recovered and reinstalled.)

*See: Legend of St. Korbinian, founder of the diocese of Freising. Bishop Korbinian embarked on a pilgrimage to Rome, encountering an enormous and terrifying bear. The bear mauled a beast of burden belonging to Korbinian, but the bishop – channeling the power of the Lord – was able to tame the animal. As a punishment, he then strapped his burden to the creature and led him to the Holy See.
B.L.

\* \* \*

"You him?" he says, opening the door three inches, one eye peering out.

"Yes, I'm him." Then, "I *think* I'm him."

"You're the fella? The head doctor?" the eye asks more insistently.

"The psychiatrist. Lt. Col. Douglas Kelley. You're Colonel Andrus?"

"Come in." One eye becomes two, then a whole face as Andrus swings the door open. He slaps a hand on Kelley's shoulder, part 'welcome aboard', part 'get the fuck in here quick,' and slams the door behind them.

Conspicuously, in the centre of the room stand twelve suitcases. They are stacked in four columns of three. Each one is of high-quality red leather; each bears an embossed gold crest in its centre. Each one also has a luggage label tied to the handle with a number written in thick black ink.

"Gotta be circumspect. Fact of the matter is that we've had some theft," explains Andrus."

"Theft?"

"Not sure how or when but a few items are missing."

"Missing from…?"

"Fat Hermann. This is all Fat Hermann's stuff," Andrus says waving a hand dismissively at the cases that almost fill the meagre storeroom. "And I don't want whispers and finger pointing to begin. I know how things like this can fester. Don't need suspicion among my ranks."

"What is all this?"

"Fat Hermann's booty. Should see this stuff. He's got gold Luftwaffe badges with diamonds; gotta traveling clock by Movado; brought five silver pill boxes with him, too. He's got diamond rings, ruby rings, emerald rings, every kind of god damn ring going. Semi-precious buttons – one of these cases is chock-full of semi-precious buttons," says Andrus giving one case a kick. "Brought his Iron Cross 1st Class with him, plus three or four wrist watches as well as lapis lazuli cuff links. And to top it all – get this – somewhere in here there's a gold cigarette case, inlaid with amethyst and monogrammed by Prince Paul of Yugoslavia!"

"And some of the items have…"

"It looks as though we've got at least one light fingered soldier in the party," he says under his breath. "You can imagine. Some of these boys are a long way from home, not much money in the bank and mouths to feed. Well, they see a pair of gold cufflinks and think 'Well why not? He likely stole 'em, why not me?' Least I hope that's what it is."

"What do you mean?"

"I mean, I'd rather have a soldier who made a dumb decision than a – God help me – fan.'

"A fan?"

"Someone who actually likes the guy. Admires him, even. See, Fat Hermann's a manipulative SOB. Why, he'd run rings around most of these boys if he set his mind to it. I can imagine him getting them into all sorts of trouble. Kinda 'You scratch my back an' I'll spruce up your tableware with a solid gold tureen.' Geddit?"

"What exactly is missing?"

"Hair net, gold collar pin with swastika and a watch."

"A hair net?"

"Don't ask," says Andrus rolling his eyes. "With the war over, this stuff would be quite a treasure for the folks back home. And worth a fortune, what with Fat Hermann's infamy."

Kelley looks at each of the cases. He can only imagine the eccentric, decadent treasures that each one holds. He ponders the fact that their contents would likely reveal a great deal about their owner. A mine of riches for a psychiatrist like Kelley.

"That's not the reason I asked to meet you here," says Andrus. "As a medical man, there's something you need to see."

Andrus then slides out suitcase number four. He lifts it, straining in the process. The latches click simultaneously, and suddenly a tidal wave of small white capsules pours out, cascading onto the tiled floor, rattling like hailstones as they spill out and bounce around. Kelley looks down at his feet. He's standing in a sea of pills, thousands of them.

"Good God, are these Göring's?"

"Absolutely they're his. He arrived here three months ago with two suitcases full of them. If I didn't know better, I'd have thought the guy was a drug salesman. It's paracodeine. Know it?"

Kelley nods. "I'm surprised to see it though because this stuff's in extremely short supply."

"Ha, no wonder!" scoffs Andrus. "They tell me that this is the whole German stock of the stuff – and since paracodeine isn't produced outside Germany, you're looking at the world's entire supply. There are 20,000 pills between the two cases, Dr Kelley."

"I read his medical notes so I know something of his addiction."

"Well, I wish you medics had told me a bit more about it before he arrived. What do you know, exactly?"

"That his addiction dates back well over twenty years," explains Kelley. "It finds its roots in the attempted coup at the Bürgerbräukeller Beer Hall in '23. When the violence erupted, Göring was at the head of the mob and took a bullet. Accounts differ. Some say he was shot in the thigh, others the groin and one suggested it was in the stomach. Anyway, a local furniture shop owner who was, er, Jewish by the way, likely saved his life. Ironically. This guy dragged him into the shop where his wife treated the wound as best she could. From there he was smuggled to the clinic of a Nazi sympathizer who did a patch-up job. Then, some days later he and his wife slipped the border into Austria where he was finally able to receive proper treatment at Innsbruck Hospital. Apparently, the wound was festering and he was in unimaginable pain when he was seen by the doctors. At the end of December he was discharged, but by then he was addicted to morphine. The report I saw claimed that his addiction was accompanied by the massive weight gain which has come to, well, sort of define him. No trace of the handsome, athletic flying ace of the First World War."

"Fat Hermann."

"Fat Hermann," he says, nodding. "Göring was injecting himself with morphine on a daily basis and by 1925 he'd developed the worst kind of symptoms. He was lethargic, erratic in his behaviour and was prone to violent outbursts. In fact, while under hospital observation, he attacked a nurse so violently that he was committed to the Långbro Institute of Nervous Diseases in Sweden. He was confined to a padded cell and forced to wear a straitjacket."

"Jesus," says Andrus slowly. "And this nut job became the second most powerful man in Germany. That figures."

"Years later even Hitler's personal physician, a Dr Morell, observed that Göring was a slave to his habit. Interestingly, the doctor noticed how he would be slumped in a chair and would then get up and leave the room with no explanation. He'd come back a few minutes later seemingly revived. Morell was convinced that Göring was dosing himself up whenever he felt his opium count had dropped."

"Well, I can tell you that when he got here, he was a simpering slob weighing in at 280lbs. Looked like absolute shit. His hands were shaking and he was sweating like a bishop in a whore-house. He was popping over a hundred and sixty of those pills. Daily. He told Miller – that's Captain Miller, our prison surgeon – told Miller that he'd had a series of heart attacks. I dunno myself. Like I say, he's a slippery devil. Couldda been vying for a sympathy vote. Either way, it's true that he was in bad shape. However," Andrus continues, hitching up his belt and adjusting his tie, "I take pride in the fact that I run a tight ship and I'm not about to tolerate a junkie in my camp. I told Miller to reduce his dosage of the stuff pronto."

"Well, the good news is that paracodeine is about one-fifth as strong as morphine. But on a daily dose of that scale....well, one needs to be cautious. Opioid withdrawal symptoms are nasty. Mood swings, insomnia, tachycardia, hypertension, nausea. A sudden withdrawal can have catastrophic consequences. And given his history of violence..." he doesn't bother finish the sentence.

Andrus and Kelley look down gravely at the sea of pills. They're both thinking the same thing.

'160 daily. 22,000. The world's entire supply.'

Ten minutes later Colonel Andrus is clip-clopping down an echoing tiled corridor with Dr Kelley a step behind him. They're somewhere in the belly of the former Palace Hotel. Andrus comes to a stop outside a door with a large opaque glass pane bearing the words 'Palace Hotel Manager'.

Like the rest of the hotel, the office is a shadow of its former self. As Andrus rifles through a dozen buff-coloured files stacked on a characterless heavy-duty steel shelf, Kelley sits, taking in the surroundings. The net curtains in the window have a gloomy, nicotine hue. Opposite Kelley stands a limp, sickly-looking plant clinging to life on the windowsill. Andrus' pedestal desk is smaller than befits his rank; it's functional and topped with a leather writing pad that's blotched with ink and faint circular cup stains to one side. 'A right hander,' observes Kelley.

"Here it is." Andrus loosens his tie and sits behind the desk, sorting through several sheets of foolscap paper within a bulging file. "Forewarned, forearmed."

"Don't worry, Colonel, I'm used to dealing with challenging patients."

"Not like this," Andrus says gravely. "Göring's a dark horse. Do you know, I've watched him every day for the last three months and I can't read him any better today than I did when he arrived. He's like a shark. Wouldn't like to play poker with the guy."

"It sounds like he's made quite an impression on you."

"Don't take my word for it," he says, drumming his fingers on the file. "Do you want to know his earliest memory?" Andrus looks down at a piece of paper, squinting. "Quote – 'bashing my mother in the face with both fists when she came to embrace me after a prolonged absence.' He was three years old." Andrus places a hand lightly on the

139

file. "This here contains some of the case notes from Gustave Gilbert. Another head doctor. PhD from Columbia."

Andrus leans back in the chair. He slides a pair of metal rimmed spectacles out of his top pocket and, perching them on his nose, flicks through the pages picking out morsels to feed to Kelley.

"Did you know that as an adolescent, Göring had some kind of vivid fantasy life – says so right here – and he explained to Gilbert that somehow reality and fantasy would get kinda blurred. Didn't know the one from the other. He used to have powerful visions of castles coming alive, medieval knights on horseback, Roman chariots crashing through the landscapes." He shakes his head and lets out a snort of disbelief.

"Hmm," counters Kelley, "but – forgive me – you're focussing on the more lurid details that play into the narrative established by the allied forces, of some kind of crazed, drug-fuelled lunatic, little more than a millionaire fantasist."

"S'what it says here, young man," says Andrus waving the file at Kelley. "Don't take my word for it, Gilbert's done his homework."

Kelley presses on.

"Did you know that in 1918 he was awarded the highest military award that the German state can bestow? *Pour Le Mérite*. And not for one isolated moment of bravery," Kelley adds becoming more animated, "but for continuous courage in action. He won *twenty-two* dogfights."

"Course I know! That piece of shit medal's in my storeroom, together with his solid gold soap dish and a diamond encrusted nail file!"

Both men take a breath. Andrus leans in.

"You sure you're not a fan, Kelley?" his eyes narrowing. "Do you realize I've had months of shrinks seeking permission to come and meet our guests here. Seems everyone wants a piece of the Nazi top brass. One fella sat in that chair where you are sitting, right now, and asked me quite seriously if he thought the American government would agree to him dissecting their brain tissue after execution with a shot in the chest. So, Dr Kelley, I'd like to hear from the horse's mouth what it is you have planned for my most infamous guest.'

The answer comes quickly. It ought to, because it's one that Kelley has asked himself twenty times in the last two weeks since receiving his orders.

"The signs of a flaw."

"What does that mean?"

"I want to know if there's a common flaw in the likes of Göring. A flaw that resulted in his willingness to commit some of the most evil acts in human history. Do people like Göring share a mental disorder or is there such a thing as, for want of a better phrase, a 'Nazi personality'?"

"A fruit cake, every one of 'em!" snaps Andrus. Not quite sure what to do in the face of this erudite evaluation, Kelley manages a blink.

"I am well aware of what you – we – are dealing with, Colonel Andrus. On the one hand we have Fat Hermann, a drug-addicted, violent, ruthless, grasping fantasist. On the other, we have a brilliant, brave, shrewd military strategist. He's highly intelligent and has a capacity for cold-blooded pragmatism when required."

Andrus sets the thick file down on the desk between them. Kelley looks at the bulging pages, full of portent.

"Well Dr Kelley, it's about time you met the famous Reichsmarschall."

Kelley nods and stands.

"And remember," Andrus adds, "Göring scored a 138 on the Wechsler-Bellevue Test. Most people get –"

"Between 90 and 109, I know."

"Right. So you'll also know that it ranks him in the top category, and makes him just about the most intelligent man in the building. So watch your back."

Before meeting Göring, Kelley manages a quick shower. As the hot needles of water pound his shoulders, he reflects on what he's learnt about the Reichsmarschall from the medical records. As he glugs a lukewarm coffee (disgusting) and chews down a salami sandwich (mediocre) he considers the few additional lurid details he's gleaned from Andrus. The rest is in the file. He'll read it later.

He then stands in front of the steamy bathroom mirror combing his hair and wondering why he has the same querulous stomach that he did when he took his medical finals.

Three minutes later he's walking along a carpeted corridor towards Göring's room, accompanied by a private soldier. They draw up outside an innocuous door and the private jerks his thumb, as though hitching a ride.

"This'll be the one, sir." He offers a half-hearted salute and departs.

Another soldier, one that seems a little more conscientious, is standing guard.

"May I?" asks Kelley, and without waiting for an answer, his thumb slides the teardrop-shaped metal cover on the peekhole an inch to the left, and he peers inside. In the concave of the miniature glass, Göring's girth looks even more pronounced. He's slumped on the bed leafing casually through a magazine. Deciding that this is no time for faintheartedness, Kelley knocks firmly and enters directly.

"Reichsmarschall Göring?" he says brightly. It's a rhetorical question.

"Who are you?" asks Göring with total indifference, shooting a cursory glance over the magazine.

"The name's Douglas Kelley. I'm a military psychiatrist. I've been assigned."

"To me?" he says with interest, lowering the magazine slightly and peering over.

"To Ashcan."

The magazine rises, the face hidden.

"I wondered if I might speak with you."

"What is it that you think you're doing now?"

Kelley doesn't move. Göring shrugs and hauls himself up.

"Well, *I'm* sitting here." He gives a little bounce on the bed, tossing the magazine aside. "You can either stand or get your own chair. Up to you."

Kelley leaves the room for a moment, returning with a wooden stool. As if to emphasize the disparity, Göring stretches and reclines languidly on the bed as though it were his mustard chaise longue at Mauterndorf. The bed lets out a prolonged squeak. Unlike the chaise longue.

"C'mon then. I see you have your file."

Kelley is clutching a trove of bulging papers; bundles of foolscap sheets, manilla envelopes and green dividers, all wrapped in a rubber band. It's all the medical records that the allies have gathered on Göring: a pre-existing medical file on the Reichsmarschall, Gustave Gilbert's psychological profile, as well as Captain Miller's daily medical records from Ashcan.

"I hope you've got plenty of pencils as well," continues Göring. "Shall I unburden myself of the woes of my tormented childhood? I was never loved, you see! Mother never let me have a train set. Boo hoo. Blah, blah. How am I doing so far, you getting all this, doctor?"

"You have a train set now though, don't you, Reichsmarschall? Two in fact."

*Touché. You smug little prick.*

"You're absolutely right. I do indeed. The Duke of Windsor said it was magnificent. That was the actual word he used, magnificent."

"You enjoy trains?"

"Trains and toys. I enjoy toys. My attic room above Carinhall contained a Marklin O and I Gauge railway set. The thing was so vast that it covered 240 square metres. Specially made. Rheingold livery, 1930s Super-Modelle locomotives all specially designed in I Gauge. I once showed it to Herbert Hoover, too. My enduring memory is that he bashed his head on the attic ceiling and the staff had a devil of a job getting the blood out of the post office."

"The post office?"

"At Schmilka. The Schmilka post office. On the train set. As he leant over the gash – you know how head wounds bleed – was dripping all over the miniature village."

Kelley scribbles a few thoughts down on the pad. This is his custom, but if his year as a fully-fledged psychiatrist has taught him anything, it's that most people baulk at the idea of being scrutinized like a lab rat. Most people. So it's disarming when Göring proclaims loudly,

"I really do hope you're getting all of this down, Dr Kelley because I'm not in the habit of repeating myself and there's going to be an absolute gold mine here. Perhaps you don't realize how important your work will be, but in fifty or sixty years there'll be statues of Hermann Göring all over Germany. Little statues maybe, but one in every German house nonetheless. I could make you famous. Rich."

Kelley stops writing and looks up. He's waiting for a glimmer of irony in Göring's face. When none is forthcoming, he presses on.

"Well I'll, er, certainly try to be as comprehensive as I can. What about other toys?"

"Well games, really. War games I've always enjoyed very much. I used to re-enact the siege of Veldenstein with my lead figures."

"Would you like to play a game now, Reichsm –"

"Oh, Hermann, Hermann, please," he insists flapping a hand airily, cordiality personified. Perhaps he's glad of some intelligent company or perhaps he really does see Kelley's work as future posterity. He stops. "What's that? A game you say?"

"A game. Well, it's really a test."

If Göring was charmed by the idea of a game, he's positively delighted by the thought of a test.

"Pray tell."

"It's called a memory span test," explains Kelley as he begins organizing his papers, slowly becoming aware that Göring is watching him more intently than before. Kelley stands and starts to clear a few toiletries from the small table.

"May I?" he asks.

"By all means."

As he drags the table to the centre of the room, Kelley continues his explanation.

"Now, although the origins of memory span can be found in the work of Gottfried Leibniz, it was the 19th Century psychologist Herman Ebbinghaus who was the first cognitive scientist to develop how span might be employed to investigate the human memory and our capacity for learning."

Kelley has now set his bundle of papers down on the floor next to his stool. On the desk before him he has a small pile of cards, his pad and a pencil.

"Here's how it works." He shuffles a little on the stool and swallows hard. "I'm going to show you a series of random numbers and letters," he explains, laying a palm on the small pile of cards. "I'll read each one aloud at a rate of one per second."

Göring is riveted.

"Quite fast then," he nods eagerly. His furrowed eyebrows suggest to the doctor that success for Göring is a matter of pride.

'What will happen if he flunks it?' wonders Kelley, before remembering the words of Andrus: 'He violently attacked a nurse who refused to give him morphine.' He casts the thought from his mind and continues.

"I'll read two to three numbers at a time. At the end of a sequence, I'll ask you to recall the items in order. I'll increase the amount of letters and numbers until you start to commit regular errors. Okay? Understand?"

"Excellent!" Göring is rubbing his hands together, the bed springs letting out little squeals of delight as he bounces up and down impatiently.

The test begins.

Kelley has a well-practised system of sliding each card neatly from the pile, turning it over, holding it up and then announcing the digit or letter. His voice is clear and focused. After each sequence is shown,

Göring repeats it back flawlessly. His eyes are in a fixed glare, ignoring Kelley and focusing entirely on each card. After several minutes, and two mistakes, Kelley lays down a final card and relaxes into his usual voice.

"Really, very good Hermann. Bravo."

"Again! More!" barks Göring. "I was distracted on that last one by the tea trolley in the corridor. Come on, we go again."

Kelley is cautious but sees no reason why he shouldn't give Göring another sequence.

"Tell you what, let's try the backward digit span test. It's basically the same, except the object is to recall the digits in reverse order."

Göring is giddy. He slaps his hands together; another bounce, another squeak.

"Yes, yes. Come on. Wait! Let me just –" and he reaches for a small paper cup that sits on the windowsill. With every ounce of concentration, he slowly sips his water, as though in doing so he is imbibing some magic elixir that will enhance his powers. He slams the cup down, empty. "I'm ready." He wipes his lips, slaps his hands on his lap and then moves his head in, resuming the same position as before, his eyebrows furrowed.

The doctor begins.

"9, 5, 2."

Göring fires off the sequence like a machinegun '*nighfightoo*'.

The game continues for another minute. Two. And a half. Almost three minutes.

"Ah, well done, Hermann! I'm really most impressed."

"*No*! I was doing so well! One more. One more go!"

Kelley's thinking again about a Swedish nurse on a gurney with a broken jaw and a bloodied nose. Nevertheless, he stands firm.

"I'm sorry, Hermann. I have a meeting to go to I'm afraid."

"What meeting!? Surely it can wait another few minutes."

But Kelley has already collected the cards and replaced them in the folder. He places his pad on top and slips the pencil into the folder, snapping an elastic band around the bundle. He drags the table back to where he found it while Göring continues to whine petulantly.

Kelley now sets the toiletries back in place on the table and suddenly Göring notices that each item has been replaced in exactly the same place that it held before. Impressed by Kelley's feat of memory precision, he subsides into quietness.

"You will visit again? When will you come?" he asks.

"We'll see."

Thus, Kelley has established a small but significant boundary between them. He nods to Göring with a polite rather than friendly smile, then turns and leaves. Before he can knock for the door to be opened, it swings back to reveal a smartly dressed lieutenant with wavy black hair.

"Help you with something there?" asks the soldier, shutting the door behind Kelley and eyeing the case file in Kelley's arms.

"Er, actually yes. Could you take these to my quarters? I have an appointment with Colonel Andrus. It's Dr –"

"Dr Kelley. Yes, I know. Happy to help, sir," the soldier says, hugging the bundle of papers to his chest.

"And you're Lieutenant…?"

"Wheelis, sir. Jack Wheelis."

Kelley turns left and heads towards reception while Wheelis walks in the opposite direction and towards Kelley's room.

He decides to make a stop along the way.

* * *

Kelley slides the peekhole cover to one side with a squeak. Expecting to see Göring either napping or reading, as is his custom at this time of day, he's surprised to see him standing in the centre of the room with his back to the door. He's speaking to someone but, given Göring's bulk, it's difficult to see exactly who. His voice is low, soothing.

Kelley opens the door. Göring takes a sidestep towards the bed and continues facing away from the door. There, standing before Kelley is Lt. Wheelis.

"Morning, sir," says Wheelis with a curt salute.

Kelley looks from Wheelis to Göring. Wheelis says nothing but walks past the doctor and out of the room, closing the door behind him. Göring turns around. He's holding a tub of hand cream.

"I wonder," Göring begins melodically, "if you've ever had occasion to visit Karlsruhe, doctor?"

"I don't think so, no."

"Well just off the market square you'll find the most exquisite emporium called F. Wolff & Son. They used to supply all my toiletries. I do hope it's survived. They say that 12,000 tons of explosives fell on the city. A terrible tragedy."

'Entirely of your own making,' Kelley wants to say but doesn't, not wishing to bite the hand that's currently feeding him content for his article for the *American Journal of Psychiatry*.

Göring now sets the cream down on his table, turns and smiles at Kelley expectantly.

"Well?"

"Let's talk about Judith," says the doctor.

Goring's interest is piqued. He tilts his head.

"Judith? Don't think I know a Judith." Unable to resit a barb he adds, "Jewess, no doubt."

"Definitely a Jewess, yes. You sure you don't know her because I understood she was quite sought-after. In fact, I was under the impression that you prized her for yourself at one time."

With a silent chime, the penny drops and Göring smiles.

"*Judith*. Yes. Not my type, alas, in life – but in *art*, well that's another story. Why do you want to talk about her?"

Suddenly the conversation catches fire and Kelley sits on the chair that has become customary for their conversations, usually set in place beforehand by Lieutenant Wheelis. Kelley has the now ubiquitous buff

148

folder on his lap together with his pad and pencil tucked under the elastic band. The notepad is shorn of its pages which now thicken the burgeoning folder with Kelley's reflections. From within the file, he slides a black and white photograph which he hands to Göring. Judith.

"I'm right in thinking that when you first encountered her she was – how can I put this? – in the arms of another. You coveted her, correct?"

"Most emphatically *incorrect*," counters Göring.

"Jacques Goudstikker," suggests Kelley.

"Never saw. Never met. Died on a boat to England if I remember well. May 1940. An avid collector, but was no more to me than a name in a ledger somewhere. You'd have to speak to Walter Hofer or Bruno Lohse."

"Hofer. It was Hofer who introduced you to Judith in 1940."

"If you say so. I'm sure you're right," then just for good measure he adds, "you do have three degrees, doctor."

"'Now is the time to recover your heritage'," Kelley closes his eyes and continues "'and to further my plans to crush the enemies arrayed against us.'"

Göring is frustrated by his inability to follow the direction of Kelley's gameplay.

"Hmm? What?"

"That's what she said. It's Judith's prayer to the Almighty. The Book of Judith, Chapter Thirteen, verses four to five. Judith prays to God before she slays Holofernes. I thought the story would be familiar to you, Hermann."

Goering feigns exhaustion, rubbing his face with his hand and sighing.

"I have little interest in Jewish literature."

"Yet you paid handsomely for a painting depicting a Jewish femme fatale beheading her lover."

"As to whether I paid handsomely for it, you surely know that this painting was but one of a wider collection. Hofer got a job lot from

Goustikker, some of which were absorbed into the Goring collection while others were…not. Furthermore, her Jewishness *per se* is of no consequence. I was far more interested in the painting's aesthetic qualities as a Cranach."

"You seem to have a passion for Cranach."

"The Elder, yes. I must say, doctor, I'm somewhat surprised by your sudden interest in art. While I'm thrilled at the prospect of discussing my collection with you, I suspect that your superiors in the military may be of the conviction that there are more pressing matters at hand. Should you wish to talk about my collection of Persian rugs as well, I'd be only to happy to oblige."

"I have free reign, a blank cheque as they say. *Carte blanche.* According to my superiors I can discuss whatever I want."

Goring flashes his teeth. Like a shark.

"Whatever *I* want, I rather think," parries Göring. "However, luckily for you doctor, today I am in the vein to speak about all things art and share with you something of my collection that I built for the German people."

"Very magnanimous."

"To speak, or the collection?"

"Both. Let's talk about decapitation." This immediately provokes a guffaw from the Reichsmarschall.

"Good God! What's got into you today?"

"Judith. Tell me about the painting."

"What would you like to know?" he asks, delving deeply into his mental inventory. Less reliant on paracodeine, Göring has reclaimed the power to recall every item lining the walls of Carinhall; every oil on canvas, oil on wood, every watercolour, lithograph and tapestry. "16th Century, oil on wood," he remembers.

"I was thinking more about the subject matter. What drew you to it, given that you're not religious and your views on Judaism are – fervent shall we say."

"Objection! Now, now, doctor, you automatically adopt the position that because I am a high-ranking National Socialist it follows I must be a fervent anti-semite. In point of fact, my views on this matter have always been unambiguous. The issue of European Jewry was, as far as I was concerned, a means to an end. When it comes to the Cranach, its Jewish subject matter is utterly redundant. Tell me doctor, do you know the story of Judith and Holofernes?"

"I didn't. I do now."

"And what did your research reveal?"

"That Holofernes was an Assyrian general whose army had besieged the city of Bethulia where the widow Judith lived. Judith was filled with the power of the Holy Spirit. She went to see Holofernes – dressed to kill, I might add – on the pretence that she had useful information to give him. Well, she then used her, er, feminine wiles to get him drunk, seduce him and, following a pious outpouring to the Lord, 'smite him', as the Old Testament might put it."

"So why the interest in Judith, when I have hundreds of other paintings which are of greater artistic and cultural merit?" Goering's antennae are twitching.

"My interest was piqued more by the symbolic possibilities rather than anything else. It's a well-worn subject in art history, is it not? The oppressor vanquished by the oppressed. Judith, David, Jael. What I can't for the life of me figure out is why it should interest *you*. It speaks of female emancipation and yet you strike me as a man more interested in patriarchal authority and brute strength." He looks at Goring who remains unresponsive, then continues. "Then there's the obvious inspirational tale of the Hebrews defeating the tyrannical oppressor. The contemporary allegory will not be lost on you I suspect. But it can't be that, can it? So, my question is simple: what's the appeal?"

"Your trouble, doctor, is that your default position is that of the psychiatrist. You look for symbolic meaning in everything. Did it occur to you that perhaps I like the brush work? Perhaps I'm a hoarder and I want the monopoly on Cranach. Maybe I saw its potential for

resale, or trade. Or perhaps, Dr Kelley, I just like a girl with small tits."
Göring looks bored and, with a sigh, brushes down his tunic and
reclines on the bed. "If you want the truth, it's that Cranach is quite
my favourite artist and I have amassed many of his works. I consider
myself the humble custodian of the artworks in my collection. My
hope is – was – that the art would be enjoyed by the masses instead of
floundering over an Israelite's mantlepiece, its delicate colours cracked
in the afternoon sun and warped by the heat of a blackened fireplace.
I was only too happy to save our cultural heritage from a despicable
fate." On this note, Göring purses his lips and sniffs. "I wish to say no
more about this." His folded arms emphasizing the point.

Kelley opts for an alternative approach.

"I was thinking about Cranach. He had something of an obsession
with decapitation, did he not?"

"There you go again, doctor. School of. Style of. It may very well be
that not all of the paintings attributed were created by the hand of
Cranach himself. Some could quite have easily been by his students,
or a contemporary trading on the name. Nevertheless, one of his
preferred subjects does seem to have been nubile young maidens
wearing little to shroud their modesty juxtaposed with a severed head.
Sex and death. The two immutables."

A silence descends on the room. Kelley can hear the familiar rattle
of the tea trolley in the corridor. Göring closes his eyes.

*Carinhall. Jeu du Paume. Those lost afternoons in the Louvre. My Golden Age.*
Kelley sits patiently until Göring breaks the silence.

"Decapitation," he begins. "The Feast of Herod, oil on limewood,
1530; The Beheading of St. John the Baptist, oil on canvas, 1515;
Judith with the Head of Holofernes, 1530. Two of those, one on
wood, one on canvas. Then there's Salome, another oil on wood. I
don't recall the year. There were others of course but – alas!"

Opening his eyes, Göring is drawn back into the dampness of
Ashcan. Now, in his nostrils is the faint odour of his excretions,
emanating from the bucket that sits behind the door.

"Well I think Cranach's a psychiatrist's dream," says Kelley.

"You would. I imagine that such art is disturbing to effete modern sensibilities," Göring replies with disdain. "Those were dark days, doctor. Cranach lived in an era when terrible deeds were commonplace. Remember, Europe was in a parlous state. Perhaps these paintings of beheadings speak to the grim times in which he lived." After a pause he adds pointedly, "I could have weathered the storms of his age. I would have thrived even. These are weakened times, I'm afraid. Everyone says they want progress but they haven't the stomach for it."

There is a pause which Kelley is suddenly anxious to fill but without the vaguest notion of what to say, he simply sets down his pencil. The two men are motionless in the stillness of the afternoon; Göring looking at the ceiling, Kelley staring out of the window and down at an army private collecting cut grass on the lawn below.

There is a knock and the door opens. Lieutenant Wheelis paces softly into the room with an aluminum mug and a pitcher of watery coffee. Göring presses on.

"Do you know *Melancholia*?" he asks Kelley.

"I'm sorry?"

"Painted in 1532. *Melancholia*. Many consider it to be Cranach's masterpiece."

Kelley picks up the pencil and listens carefully. But not as carefully as Wheelis does.

"It's a painting of a woman, an angel in fact, sitting on a cushion. As she sits, she fashions a toy for two children who are sitting at her feet playing with a globe. They're joined in the scene by a spaniel and a pair of partridges. All very symbolic I'm sure, but it's not those details that I'm drawn to. You see, to truly understand *Melancholia* you must look beyond the window and see behind the angel." Göring is staring at Wheelis who can feel the Reichsmarschall's eyes on him. "It's the background that's captivating. You see, through the window in small detail we see a Saxon landscape filled with a tumult of armoured figures slaughtering one another. Above this horror of warfare, there are strange deities riding the storm-filled skies, embarked on a hunt with boars, hounds and other beasts."

Kelley scribbles on the pad. Wheelis sets down the mug. Göring speaks over the scratching of the pencil, the pouring of piping hot coffee.

"*Melancholia* says to me that there's a darkness that lies just under everything we do."

*Wheelis, are you listening, boy?*

"Cranach is showing us ourselves as we really are just below the surface. On the periphery of polite society – just beyond the window, as it were – there is ugliness and there is death. Man slaughters man and the gods are indifferent, embarked on a hunt all their own." He snorts. "The notion that there's a benevolent deity waiting to scoop us up into his loving arms…it's a fallacy, poppycock! I just wish more people could see it," he adds wistfully.

The pencil stops. The coffee steams.

The rubber band snaps the pencil and pad back into the bundle and Wheelis slips file from the doctor's lap.

"I'll get this to your quarters, sir," and the door gently closes.

# An Allegory of Vanitas

## Inventory of the Art Collection
## of
## Reichsmarschall Hermann Göring

Owner: Jacques Goudstikker — Amsterdam, Netherlands
Collection: J. Goudstikker, Amsterdam
Artist:        Willem de Poorter
Medium: Oil on panel
Title:        *Grave Robbers* or *An Allegory of Vanitas: The desecration of a tomb*
Measurements: 39 x 30 cm.

Note: De Poorter was a specialist of history and still-life painting, though only a few of the latter survive. Like Rembrandt and Lastman, De Poorter set his scenes in large, dark interiors with a central grouping of figures differentiated through animated expression and pose. Scholars have attributed these similarities to the proposition that De Poorter studied with Rembrandt in Leiden around 1629–30. Besides a vanitas still life in the foreground, the motif of the robbers breaking open the tomb of a general alludes to the transience of earthly possessions including one's own body. De Poorter often treated themes that provided him with the opportunity to render different textures, such as shimmering armour, silverware and the marble of the sarcophagus in this work. He had a particular interest in painting still life and capturing the effect of chiaroscuro.

"Vanity of vanities. All is vanity." *Ecclesiastes 1:2* succinctly describes the vanitas movement that began in response to the prosperity in 18th century Holland. Vanitas or "vanity" paintings were created as *memento mori*, reminding us that our material possessions and pursuits do not preclude us from the inevitability of death. The nature of life and the world is fleeting, finite, and temporary.

Ref: Alois Miedl
B.L.

* * *

The tired green Büssing omnibus makes slow progress along country lanes. Linnie stares out of the window, quietly triumphant about her victory over the American investigators who apprehended her just two miles from *Landhaus* Göring. Having an almost photographic memory, she can recall the conclusions of their report. They decided that she was little more than a functionary of the German state. She 'made an excellent impression on her interrogators'; 'Reserved…her story consistent,' they said. 'Her role was limited to purely administrative tasks'; 'No personal responsibility'. Notwithstanding her excellent performance in the role of hapless functionary of the Reich, Lt Rousseau made one thing clear: remain at the disposal of the United States Army pending Reichsmarschall Hermann Göring's trial. The Recommendations for Action in the report were unequivocal: 'The information she has provided is only a minor part of what she knows. She is an important source of further information.'

By the time the omnibus draws into the cobble stone market square her nerves are frayed. When she boarded an hour ago, she managed a weak smile at the driver and made directly for the back of the bus for the best vantage point of the other passengers. Alighting now, she paces slowly over the cobbles and past the small collection of sad market stalls. At any other time, the view from St Bartholomew's church over the Königsee Lake would be captivating. The deep red onion domes of the 17th Century baroque church contrast with the lush green pine trees that climb high up into the snow-capped Bavarian Alps. The white-washed walls have a rustic, weathered appearance that speaks of the church's long history. The air is crisp and fresh, filled with the sound of gentle waves lapping against the lake's shore. Linnie checks her watch – 10:33 – and hastens inside to have her confession heard.

St. Bartholomew's exudes an ambiance of sanctuary and solitude. The walls are adorned with small depictions of the stations of the cross. The altar is backed by a small stained-glass window of Bartholomew's martyrdom that filters soft red and orange coloured light which reminds Linnie of Göring's face in the glow of the firelight. The air inside the church is cool and still. There is a faint scent of incense mingling with candle wax and the musty aroma of old wood

157

and damp stone. To her right she hears the creak of wood and turns to see a large ornate oak confessional with red velvet curtains on each side. She notices the tips of a pair of black shoes peeping under the curtain on the left which say, 'You are expected'. Sliding the right-hand curtain aside, she steps into the confessional and sits. There is a square aperture covered with a brass plate perforated in a cloverleaf pattern. Behind it, she makes out the shape of an elderly man with tufts of white hair and thick black glasses. She begins, as instructed, giving him the code word. The priest now turns to face her, his thick glasses staring through the perforations. She can feel black lenses peering through at her. She hears his curtain draw back and footsteps on the stone floor walking slowly away.

At least two minutes pass before she hears the slow, steady footfalls of the man returning. There is the sound of the heavy lock on the door being bolted twice and finally the priest draws the curtain back and resumes his seat. For the next few minutes he speaks quietly but urgently. He tells her about Maria Alm in Salzburg. He speaks of friends in Munich, ones who'll know what to do with the Inventory. He slides an envelope under the screen and bids her open it. He tells her not to worry, that he has helped many like her. She slides out a small cluster of documents. She is confronted by a face she doesn't know, a half-ghost. A *doppelganger* who could be her in another life. The priest is still talking, explaining what she must do, but instead Linnie is acquainting herself with the stranger in the photograph; her but not her. The face staring out at her is a remarkable likeness, the hair is even dressed in a French twist. The priest doesn't tell her about the stranger, Fräulein Gisela Weschler. An innocent casualty of war.

Linnie realizes that he has stopped speaking and has disappeared. She hears the bolt of the door turn twice and then his footsteps return to the confessional. He resumes his place silently in profile against the screen, immobile, like a coin-operated fortune telling machine in a fairground once the money's been spent. She draws back the velvet curtain and leaves.

At the market square another bus is waiting to convey her to another life.

As doubtful as the future seems, Linnie has made provision for the uncertainty.

\* \* \*

Provisions have also been made for the Reichsmarschall. Colonel Andrus is wary of troublemakers and sees to it that he will be held in isolation in the prison that is now home to all of the defendants awaiting trial. They are housed on the bottom floor of the prison wing attached to Nuremberg's Palace of Justice. The wing contains twenty-nine cells, of which eight are unoccupied. Of the remaining rooms, one room has been used for the prisoners' possessions, and it is here that Göring's red suitcases are held. Few officers have access to it. One of them is Jack Wheelis.

Göring has been assigned Cell #5, measuring 4 x 2.5 metres. Prior to his admittance, the cell was thoroughly searched, including walls, floor, toilet and mattress. Its only furnishings are a metal bed which is bolted to the floor, a small, light-weight table, and a chair that remains in the cell only during daylight hours. A basic toilet without seat is squeezed into an alcove to the right of the door. Any small protrusions such as hooks have been removed from the wall, as has as all electrical wiring. The glass in the small windowpane has been replaced by a plastic screen. It is forlorn, having not been maintained during the war years. The whitewash on the rectangular bricks has dimmed and, in the trickle of sunlight, appears grey. Patches of the wall and ceiling peel and bubble in the musty air. Göring is separated from the outside world by a large metal door that contains a large round black eye, a Judas Window.

*All the better to see you with.*

It is in this unhappy chamber that the Reichsmarschall now sits, perched on the edge of the bed while Wheelis sits facing him on the wooden chair and slowly, carefully, delicately painting Göring's fingernails. The Reichsmarschall sits perfectly still, one moment staring at the shiny Brylcream on the top of Wheelis's head, the next inspecting the quality and sheen of the crimson liquid adorning his nails.

*Red like the banners lining our rally grounds.*

'Goddam gaylord if you ask me,' bellowed Andrus, when he first clocked eyes on Göring's nails in the dining hall two weeks ago. Notwithstanding his dismay, the upper echelons have reasoned that this is a peccadillo that the system can indulge as long as Göring remains compliant. No one quite knows from where the gloss materialized, but Wheelis has been appointed as guardian of the offending make-up and sees that it is returned when Göring has finished with it. That Wheelis has been promoted to the Reichsmarschall's personal beautician, no one knows outside the two men. Andrus sees the whole spectacle as clear evidence of deviancy; Kelley sees it as a small rebellion worth indulging. Kelley's reasoning convinced the decision makers.

When the doctor arrives at the door of Cell #5 this morning, he does not react to the sight that greets him through the Judas Hole: the Reichsmarschall play acting. Who can say where his fancy has taken him. Perhaps the extended painted hand is reaching out to a make-believe dignitary arriving at Carinhall? A hand is taken – let us say that it is kissed – Göring feigns a modest smile and bows his head and then with a sweep of his arm, bids his guest enter within. Kelley watches Göring's arms drop to his sides and the imagined scene dissipates into the damp air. The Reichsmarschall has returned to Nuremberg. This is his cue to enter, and he swings the door open.

"I heard that you attended matins in the chapel this morning," says Kelley breezily. Such is their relationship that they have long since dispensed with customary pleasantries.

"I did." Is it Kelley's imagination, or is Göring wiggling his fingers just a little, to catch the doctor's eye?

"You were the first to arrive, sitting in the front row so Fr. Gerecke tells me.

160

"Correct."

"I didn't know you had faith."

"Oh but I do, Kelley, I do," he says enthusiastically, "I have complete and unfailing faith in the chapel's heating system. Stay up here freezing my arse off? No thank you. Speer mentioned the other day that the chapel was the warmest room in the whole damn place. My curséd sciatica has been intolerable of late," he says bitterly, massaging his thigh. "Can't warm up in here at all. Look at the condensation on that window this morning. I decided to sit myself slap bang in front of that lovely heater they have by the altar. After fifteen minutes I was toasty-warm," he says rubbing his hands. "You know, the chaplain might just make a convert of me yet – if he can stretch to ground coffee and pastries, too." The bed squeaks as Göring bounces up and down with mirth. "As for that drivel he's spouts. Know what I do? I close my eyes and I imagine my beautiful altar piece I bought from the Goudstikker collection."

"'Bought'?"

"You know, I wondered about having it transported to the chapel here to spruce the place up a bit. Wondered for about thirty seconds, that is. That arsewipe Andrus hasn't got an artistic bone in his body. Have you seen his hands? Why, they're the hands of a navvy, gnarled and calloused. I'll bet he's never run taffeta through his fingers, or held a chilled champagne coupe."

"About the altar piece, I understood that you and Hitler had something of a spat over it."

"A what? No, no, that was the other one. The Van Eyck. Hitler was desperate for that for his collection in Linz but it would have really set off the entrance at Carinhall."

"But it wasn't yours. Or his."

"Oh here we go! Come on, say it. 'Looting', that the word you're looking for?"

"Well, what word would you use for it? Stealing priceless art the length and breadth of Europe."

"Poppycock! Balderdash, man!" He wipes the spittle from his chin. "I'll have you know that every bloody nation has looted at one time or another. Please don't try to lecture me about looting, as if we're the only nation that's ever seized cultural objects during times of conflict. How quick the victors are to seize the moral high ground. Sniveling little shysters."

Beyond the door they can hear the rattle of a trolley and the slopping of a mop on the flagstone floor before the sounds die away.

"You speak so rarely of Hitler."

They both sit and savour the silence.

"I was never in awe of him in the way others were. You must understand; I was always Hermann and he was always the Führer."

"You called him Führer?"

"That's not what I mean, I'm referring to the people. The people called me Hermann. They could hardly call him Adolf. Can you imagine Hitler sat down in some bierkeller with a stein in his hand? That was my role and I played it beautifully. That's why we complemented each other. He could be taciturn, introspective. He was awkward while I was ribald, extroverted."

"Did you share the same tastes?"

"Hitler preferred 19th Century stuff. Favoured Rembrandt. Hated Durer, whom I adore. Michelangelo and the Renaissance artists were his bag. Me? I prefer the German masters."

"Like Cranach, we've spoken before about him."

"Cranach, yes."

This provides Kelley with the segue he has been awaiting.

"They say that you had nine versions of *The Rape of Lucretia*, all by Cranach."

"Who says?" he sniffs suspiciously.

"Jeu de Paume people."

"Oh, pay no attention to them," says Göring dismissively. "Thirty-five."

"Thirty-five what?"

"That's how many versions of *The Rape of Lucretia* that Cranach painted. In total."

"Why so many? And why do *you* have nine of them? What is it about her?"

"Ever the psychiatrist, eh Kelley? Why settle for one simple meaning when six convoluted ones will do."

"Well, the facts of your interest do bear closer scrutiny, don't they?"

"Ah! You have a theory. Goodie," and then the Reichsmarschall hoists himself further onto the bed to enjoy the cross-examination.

"Well in Ovid's account –"

"Someone's been doing their history homework. Good boy."

"In Ovid's account Collatinus welcomes his enemy Tarquin into his home as a guest. Lucretia prepares a sumptuous meal to welcome him, but then, later on –"

"In the dead of night," says Göring, picking up the story and narrating it like a children's bedtime ghost story, "he sneaks into her bed chamber, frees his sword from its golden sheath and advances on the sleeping Lucretia. In fear of her life, she lays there, speechless as the vulpine Tarquin ravishes the trembling lamb lying helpless beneath him."

"Titian, Rembrandt, Shakespeare. What drew them to the story of the rape of a Roman noblewoman, I wonder."

"Who knows why these things capture the imagination," mutters Göring. He stands, moves towards the window and turns his back on Kelley. The gesture is deliberate and its significance not lost on the doctor.

"It was a letter from my wife that made the connection for me," says Kelley, awaiting a flicker of a response that never comes. "She wanted to join me here for a few days but I told her, 'Alice,' I said, 'this is no place for you'. So, she decides perhaps she'll summer in Rome, maybe Paris, take in a little bit of England. Now, one thing you should know about my wife is that she's an opera buff."

Göring stands perfectly still with his hands clasped firmly behind his back, looking up at the window.

"She's always been interested in Glideborne," says Kelley, deliberately dropping a crumb for Göring to pick up. The Reichsmarschall obliges.

"*Glyndebourne*," he growls.

"Well anyway, it turns out that Benjamin Britten premiered a new opera there. Guess what it was?"

"Lucretia," Göring whispers.

"Right, *The Rape of Lucretia*. But here's the thing, my wife sends me a few clippings from the London Times. They'd done this interview with Britten and he explained the inspiration. And that's when I thought of your collection."

Kelley waits to see how hungry the shark is to bite.

"Well?"

"Britten is a Christian pacifist, did you know that?"

Göring shrugs.

"A registered conscientious objector as well. Naturally he responds to war the only way he knows how, through his art."

"I thought we were talking about painting, not opera."

"Doesn't matter, it's all art. For Britten the rape of Lucretia is an allegory. It's not about the sexual act, it's a question of power. A story of subjugation."

"Cranach was painting in the early part of the 16th Century," says Göring irritably. "Are you suggesting that any of this was relevant to him?"

"Not him. *You*," says Kelley softly. "I'm talking about power. I'm talking about the subjugation of nations. I'm talking about coveting and possessing. By force. I'm talking about nine paintings by Cranach hanging in your collection, Reichsmarschall."

In circumstances such as this, Göring responds the only way he knows how.

"Let's take a break, doctor. I need a shit."

* * *

"What might this be?"

"Think of it as another game."

The day has surrendered, evening ascends. Kelley has positioned a small table between them. On it he has placed ten cards.

"What kind of game?" demands Göring suspiciously. Neither man has returned to the subject of their conversation this afternoon.

"Have you heard of Bruno Klopfer?"

"Psychologist."

"The very same," says Kelley, casually shuffling the cards in his hand. "He's been developing projective testing."

"You are referring to The Rorschach Technique, yes?"

"Correct. Created by Hermann Rorschach in the Twenties."

"I know of it, of course," says Göring. "We used it to weed out disruptive social and racial elements."

"Well I've used it to establish if there is such a thing as the Nazi mind. Speer, Hess and Ribbentropp, they've all taken it. Frank, too."

"Good God, I hope you don't rank me in the same class as the Butcher of Poland. I'll take Fat Hermann over that sobriquet any day."

Kelley slaps a card on the table.

"Shall we?"

Göring looks down, studying the image for a moment.

"It is a mask," he asserts quickly. "Here are its eyes." He tilts his head a little and adds, "Here are horns. The horns of a ram."

Kelley nods and flips the second image over.

For a moment Göring's crimson nail scratches at the card.

"Clowns. Or bears. It is two bears fighting."

"Is that all?"

"Perhaps clouds. Yes, clouds. There is a storm coming."

Göring waves his hand and Kelley reveals the third card.

"Two men in a fantastical dance. See? They are like whirling dervishes," he adds with a chuckle.

With the turn of the fourth card, Göring raises his eyebrows.

165

"Ah, this man is a giant. He is towering over us. You can see the enormous feet."

Kelley is about to slide it away when Göring snatches it back.

"Wait. Here, see? Ha," he laughs, "A huge prick, too!"

So it continues, with Göring gradually losing himself in a menagerie of birds and butterflies as well as genitalia and musical instruments. In card #6 he sees a U-Boat; in #7, two gossiping women. His delight is palpable. Sometimes he's intrigued, offering well-considered and intricate readings; sometimes he finds amusement in trying to shock Kelley by offering lengthy vulgar and anatomically detailed descriptions of fornication.

When they finish Göring looks at the doctor expectantly.

"Well? How did I do?"

"It's not a question of how you did. There are no correct answers. The responses are intended to offer some insight into your mindset."

"What about my mindset?" says Göring looking squarely at him. "Look here, Kelley. For – whatever it is – seventeen months now, you have been entering my private dwelling, the only place I have left in the world. We have had frank conversations. I have accepted your little parlour games, answered your questions honestly and told you everything about myself. Surely, after all this time together, you can offer me some insight about what it's all been for."

Kelley looks at him. Göring is right. So, he reasons, why not share what he has learnt with the man he has been studying.

"You betrayed yourself with one particular gesture," Kelley says, opening a doorway.

"Go on," says Göring, entering it.

"Remember this one?" Kelley holds up card #2. It contains small red dots. "You see these? Morbid neurotics see them as droplets of blood. Do you remember your reaction to them?"

"I don't." He does.

"As soon as you saw it, you scratched that red spot with your finger. Why did you do that?" But he doesn't wait for an answer. "You thought you could wipe the blood away. You can see where I'm going?"

"I can't." He can.

"I believe that you did the same thing this morning. When I was speaking about *The Rape of Lucretia*, you moved towards the window and turned your back."

"I was merely —"

"You do the same in court, have you noticed? You swipe the headphones from your head. You refuse to listen. You've always tried to brush the blood away, as it were. I wonder if you haven't been doing the same thing since 1933. The blood on the card; the window; the headphones. The morphine and then the paracodeine. The art. All this time you've been pathologically unable to face the consequences of your actions."

"And that's what these little games have taught you is it?"

Kelley waits a moment, weighing it all up. Seventeen months.

"That. And worse."

"How worse?"

"I've learnt that unfortunately you're not exceptional. That all of you in here, including your friend the Butcher of Poland, you're not aberrations. Colonel Andrus," at the mention of his name, Göring tuts and rolls his eyes. "Andrus was convinced that we might use these sessions to unlock some secret mindset unique to the Nazi elite. To find some fatal flaw that binds you together and alienates you from the rest of polite society."

Göring nods slowly. "But that's not what you found, is it doctor?"

"No. That's not what I've found. The truth is more prosaic and much more troubling.

You're not Shakespearean villains. You're not moustache-twirling hoods straight out of a B-movie. You're unremarkable. That's what scares me."

"I scare you?"

167

"Not you personally. What scares me is that so many people out there would have behaved – would still, *will* still – behave like you. You're everywhere. In the military, in government, even in ordinary office buildings. That's what scares me."

Göring places a hand on Kelley's shoulder.

"Who would have guessed that all this time you've been looking in a mirror."

Göring can't resist one final thought.

"You're wrong about one thing though," he says reclining and heaving his trousers over his belly. "I'm anything but ordinary. 'I make the south wind blow.'"

"The south wind?"

"Book of Psalms 78:26. Look it up."

The Reichsmarschall stands, walks to the window again and turns his back on the doctor.

*Dismissed.*

# The People of Justice

Inventory of the Art Collection
of
Reichsmarschall Hermann Göring

Collection: Walter Strauss – Paris, France
Artist:     Honoré Daumier
Medium: Works on Paper
Title:      *Les gens de justice* – Nr.38
Measurements:

Note:  Item retrieved from Walter Strauss' apartment in March 1942 which was raided for cultural objects by The Dienststelle Westen.
Honoré Daumier mastered the technique of lithography early on in his career and published his first plate in the satirical periodical La Silhouette in 1829. He was dubbed the "Michelangelo of caricature," famously satirizing France's bourgeoisie.

Grotesque caricatures of government officials endeared him to the public. He frequently derided professionals such as doctors, professors, and especially lawyers and judges, whom he deemed cruel and pretentious.

This item comes from a collection of 38 lithographs that were published between March 1845 and October 1848, entitled to *The People of Justice*. Throughout the collection, the cantankerous artist casts a mocking eye on the innumerable types of lawyers: greedy and grasping, idle and bumbling. B.L.

\* \* \*

1st October, 1946

His mouth dry, Sir Geoffrey Lawrence takes two sips of water, and begins.

"Hermann Göring has been indicted on all four Counts: The Common Plan or conspiracy; War Crimes; Crimes against Peace and Crimes against Humanity. The evidence shows that after Hitler, Hermann Göring was the most prominent man in the Nazi regime, and had tremendous influence, at least until 1943, when his relationship with Hitler deteriorated, culminating in his arrest in 1945. From the moment he joined the Party in 1922, he was the adviser, the active agent of Hitler, and one of the prime leaders of the Nazi movement. After his own admissions to this Tribunal, from the positions which he held, the conferences he attended, and the public words he uttered, there can remain no doubt that this man was the moving force for aggressive war, second only to Adolf Hitler himself.

He was the planner and prime mover in the military and diplomatic preparation for war which Germany pursued."

*True. 'Tremendous influence', 'second only to Hitler'. Perfectly true.*

"There is nothing to be said in mitigation. Göring was often – indeed almost always – the moving force, second only to his leader. He was the leading war aggressor, both as political and as military leader; he was the director of the slave labour programme and the creator of the oppressive action against the Jews and other races, at home and abroad. All of these crimes he has frankly admitted."

*I would do it all again.*

"His guilt is unique in its enormity."

*One man's guilt, another man's accomplishment.*

"The record discloses no excuses for this man."

*I have never asked to be excused.*

"The Tribunal finds the Defendant Goering guilty on all four Counts of the Indictment. The Tribunal will now adjourn and will sit again at 10 minutes to three."

Cooly staring straight ahead, Göring resumes his seat.

* * *

Ernest W. Michel sits on a wooden bench outside Courtroom 600 scrawling phrases, refining his latest dispatch. His pencil glides across thin yellow sheets of paper, recounting the verdicts. For the last seven months his copy has provided the American public eyes on the proceedings at Nuremberg. Over time he has developed the journalist's art of shutting out peripheral distractions. It is for this reason that he is oblivious to the elderly gentleman standing over him repeating his name. Finally, without moving his head, his eyes lift from the pad to a pair of shoes before him. Wide woolen grey pin-striped trousers gather in folds where the laces should be, and he looks up directly into a thin, jowly face bearing a serious expression. Though he knows the face well, he is more familiar with the man's shoulders and back, having spent the last three months sat a few rows removed from him in the courtroom.

171

"It *is* Herr Michel isn't it? I believe yours was the description I was given. My name is Otto Stahmer, but at the risk of sounding presumptuous, I suspect you know that."

"Indeed I do."

"I wonder if I could have a moment of your time?"

DANA will be expecting his copy in the next two hours. Notwithstanding the deadline, he would be mad to pass up an invitation from Göring's lawyer.

A few minutes later, the pair are in a small office room, shielded from the brouhaha of the courthouse.

"You're probably wondering why I brought you here."

"You could say that."

"I've found your reports on the trial well written and for the most part, accurate," says Stahmer. "But I was wondering about the byline on your articles."

It takes Ernest a moment, and then he remembers.

"Auschwitz number 104995."

"Yes. You were imprisoned at Auschwitz?"

"And Buchenwald. I escaped the death march though." Unable to resist, he adds, "I seem to remember that your client was under the misapprehension that the footage of the concentration camps was somehow, er, embellished. I can assure you, if that were the case, I would have known." He resists the temptation to lift the sleeve covering the smudgy blue number tattooed on the soft pale forearm.

"If you'll forgive my asking, Herr Michel, how did you manage to survive when so many perished?"

"I was hospitalized at Monowitz and by chance – I won't say luck - I was in the ward when a man arrived wanting to know which patients had decent handwriting. I copied out three sentences and they said 'He'll do nicely'."

"For what purpose had you been selected?" asks Stahmer.

"Administration. The issuing of death certificates mainly. We were never allowed to write 'gas chamber' of course."

Stahmer takes the conversation in a different direction.

"Like me, my client has been reading your reports of the trial. He appreciates your turn of phrase and would like to meet."

Michel sits in stunned silence. He's not sure whether to burst into laughter or tears as he tries to comprehend that one of the engineers of the Holocaust is – how can he put it? – an admirer.

"I appreciate that this may strike you as a rather unusual request," says Stahmer, "but I hasten to add that this would not be a formal interview in your capacity as a member of the press."

Despite words being the tools of his trade, all possible utterances elude him. Stahmer speaks into the emptiness.

"Now that we have a recess until just before 3pm, Göring is at liberty to meet should you be available.'

Suddenly realizing the implication of this remark, the power of speech returns to him.

"*Now*? He wants to meet me *now*?"

"Well, if not now, when? I mean…who can say how much time he has left?" which is followed by an embarrassed chuckle.

A short while later, Ernest Michel is facing an anonymous grey metal door within Nuremberg prison. 'Within this room is the manifestation of evil,' he tells himself. The door opens and Evil stands before Ernest. He looks into its eyes.

Evil knows what a smile is. It is aware of the convention. It opens its mouth and bears its teeth. 'I am smiling', it thinks to itself. The eyes, like a shark's, are black.

Ernest falters so Evil seizes the initiative and takes a step towards the young journalist, its arm outstretched in the customary gesture of welcome.

Impulsively, Ernest turns and runs from the cell. He slams against the wall outside, gasping for air and choking back tears. Stahmer has followed him out, and stays by him for a moment before returning to Cell #5.

"Apparently, Herr Michel says he just couldn't bear the thought of meeting you after…everything."

"Ah, well. Yes. Quite understand," says Göring. He adds magnanimously, "Please tell him, no hard feelings, won't you Stahmer?"

* * *

"In accordance with Article 27 of the Charter, the International Military Tribunal will now pronounce the sentences on the defendants convicted on this Indictment:

Defendant Hermann Wilhelm Göring, on the Counts of the Indictment on which you have been convicted, the International Military Tribunal sentences you to death by hanging."

It takes only one word to strike despair. It is not the sentence of death that causes him consternation. Why should it? It is what he has been awaiting for the last 216 days.

*I have never feared it. Even when the avalanche thundered around my ears as a boy. The true German faces up to the ultimate sacrifice with sovereignty and peace of mind. I told my men the same.*

It is the ignominy of the manner of death. No firing squad, but hanged like a common criminal.

"Life on this planet has just been an intermission during which I have had to perform as best I could. No more, and no less. . .The devil take it, before I allow any man to drag me down and make me grovel just to cling on to this tattered thing called life."

"A quotation?"

Douglas Kelley is now standing in the doorway of Göring's cell a few minutes after sentencing.

"A quotation," says Göring, as he peels a small photograph of his wedding day from the wall and smooths it with his fingers. "It's a line from a speech I gave to my men. It seems apposite."

Kelley steps into the room. "I wanted to see you. To offer my –"

"Condolences?" Göring turns sharply. "Can that be correct? I mean, strictly speaking, can you offer someone condolences *before* death? Especially if it's *their* death you're referring to. Perhaps you might wait and offer them to my wife. Or my little girl."

"I was going to say sympathy."

The room suddenly seems smaller than ever.

"I really am very sorry." He draws up a chair while Göring slumps heavily on the bed.

"While I was awaiting this morning's verdict, I was staring out of the window behind the judges. You can't know how many times I've looked out there over the last few hundred days, watching the skies and seasons change. Always in my view was part of a stone column. There was something I recognised about it, I mean I'd seen it somewhere. Sitting there today for the very last time, I remembered where I'd seen it."

"In Germany?"

"Frans Floris. His *Allegory of Justice and Peace*. In the centre of the painting Justice is seated on her throne holding the old sword and scales, of course. On either side of her are two women, Peace and Victory, and behind *them* are columns. *That's* what I recognized." Göring gives a derisive snort. "The pillars of society."

"It's not a painting I know, I'm afraid," replies Kelley, at a loss.

"There were other details in it. Some that were absent."

"Absent?"

"Absent from the trial. For one thing, Floris clothes Peace and Victory in white and blue for purity and trust. Don't you think it's ironic that our most esteemed judges spent the last six months clad in the clothes of death?"

"Your judges, too. In Germany they also wear black."

Göring doesn't hear. Or doesn't want to.

"There are books in the painting. The symbols of wisdom and the law. Do you know, Kelley, I cannot think of one single day when I saw anything more than revenge out there in the courtroom. The United States, preening itself as the bastion of modernity, thinking it's dragging the whole fucking globe out of self-imposed Dark Ages.

175

Then you've got the supine, sycophantic British, ruing the loss of an empire that slipped through its fingers while it was looking the other way."

"Don't forget the French," chimes in Kelley, in a rare show of sarcasm.

"That lot have been no fucking use to man or dog since…when did Napoleon die?"

"1821," says the doctor, plucking the date from his mind.

"Worst of the bunch are the Bolshies. Thugs to a man. With any luck your lot will rain hydrogen bombs on those bastards and send the whole sorry bunch to kingdom come." Göring harrumphs, folds his arms and stares at his shoes. "So this is what passes for justice in the new post-war world does it? Sending the Reichsmarschall of Germany to a shameful death by hanging?" he asks glaring at Kelley, then spits, "Victor's justice." He closes his eyes and folds his hands over his belly.

*Well since they have denied me a death that befits my status, it follows that I must deny them the pleasure of my humiliation.*

*Seeds have been sown that are almost ready to bear fruit.*

"Well," says Kelley, standing to take his leave.

"Yes." Göring doesn't move. His eyes remain closed.

"I suppose…Should we? Or, what? What should we…?" He holds his hand outstretched. Göring remain impassive, his eyes still closed.

"Goodbye. Reichsmarschall."

# The Liberation

Inventory of the Art Collection
of
Reichsmarschall Hermann Göring

Collection: Jacques Goudstikker — Amsterdam, Netherlands
Artist: Hendrick van Steenwyck the Younger
Medium: Painting
Title: *The Liberation of Saint Peter from Prison*
Description: Panel, 21.5 x 26.5cm.

Hendrick van Steenwijck the Younger was a master of the architectural motif, painting everything from church interiors to palaces and prisons. This particular panel is one of twenty-five he is thought to have painted on the subject of Saint Peter's liberation from Holy Monastery of Saint Nicodemus in Jerusalem, where he was imprisoned on the orders of

King Herod. Retold in the *Acts of the Apostles*, the story tells of an Angel of the Lord appearing in timely fashion, and the shackles miraculously falling from Peter's hands.

Here, the dimly lit vaulted interior is typical of Steenwijck's work. There's an extraordinary sense of space and texture that evoke the dark recesses of the prison setting. It was a particularly popular subject during the Baroque period, inspiring the likes of Ghisolfi, Lanfranco, Murillo and Il Ticinese. Its enduring popularity might be explained by the fact that it speaks to the idea of freedom from our temporal constraints; there is no gaol too fortified, no restraints too strong that we might not have the means of escape.

B.L.

\* \* \*

Tuesday 15th October, 1946

"Mind your footing, sir. Forgive the insalubrious surroundings but I don't think you'll be disappointed," says the jester with a wave of his marotte. Göring edges slowly into the darkness of the barn in trepidation. Outside an owl emits a deep, soft cry. The small cluster of bells on the marotte jingle in the still air, drawing attention to a horrific tableau lit by candlelight before them. On a gibbet hangs the gaping carcass of a pig. The jester gives it a playful nudge and steps back as it sways gently by its hind legs. Heat rises from the hirsute pink skin in the cool night air.

"He's quite harmless now," chuckles the jester, his face illuminated by candles below the body. It is a familiar face. Bruno Lohse.

"Van Ostade has employed generous impasto brushstrokes to the body, adding such depth, such texture."

*I know this barn. It is my godfather's, in the woods at Burg Veldenstein.*

There is the sound of a waltz drifting through the darkness.

"Death is transformative," says Jester Lohse. "Once Reichsmarschall, now cadaver."

The jester reaches out to take Göring's hand. In it he places the hilt of a large hunting knife.

*Scandinavian. Geometric. Sámi. An inscription: 'From Eric to Hermann'.*

The jester directs his hand up towards the pig. Göring wants to withdraw, but Lohse clamps hold of his wrist, guiding his fist, pumping it back and forth into the hard, warm flesh of the animal again and again, a frenzy of jerking thrusts with the dagger.

"Historically, the slaughter of swine was a popular subject in 17th Century Dutch art," the jester explains as thick, syrupy blood trickles over them both. "Rembrandt and van der Poole explore it as a metaphor for the transience of our existence."

With a final prod from the jester's marotte, a bulbous protrusion of brown entrails plops through the stomach lining. From somewhere behind them the waltz stops and there are unrestrained cheers and applause in the distance.

"Do not let your hearts be heavy, friends," says Lohse taking a bow. "No one loved the sheer theatre of it all more than Uncle Hermann himself. Hipp, hipp, hurra!"

Göring wakes in a cold sweat with the image of pendulous entrails in his mind. He opens his eyes and in the moonlight, sees the blistered paint forming dark blue veins across the grey skin ceiling like a dead hand. He imagines gallows somewhere in the distance. He imagines the smell of freshly cut beams of untreated wood, each joist harnessed by five-inch silver nails that glisten.

*Where did my Van Ostade go? To Altausee with the rest, perhaps. The inventory will have it. She will know.*

He draws the khaki United States Army blanket up to his neck and waits for the solace of sleep's embrace. It never comes.

* * *

Wheelis shoves open the swing doors of the gymnasium and hears curt bangs behind him as they swing shut. He has made sure he is alone. The gym is attached to the far right of the prison complex, a short walk from the wing holding the guilty men. Its smell is distinctive and typical of every sports hall he's ever known; sweat mingled with rubber plimsoles and wood polish. The parquet floor is etched with faded white lines that mark out the basketball court.

In the centre of the room are eleven newly constructed wooden coffins set out side by side. He makes his way towards them, aware of the squeal his boots make on the floor. He drops to his haunches, unbuttons them and then places the pair carefully on a bench. He stares at the coffins wondering which one. Likely the first, he reasons, given the Reichsmarschall's status. They'll do him first to make a show of it. Or last perhaps, a big finale. No, it's the first one, far left.

He looks over his shoulder and checks the doors. Shutting his eyes allows him to focus his attention. The distant rattle of a trolley and more squeaky boots, this time accompanied by the lick-slop sound of a mop hitting a tiled floor somewhere out there. He bends on one knee and allows himself a furtive touch of the oak lid of the coffin. His one. He nudges the lid. It's heavier than he thought. He is disappointed to see that there is no lining within. He leans over and smells inside the box. A deep, savouring breath of fresh pine. He runs his fingers along the almost white surface, nicking a finger on a splinter as he does so. He musters his courage and then slides the lid over and climbs inside, shuffling into position.

He's too tall. His stockinged feet hit the end so he writhes slightly until he can slide the lid across. Now he can smell the wood more fully.

180

He runs his fingers around inside, across the cold metal heads of the nails. He closes his eyes. Indescribable currents of excitement run through his body. He doesn't even hear the bang of the doors as someone enters the gymnasium.

Problem. Who?

Andrus and someone else. Squeaky boots. Step, two, three, four, stop. Squeak. Muttering something. Creaking of wood, but not the gymnasium floor. The gallows. They're inspecting them. More creaking. Andrus mutters something and the other man laughs. Something dark. The proverbial gallows humour.

Wheelis can hear the thumping footsteps reverberating around him now. Through space between the planks over his face, Wheelis can see Andrus's paunch and two hairy nostrils almost directly over him.

He realises that he's holding his breath and so slowly exhales, gently.

"Whassat?" Andrus says, pointing.

Suddenly the footsteps quicken and march away, towards the other side of the room, away from the coffins. He can hear Andrus bark the word 'Boots' and realizes that they've discovered his shoes sitting on the bench. Andrus grumbles something inaudible and then a moment later, Wheelis hears the gymnasium doors slamming shut.

* * *

Göring has refused to leave his cell since Emmy's visit just over a week ago. Unable to touch her hand, he sat trying to muster a smile, his chest tightening at the sight of her.

*She'd lost weight. I saw it instantly. That blue dress hanging limply on her.*

As good spouses, they both knew that the truth was something to shield one another from. She hadn't told him that her scuffed shoes were the only ones she has left; he hadn't told her about the dreams.

Times passes agonizingly. Sometimes he reads and sometimes he writes. Often he sleeps. He feels angry about the absence of Dr Kelley who has, it would seem, turned tail and scurried back to his masters with copious medical notes, happy to find fame riding on the Reichsmarschall's coat-tails.

Now he sits staring at the blistered paintwork as he peels off the four black and white pictures that have provided some small solace over the last few months. Item one: his wedding day, in full *Reichsjägermeister* attire at Carinhall. Him, Emmy and – if only his captors knew it – the right arm of the Führer edging into view. Item Two: Göring flanked by his two lion cubs. Here again, the photograph hides a secret. Standing by the entrance of Carinhall were the Duke and Duchess of Windsor. October 1937, almost exactly nine years ago to the day. Lifting another picture from the wall, he smooths its curled edges between his thumb and forefinger and stares into the past. Item 3: Edda, aged eight in a misty portrait lovingly enhanced by small brush strokes on her kiss curls. He turns it over. 'Dear Daddy, come back to me again soon. I have such longing for you. Many thousand kisses from your Edda!!!' This is too much. He snatches the khaki blanket from the bed and stuffs it over his face, smothering the despair.

Following near exposure, comes re-composure, and Wheelis makes his way to Cell #5 calming himself down. Sliding the metal cover, he peeps through the Judas window. He leans his chest against the metal and stands for a moment peeping in. 'What the Butler Saw'. Wheelis's palms are spread against the cold, grey metal of the door, a finger inadvertently picking at the paint, scratching small flakes to the floor as his nail picks at the scab. His breath has completely misted the small eyehole and he wipes his thumb over it, causing a squeal on the glass which immediately draws Göring's attention. He drops the blanket and is suddenly a model of composure.

"Ah, Wheelis. I was wondering when you might come," then, "what on earth are you doing in your stocking feet?"

He immediately notices the perturbed look on the lieutenant's face.

"My dear boy, what is it?"

So Wheelis tells him, recounting all he has learnt. Tells him about the arrival of the coffins. That last night's late night game of basketball that Rosenberg was bitching about was nothing more than an elaborate smokescreen. The incessant squeak of sneakers, the pounding of the rubber ball, toots on the whistle. This, Wheelis explains, was to cover the sound of three gallows being constructed in the gymnasium. A ruse so that the convicted men wouldn't rumble the fact that the final order had reached Andrus: do it tonight. He's seen the gallows for himself and seen the coffins too, he says, bowing his head.

"I'm really awful sorry, sir. Not right for a military man," Wheelis adds, repeating Göring's very own words back to him.

Göring whispers, his lips almost touching Wheelis's ear so that when he speaks, his breath tickles. "Seeds have been sown that must now bear fruit. Hmm?"

Wheelis looks up.

"Will you be my reaper, boy?"

Twenty minutes later, Wheelis is rummaging in the luggage room. He's sweating as he lugs red suitcases, scraping them back and forth across the concrete floor, foraging in a high stakes game of Find the Lady. He has strict instructions: "The case you're looking for also contains a brown quilted smoking jacket and a gold-mounted guilloché enamel Fabergé egg pendant." Wheelis has no idea what guilloché means, but he knows what an egg looks like. The first case reveals various undergarments and is stuffed with six pairs of silk boxer shorts by Grunschild. The second holds a silver snuff box, two repousse rose napkin rings and an ivory soap dish. In another case his attention is drawn to an Art Nouveau flask by Schleissner & Sohne and four bottles of Agua de Colonia Aneja. Despite the treasures, the hunt does not yield the two items of great importance to the Reichsmarschall.

Despite the perspiration now sucking at his shirt, he searches on and is eventually rewarded with the two containers he's been looking for. The first is nothing more than a flimsy ivory and lime green cardboard box containing a pot of Kaloderma cleansing cream. Wheelis knows it immediately; it's the same as the one he purchased for himself the day after he watched Göring applying it. The second is a tan pigskin coffin box for a wristwatch. He slides both items into the black box file that he brought to hide them in.

A few minutes later he is back in Cell #5, handing the items to Göring, who caresses each one in turn as though they were finest Lalique. He turns his attention to the cream, rotating the box over in his hands. His eyes move deviously from the box to Wheelis before he snaffles it under the blanket and picks up the pigskin watch case.

"This is for you, my friend." He does not yet allow it out of his hands, preferring to hold it in front of Wheelis and open it slowly for him. On a dark brown velvet cushion sits a large, white-faced watch with Arabic numerals and blued steel hands. Below the 12, the word 'Universal' is written in black capital letters and, below that, 'Genève'. The same is repeated in gold lettering on the ivory silk cloth that lines the lid of the hand-made box.

"A Compax pilot's watch by Universal of Geneva," explains Göring. "Here's the best bit," he adds enticingly. He snatches the watch out of the case and turns it over. 'Hermann Göring' is engraved, signature style, on the back above a sequence of numbers.

"With my warmest wishes. And thanks."

"For what?"

"The *coup de grace.*"

He sends Wheelis on his way.

It is really a question of mathematics. Like one of those problems etched in chalk on the blackboard, with which Mr Weber would torture the class at school: Hermann has a tin of Kaloderma cream with a diameter of 70mm and a height of 80mm. Hermann also has a 1cc glass vial of hydrocyanic acid (ssh! Very dangerous, boys and girls). The vial has a diameter of 9mm and a height of 35mm. How much of the cream would be displaced if the vial was inserted into a full tub of cream? How many vials of acid can Hermann reasonably fit into the pot? Mr Weber would be proud.

\* \* \*

It is 2224 exactly. Private First Class, Harold Johnson is the appointed member of the 2nd Relief of the 6850th Internal Security Detachment on duty outside Cell #5. The fates have conspired to place this inconsequential soldier on duty at a moment of history in the making. In a few hours, when the flashbulbs pop before his eyes, he'll curse himself for not clipping his nasal hair. He will dine out on this one back home. 'Tell 'em what you saw, Harold,' his wife will say at the yard party next summer.

It is 2232. Johnson knows this because he's just glanced at the hands of his service watch. The smell of ersatz coffee drifts from the guard room. He turns to his right, glancing down the corridor; nothing doing. He turns around and, closing his right eye, peers through the Judas window with his left. His eye slowly becomes accustomed to the deep blue of the room. It's an underwater scene, with Göring lying at the bottom of the deep. He is flat on his back with his hands on top of the bed covers, perfectly asleep, floating in the deep blue without a movement. His hand drifts to the wall, groping in the deep. It glides slowly across the cold white bricks, his fingers feeling their way as if searching for a secret message in braille. It is 2240. He brings his hands across his chest and laces his fingers. He turns his head to the wall and takes a deep breath.

"That's when something must have happened."

"What happened?" asks Colonel William H. Tweedy, member of the Board of Officers who is writing the report on the whole sorry affair for the Quadripartite Commission.

"Take a step back, soldier. When was this?"

"At 2244 exactly. I looked at my watch and then when I turned around, he..."

"He?" says Tweedy, tugging at the thread.

In Cell #5 Göring stiffens and makes a wheezing, choking sound.

Johnson fumbles with his chain, then the keys, then the lock, losing all control of his fingers. He's calling out for the Corporal of the Relief who's trying to look busy on the second floor when all hell breaks loose.

What ensues is a melee of bustling as Cell #5 fills, empties and refills with officers of increasing seniority as the drama unfolds. Eventually, a disbelieving Colonel Andrus stands shaking his head and cursing under his breath, seething. He is flanked by the chaplain, Fr. Gerecke, and the stooped figure of the prison physician, Dr Pflücker.

The scene progresses from 'Save him!' to a desperate 'Can he be saved?'. Thereafter comes 'Is he dead?' followed by 'Can we confirm he's officially dead?' Finally, comes the issuing of the time of death. The prison physician Dr Ludwig Plücker speaks up grimly.

"If it's cyanide, there's a vial and if there's a vial there may be glass. Look for splinters," he says prodding his fingers into the wet, fleshy mouth.

"It's cyanide," says the chaplain. "Can no one else smell that? Almonds. Look at his skin, it's cherry-red."

Pflücker suddenly thrusts his arm into the air.

"Glass!" he says triumphantly, brandishing a tiny splinter.

Into the vacuum of silence creeps anger.

From the corner of his eye, Pflücker notices Andrus's hands curling into fists and his cheek muscles tighten. Taking a step forward, he leans over the body and reaches down, slowly seizing Göring's tunic and squeezing the fabric which slowly contorts in his ever-tightening grip. Andrus is whispering something bitterly and his words pour from lips mingling with spittle as his face reddens. Then, he notices something. He takes Göring's limp fist and peers at the white within it. Unpeeling the fingers, he removes the white carnation of crumpled paper and slides it into his pocket. He has an idea.

"We – we could get him out. Get him to the gallows. Hang him," he says in bare-faced desperation. "Strap him up on the gallows," he urges, warming to the idea.

"Might you be suggesting that we kill him again?" asks the chaplain dryly.

"I'm suggesting that we avoid the hatred of the entire world by not having to announce that the biggest war criminal of the whole poisoned bunch has cheated justice! Have you any *fucking* idea what this will do for my career?!"

"Sir," says Gerecke, "take a moment. There are too many people that have been through this room in the last ten minutes to even begin to keep a lid on this."

Andrus does not respond. He stands for a moment, red-faced, then storms out.

The clip clop of military heels echoes down the corridor, and an echo accompanies Andrus past the cells of the condemned and beyond, clanking up the metal staircase alongside him. For a moment the chaplain wonders if it is the Reichsmarschall's ghost goose-stepping beside his tormentor, exacting a cruel revenge.

Over hot coffee in the guard room, Jack Wheelis wonders if he should feel bereaved. Perhaps. But it's hard to be gloomy when you've just got your hands on a brand-new watch.

He leans against the wall of the guard room rhythmically winding the crown between his finger and thumb, to no avail. Lifting it to his ear, he gives it a little shake and then hears the soft jingle of broken components rattling within.

Nothing says 'Adieu' like a broken watch.

"Bastard," he mumbles.

\* \* \*

In the Thalkirchen district of Munich, there is a leafy villa colony called Prinz-Ludwigs-Höhe. Within it, Heilmannstrasse is indistinguishable from the other streets of well-tended gardens and manicured facades. Few Munich residents have a reason to visit Villa Oberhummer, but to the occasional dog walkers and Sunday strollers who pass it, it exudes a feeling of stately comfort in the English country house style. Since the end of the war, it has been a U.S. Army mortuary.

On this cold, bright October morning, a low mist sits over the lawn beyond the terrace. A side door yawns open and a group of eleven army officers emerge slowly, making their way silently across the dewy lawn, heralded by the rhythmic call of a wood pigeon somewhere in the dense wood above them. Each man carries a bright urn, sixteen inches high. At the bottom of the garden, they reach a tiny stream that runs into the Isar River and the soldiers arrange themselves into a line by the water's edge. In wordless consent, they kneel, setting the cylinders down in the wet sand. One by one they smash their boot-heels onto the urns, following this with piston-like footfalls until the urns are ground down and their contents indistinguishable from the silt and sand of the riverbank. They kick the detritus into the stream that bubbles around their feet.

So it is that in quiet obscurity, the remains of the Reichsmarschall mingle with sand and stone before being carried downriver into oblivion. Overhead the rhythmic call of a wood pigeon resumes.

* * *

A few miles away, Colonel Burton Andrus makes his way sullenly towards the world's press corps who are waiting to turn rumour into publishable fact. None of them know anything about the suicide in cell #5. As Andrus leans towards the microphone, a shrill whine whistles painfully through the speakers before he begins.

"Hermann Göring was not hanged. He committed suicide at 10:45 last night by taking cyanide. He was discovered at once by the sentinel who watched and heard him make an odd noise and then twitch. An investigation is now going on to learn how he could have obtained the poison, since he was subject to daily and rigorous searches, both of his clothes and his person."

The small room erupts, but with a wave of the hand and a "Thank you gennelmen," Andrus squeezes between two guards and out of the door before he can suffer scrutiny.

Five minutes later he is in his office reeling off orders to his adjutant.

"And shut the door on your way out," as finally, silence embraces the room.

Andrus sits rigidly in his chair and takes a very slow and deliberate breath as the words of Justice Robert Jackson ring in his ears, "Göring's wiped out everything we did at Nuremberg," the lawyer had whispered bitterly down the phone to him late last night.

Andrus splays his palms on the desk-top and sits staring at the remnants of a career that began on 25th October 1917 at Madison Barracks New York and ended in cell #5 at Nuremberg.

Summoning his courage, his hand reaches down into his pocket and feels for the crumpled white carnation. Delicately pulling at the crumpled sheet, he lays the paper down and smooths it out. It is only now that he sees that the letter was always intended for him, it bears his name in dark blue ink. Reichsmarschall Hermann Göring reaching out from beyond the grave.

He reads.

It's every bit as bad as he expects. Career-ending bad. The Quadripartite Commission will slaughter him and then let the press feed on whatever scraps are left after the mauling.

# Epilogue

Title: *From the Unholy Organist, a Hymn of Hate*

From the portfolio of seventeen plates Écraser l'Infâme

Artist: Baron Rudolf Charles von Ripper

Medium: Etching

Dimensions: 39.8 × 29.6 cm

Note: In January 1939, Time magazine used von Ripper's picture captioned 'From the unholy organist, a hymn of hate', from *Ecrasez l'infame*, on the front cover of the issue which named Adolf Hitler as 1938's Man of the Year.

The central figure of the organist at his instrument traditionally symbolizes the creation of music and harmony. However, labelled as 'unholy' and with a 'hymn of hate' it suggests a perversion of this traditional role*. The large wheel with human figures attached to it evokes the medieval *Rota Fortunae*, a symbol of the arbitrary and fickle nature of fate. Meanwhile, the figures around the organ are in different states of distress and the skeletal figures suggest a Danse Macabre, reminding us of the universality of death.

The original title– *Les Chrétiens allemands – The German Christians* – suggests the contamination, seduction and influence of Nazi liturgy on clergymen.

*It is interesting to note that while Hitler plays a symphony of death on the monstrous organ, to the left we see Reichsmarschall Hermann Göring depicted as a clown on a fairground swing.

\* \* \*

Munich
Monday 4ᵗʰ September, 1972

The tram lines stretch down Barer Strasse and into the distance, threading the spindly, pastel-coloured buildings. The jaunty rattle and chime of the tram creates a jollity that is reflected in the sage, peach and corn facades. Wagner said that Munich is the capital of German art, and the Schröder Kunst auction house believes it. Its façade remains one of the more stately tenants of the street. As if to emphasize the fact, a dark blue standard bearing the family crest hangs ostentatiously from a flagstaff above the door, belittling the meagre painted hoardings of its neighbours; a café to the left, a small bookshop on the right.

There are two types of auction house in Germany. The first is at pains to emphasise its grandeur and exclusivity, warning the consumer that art is not for the faint-hearted. Its patrons are aloof, eschewing polite conversation in favour of transaction. The second says 'come one, come all' and is a charming assortment of the bohemian. A world in which grimy oil paintings lean against once-cherished perambulators which sit behind electric teasmades that stand on plastic bar stools.

The dark oak interior and green velvet furnishings reassure patrons that Schröder's sits primly within the first category. Imperious staff float noiselessly around the building, their presence betrayed only by the occasional comforting creak of a well-polished floorboard.

Upstairs, in a small office deliberately away from inopportune glances, an elderly man is completing a purchase. Despite the warm September weather, he is dressed in a grey wool plaid two-piece suit and a Mercedes-Benz Club tie. A friend of Schröder's, he is a customer of long-standing. As evidence, note the way in which the obsequious manager fusses quietly around him, sliding a chair over the thick pile carpet; proffering a cafetiere of steaming hot coffee accompanied by the whispered suggestion of a wafer biscuit.

At Schröder's, discretion is the watchword. Herr Schröder Snr was of the old guard, following a tradition of averting his eyes from the inelegance of provenance. Business was conducted by way of a handshake and a nod. Herr Schröder Jnr is cut from the same atavistic cloth, knowing from bitter experience that too many questions are not only inelegant, but also fatal for business. This is especially true of this morning's esteemed customer.

"Hot one," says the old man, loosening the Mercedes-Benz tie.

"Set to last, they say," agrees Schröder. "Still, good for the Games. I don't recall ever seeing the city so busy."

"With foreigners," snorts the man. "I promised myself I'd be confined to the apartment for the duration, but this was too good an opportunity to miss," he says wafting the plastic folder contianing the faded, sepia envelope. "You were right to call me. How did you come by it?"

"According to our man, Andrus was obliged to submit the letter as evidence to the Quadripartite Commission investigating Göring's suicide, despite his reluctance to do so. After the tribunal, the Commission couldn't agree on where to retain the evidence and, as a result it, was one of dozens of documents that went missing. Then, two months ago that letter turned up at a black auction in Ulm. With some digging, our contact established the provenance and its authenticity: the vendor was a former employee at the National War Crimes Archives at Nuremberg looking to supplement her retirement plan. When I received the call from my associate, I knew that you would be interested. Especially considering that you used to work for the man himself."

"Excellent work, Schröder. Your father would be proud to know the place is in good hands."

The man is already on his feet and making his way to the door with a spring in his step attributable to his good fortune at purchasing the letter. Schröder opens the door as the man slides the plastic wallet into the inside pocket of his suit jacket. Schröder is caught off-guard when the man gently pushes the door closed and turns towards him.

"Got a beautful watercolour by Dürer you should look at," he says quietly. "I'm retrieving it next month and could arrange a viewing probably end of October. Interested?"

"Schröder's is always interested in your items, Mr Lohse. I'd be delighted to have Fräulein Baier set up an appointment."

"See that she does," says Bruno Lohse, tugging the black trilby onto his brow and marching out of the room.

At the bottom of the stairs he tarries for a moment in the cool darkness, bracing himself for the warm September sun and the hundreds of tourists whose interest in the Games has swelled the city. Around him people bustle, coming and going from this morning's auction of Japanese *objets d'art*. He hastens towards the light and grabs the brass door handle, pulling the it back for a lady crossing the threshold.

In that moment, time stops. She sweeps through the doors; he freezes as her perfume awakens a memory and instantaneously he remembers his Schiller: 'Not without a shudder may the human hand reach into the mysterious urn of destiny.'

He turns back and follows her as she disappears into the crowd of people making their way into the auction. They criss-cross in front of him but he keeps his eyes fixed. Despite the heat, she wears a light brown trenchcoat, its wide collar accentuating her long neck. She's retained her figure, he thinks. The hair is dressed in the same elegant French twist that it always was, only now the brown sheen has given way to white. He focusses on a detail that awoke his subconscious just a few moments ago and told his memory that it could be no one else: a handcrafted, two-prong horn hairpin with cut rhinestones in a rose gold plaited mounting.

He pushes himself forward through the doors and into the auction room. She is a few metres ahead of him, making her way down the main aisle and into row G. He takes H.

He's directly behind her and staring at the hairpin. There's a little light oxidation to the metal but this is to be expected. Some light wear to the horn itself; it's been almost thirty years, after all.

A hush descends on the room as the auction begins. It has been many years since Bruno Lohse attended an auction, preferring to deal exclusively with private sales. Any business that he has with Schröder's is conducted in the manager's office and never in the glare of public scrutiny.

The auctioneer announces the next lot and Lohse notices a change come over the woman. She shuffles in her seat and opens the brochure, running her forefinger down the page, creasing the spine. She slides a pen from her handbag and sits upright, her pen poised.

"A delightful Arita vase from the late Genroku period," gushes the auctioneer. "The hexagonal form is decorated in Imari palette and adorned with overlapping fan and chrysanthemum panels, while vibrant tsubaki flowers alternate with Edo uchiwa around the neck. This unblemished 17th Century vase is as fine an example as one can find, and will make an enviable addition to any collection."

The bidding begins (at a reasonable price, Lohse notes). While the heads of those in the auction room bob and sway, following the action, Lohse remains still, his eyes on her, leaning in to see what she is writing.

All the while as the price slowly mounts, she makes jottings. Then he realizes: she's a proxy, instructed to keep a close eye on the bidding for an interested party.

As quickly as it began, it's all over: the gavel falls, the clerk makes notes, shuffles papers and the attendants deftly swap the item for the next. As a collection of antique omamori are presented in a display case, the auctioneer makes a quip about the Japanese sprinting team needing all the luck they can get in the Games. As a wave of gentle laughter ripples across the room, she snaps her brochure shut and stands to leave, the others on the row pivoting to let her pass. Lohse waits a moment, wondering what to do. Turning his head only as much as he dares, he sees her leave the room and then stands.

They are on the street now. It is approaching midday and Lohse is aware of the tightness of his collar. He pursues her, telling himself that he has no business chasing the past, reaching his hand into Schiller's urn of destiny and rummaging through contents that no one wants disturbed. Nevertheless, he has questions that must be answered and evidence that must be seen and shared. It's *schicksal* – fate – he tells himself, dabbing the sweat on his brow. He must present his evidence; hear her testimony.

Ten minutes later he is on a tram headed towards Bogenhausen, leaving his Mercedes in the car park at Schröder's. The streetcar jerks and rattles, reminding him why he loathes public transportation. All the while his eyes remain fixed on her, sitting quite still at the front of the tram and staring out of the window, oblivious to the fact that her past has finally caught up with her. How is he going to do it? Will he wait until they have disembarked in a quiet part of some leafy residential neighbourhood? Should he grab her arm now, a captive audience, and confront her? Should he speak to her at all? These details are replaced with a more threatening one: what if she's married? How does a ghost materialize from out of the past? He will be both Banquo and Old Hamlet, here to confront the guilty. He served his sentence, why not her? However, before he can accuse her, he needs the evidence that is stuffed in a compartment of his writing desk. Does he even still have it after all this time? Where did he put the damn thing? Instinctively, his hand reaches to his left breast to feel the letter. 'Not without a shudder may the human hand reach into the mysterious urn of destiny.' Today of all days to purchase this and to see her.

Alighting the tram and now walking briskly down the quiet, tree-lined street, she turns into Titurel Strasse and Lohse wonders how a woman in her late seventies has done so well for herself on the meagre wage of a secretary. Surely there's a wealthy husband waiting. The Hügelhaus is a nearly new apartment complex. The brutalist residential building is designed so that plant troughs on the tiered balconies spill over the parapets giving the impression of hanging gardens. Lohse pauses thirty metres from the building and watches her enter. As the glass door swings slowly shut, he jogs down the road and up the path just in time to see the elevator light rest at the fourth floor. But which apartment? He turns and looks at the row of anonymous metal mailboxes, quickly locating those of fourth floor residents:

Frau, Herr, Herr & Frau, Fräulein, Fräulein, Herr & Frau.

*Ene mene miste, Es rappelt in der Kiste...*

*Eeny meeny miny moe...*

There is no hurry, he tells himself. He can do nothing without the evidence. He pushes the door open, bidding good morning to a young woman with a pram entering the building. He remembers the small park at the end of the road on Wahnfriedallee, and makes out he's just another late summer stroller enjoying the weather. He ambles across the park, glancing now and then across to the fourth floor of Hügelhaus.

It is a hot day. Sooner or later she'll open a window. Then he'll know the number.

Frau, Herr, Herr & Frau, Fräulein, Fräulein, Herr & Frau.

*Ene mene miste…*

\* \* \*

The next day, the bell on the timer makes her start and, opening the oven door, the apartment is filled with the smell of warm, freshly baked *Lebkuchen*. She doesn't have a substantial repertoire, but she likes the little ginger biscuits and, contrary to all advice, so does Aldo. She plucks them from the baking tray one by one and drops them onto a plate, singeing her fingertips in the process and causing dark brown crumbs to scatter onto the yellow worktop. True to her fastidious nature, she slides a damp cloth up and down the surface while Aldo patters on the brown tiled floor, content to lick up the crumbs.

The sing-song chime of the doorbell interrupts her and she enters the last few moments of solitude, oblivious to the fact that past and present are about to collide in the form of an old man in a Mercedes-Benz Club tie.

Aldo musters his customary bravado, scuttles out of the kitchen and down the darkened hallway yapping all the way to the front door while she makes her way in carpet slippers, drying her hands on a tea towel as she does so. No, it's not Frau Herbig returning her whisk, but the distorted figure of a man standing in profile. In a hat. His silhouette is fragmented by the taffeta glass of the small window on the door. Her very own Judas window.

"Scht," she whispers to Aldo, scooping him into her arms and sliding the chain from the door.

"Good afternoon, Linnie," says the old man, reaching into her destiny.

* * *

"Or is it Fräulein Gisela Weschler these days?"

With little choice she lets him over the threshold.

"How?"

"By complete accident," he replies. "Schröders."

She nods, holding the door open for him, as if 'Schröder' is the word code. She sets Aldo down as he emits murmuring growls while bobbing and weaving with sniffs of the stranger's shoes.

Lohse follows her down the hallway silently, double checking his pockets for the two important documents, one in each pocket.

She leads him into a spacious sitting room scented with summer flowers standing on a low coffee table. The room is pure Linnie he thinks, polished and orderly.

"Coffee?" she says over her shoulder, walking into the kitchen.

Alone now, Lohse slowly takes in the details around him, accompanied by the sound of crockery being laid and coffee made in the next room. He is used to reading a room. It is a skill he has acquired from time spent with members of the old network who, in these straitened times, have asked him to appraise a ceremonial dagger here, a few medals there. Occasionally he finds a gem that someone ferreted away during the war for that rainy day, and now, finding themselves in a torrential downpour, they flip open the pop-up address book under 'L' to enquire as to whether he might help out an old friend. For his part, the old habits remain, and Lohse has substituted robbing the Jews of Europe for fleecing former Party members.

The room is dressed in light blue and bathed in the light of a late summer's afternoon. From the fourth floor she has a good view over the Englischer Garten, the Isar River and beyond.

198

"You have a wonderful view of the Olympic Tower," he calls out to her as she busies herself in the kitchen. "I'm really rather envious," he adds, slowly probing here and there.

Is he local, she calls out from the next room.

He is. Since the French acquitted him in '50.

She continues to throw crumbs of polite conversation in his direction; he continues his examination, discovering who Fräulein Gisela Weschler is from the objects gathered around her. No photographs. No family.

Yes, he agrees there's nowhere quite like the Englischer Garten in the summer, picking up a magnificent quality silver magnum wine coaster, hand engraved in late eighteenth century style.

No, he's never admired the view from the monopteros he replies, holding up a silver cigarette case to the light; blue guilloche enamel, circa 1920.

From the background there is the clatter of spoons and the *plock plock* sound of a percolator.

No thank you, she doesn't need any help.

Art Nouveau napkin ring, decorated with repousse poppies. He turns it over: Lutz & Weiss of Pforzheim.

The Chinesischer Turm? Quite lovely this time of year, he agrees, delicately trying to slide open the drawer of an 18th Century dresser in burr ash and oak, wincing as it squeaks in protest. Aldo scurries in and recommences sniffing at Lohse's feet.

He's only followed a little of the Games, he tells her, but he enjoys the swimming.

Hasn't the American, Spitz, done well?

She murmurs assent as he's drawn towards an expressionist oil painting in vivid blues: a girl sitting alone at a table. Suddenly the voice is in the room with him. Behind him.

"I said you can switch it on if you like," says Linnie. "I enjoy the company of the television."

"You know, your Camoin is really taking far too much light hanging there," says Lohse, taking the tray from her and setting it down on the coffee table.

Linnie clicks the dial on her Porta-Colour television set and watches the ghosts of the XX Olympiad emerge from out of the grey mist. She turns the sound dial to zero. Plumping the cushion in her favourite armchair, she lowers herself into it. He sits opposite on the matching sofa.

He taps his pockets again, checking. Just to be sure that he has them both. Like most dealers in Bavaria, Lohse can instantly recognise a Nymphenburg tea service when he sees one, and he hasn't seen pearl design porcelain this good in a while. The blue and gold detailing is superb, mid-18th. As she pours, she watches his eyes rove, appraising the items before him. Lohse does not show his hand yet, instead sitting back with cup and saucer and pointing to Camoin's girl again.

"Seeing her reminds me of something," he says, refusing a *Lebkuchen*.

Taking sips from the cup, she listens as he tells her a story.

"Do you remember that time at the Jeu de Paume? That creepy fellow Miedl gave us a visit. You remember Miedl, the sweaty chap. Boss couldn't stand him."

She listens as he continues, painting the scene for her. The day Vermeer came to Paris. Yes, she remembers, *Christ with the Adulteress*. She knows it well, the one that Göring hung in pride of place behind the desk at Carinhall.

Then Lohse delivers the punchline: it was a fake.

"Göring swapped thirty-something paintings for his own Vermeer so he could to get one over Hitler. Ever heard of Theodore Rousseau?"

It's a name she's not heard in a long time. The lieutenant who interviewed her in Berchtesgarten and then let her slip away into obscurity.

"He's a chum," explains Lohse. "Former Monuments Man, who used to chase down looted art back then. Became curator at the Metropolitan Museum of Art in New York."

Rousseau has told Lohse the story of how Göring's cache was found in a salt mine in Altausee. How they found an unknown Vermeer entitled *Christ with the Adulteress*. Eventually they traced the painting from Göring to sweaty Miedl in Munich, and from him to Holland and a man named van Meegeren who was on trial for collaborating with the Nazis. Van Meegeren was so desperate to save his skin that he told all.

"An incredible bedtime story of how he alone fooled the Great Nazi Hermann Göring and all the dealers in the Third Reich by flogging them a dud, painted by mixing paints with bakelite and then cooked in an oven for good measure." He shakes his head in disbelief.

"Well Bruno, that's quite a story," Linnie says taking a sip of coffee.

"Fooled 'em all." He's looking straight at her now. "Bet he's not the only one."

He doesn't play his hand yet. He's wondering which document to draw first.

They both sit silently for a moment, turning from each other to the silent television set, grateful for the distraction.

The image zooms in and out of focus on the Lego landscape of the Olympic village, fixing itself on 31 Connollystrasse.

"I must say Linnie, I had no idea that you were a collector. All those years we worked side by side. Isn't it funny how you think you know someone," he says as they continue to stare at the muted set.

A series of black and white photographs: Yosef Romano, 31. David Berger, 28. Moshe Weinberg, 33.

Lohse stands and walks to the mantel piece. The vase is painted in cobalt blue, its tapered panels decorated with birds perching on bamboo stalks. Elsewhere, boats drift on a river below a mountain range.

"I think that this is Meiji. Is it? Is it Meiji?"

She nods.

"Miyagawa Makuzu Kozan. One of the most revered potters of the period." Frustrated by his laboured subterfuge, she adds, "It's nicer than the one I sold at Schröder's."

Momentarily his face is a picture of incomprehension. She watches as realization dawns.

"You're no secretary. All that time I thought you were a proxy, taking notes for the vendor."

She smiles.

"You *were* the vendor," he adds. "Some secretary. Look at this stuff. Christ, you're a connoisseur."

She lets him take it all in again; the Camoin, the dresser, the Meiji, the cigarette case, the napkin ring, the Nymphenburg.

"Actually it's *connoisseuse* – for a lady."

He now walks through the apartment  again but now without restraint; strolling, studying and observing like a privileged guest at a vernissage. Linnie sits quite still and watches as he circles the room, occasionally stopping, picking up an object, checking for a maker's mark. Once or twice, he chuckles to himself and shakes his head.

"You know what I was doing at Schröder's, but what were *you* doing there?" she asks, unwittingly inviting him to finally play his hand.

"I was making a purchase actually," he replies without looking at her. "Something special. Something you will be very interested to see, Linnie. That's why it was *Schicksal* that I saw you yesterday. Fate."

From the mantel piece, a Döring carriage clock chimes elegantly four times.

From the television, a ghoulish masked face peeps furtively over the balcony on 31 Connollystrasse, its black hole eyes staring towards the camera.

"They're all gone," says Bruno drawing a folded piece of paper from his jacket. The other piece of evidence, for now, remains in his other pocket.

"Who, all?"

Sliding the coffee pot aside, Lohse gently lays the paper down with his knuckles resting on it.

"Rousseau told me that Jodl took eighteen minutes to die. Remember Kietel? Keitel was hanging there for almost half an hour twitching and choking before death took him."

"I had no interest in the others. I answered to the Reichsmarschall."

"The only one to escape the hangman's noose."

"Good for him." She is the most animated that she has been all afternoon. "He was a soldier and soldiers deserve an honourable death, a military one."

"Have you never wondered how he cheated them?"

"At first I did. When I heard the news on the radio, I wondered about how. And who."

Lohse taps a finger on the paper and then removes his hand and withdraws, sipping his coffee.

"The how," he says enigmatically.

Linnie takes the paper and opens it.

Nuremberg, 11 October 1946

To the Commandant:

I have always had the capsule of poison with me from the time I became a prisoner. When taken to Mondorf I had three capsules. The first I left in my clothes so that it would be found when a search was made. The second I placed under the clothes rack in undressing and took it to me again on dressing. I hid this in Mondorf and here in the cell so well that despite the frequent and thorough searches it could not be found. During the court sessions I had it on my person in my high riding boots. The third

203

capsule is still in my small suitcase in the round box of skin cream, hidden in the cream, I could have taken this to me twice in Mondorf if I had needed it. None of those charged with searching is to be blamed for it was practically impossible to find the capsule. It would have been pure accident.

Hermann Göring

She folds it carefully and returns it to the tray.

"And the who?"

"Wheelis. The name won't mean anything to you, I suspect. A lieutenant in the American army, of all things. It seems that he was...close? Close to the boss in those final months. A valet of sorts. He's bragged as much since he returned to obscurity in...Wyoming. Or Kansas. Or Iowa or one of those places with nothing more than tumbleweed and a rusting gas pump. Imagine that, dining out on tales from the Reich and boasting about being touched by greatness."

"More coffee?"

Lohse uses the opportunity to take a lump of sugar, keen to inspect the sterling silver sugar tongs that have caught his eye. English, by Thomas Heasley of Birmingham and with a Corinthian design. They bear an engraving, 'To Beatrice', and without knowing quite why, he associates the name with horse riding in the Bois de Boulogne and a girl with a ribbon in her hair. The television coverage continues beside them, though Lohse and Linberg are oblivious.

Baying for blood, the cameraman from RTF perches precariously on a ladder, above the heads of his envious rivals who suffocate in a jungle of flared trousers and telephoto lenses. He reasons that an artistically framed sequence of an emerging cadaver, bloodied and bullet ridden, might earn him the Pulitzer. Christians in the Colosseum, Jews at the Olympics, it's all the same.

"Death surrounded him. What do you think about that? No one was immune. Did you ever hear of a man called Kelley, a psychiatrist?" asks Lohse.

"No."

"He spent months speaking with the Reichsmarschall at the prison. Made a name for himself after that, publishing the insights that he learnt about the Nazi mind, apparently. Another one dining out courtesy of Göring. The peculiar thing is – he killed himself after that. And do you know how he did it? A 1cc glass vial of hydrocyanic acid. Imagine that – cyanide. The very same. Three capsules, Göring had." Lohse lets a theory sink in.

"Wait –"

But Lohse is on the other side of the room examining the Camoin. Linnie tidies the crockery on the tray.

"Why are you here, Bruno? Was it to resurrect the past or disturb the future?"

Withdrawing the second piece of paper, he lays it on the tray, once again resting it under his knuckles.

"I'll answer your question, but first, I noticed a Goethe first edition on the shelf – also in too much sun if I may say so. I remember my teacher used to quote him often. One of his favourites was, 'Thou must be either anvil or hammer'. I've always remembered that. If I'm honest I'm not sure I've ever decided which I am, anvil or hammer."

In the summer sun, men in track suits crouch on white Lego blocks of Connollystrasse clutching H&K G3 rifles, waiting impatiently for something to happen.

Anvil or hammer?

"Anvil or hammer, Linnie?" he asks raising an eyebrow.

"Bookkeeper, I'm afraid," she replies meekly.

"I wonder if we're not all of us bookkeepers in Germany. Those of us from the old Germany, I mean. Not the new, not the bastard son from Bonn. We were all bookkeepers then. That's what did for us at Nuremberg. So many bloody records that the prosecutors had a field day. Names, dates, places. They couldn't burn that stuff quick enough at the camps. It was all there in black and white. And then there's the art."

"The art."

"Inventoried in black and white. Only, they never *did* find the records. His Inventory. You carried it everywhere for him." His finger taps the paper twice and the hand moves away. She's unable to read his blue eyes, so she unfolds the paper and reads that instead.

Owner: Gisela Limberger – Berlin, Germany
Case Nos 1–11
Artist: Various
Medium: Decorative Arts
Date: 25th November 1943

"It's extensive to say the least, wouldn't you agree?" interrupts Lohse as her eyes rove the paper.

Six two-compartment salt-shakers
Three Gravy Spoons

"How much gravy can a girl have?"

Six Decanter Coasters
Three Sugar Bowls
Two Snuff boxes

"Cigar cutter it says somewhere on there," he says stabbing vaguely in her direction. "I didn't have you down as a smoker."

Bread tongs
Three Toast Holders
Gravy Boat Holder
Two Ice Buckets

"Twenty-six dishes – twenty-six?! 'Who is she entertaining?' I thought, when I saw that, 'the Shah of Iran and – what is she – the Shahrina? Shahress?'"

Bronze Doorbell

Two Bronze Chimeras

Upwards of about a dozen Japanese vases

Tea Caddy Japan

Inkwell Japan

Two Japan Plant Jars

Linnie folds the paper, places it on the tray and disappears slowly into the kitchen.

"Port Decanter I recall, too," Bruno continues, calling over his shoulder. "I'm partial to a drop of port myself as a matter of fact. Do you favour it like the French, as an apéritif, or like the Brits, with cheese? There *were* two cases of cognac, though I imagine that they're long since...er..." he doesn't bother to finish the sentence.

Linnie returns carrying two balloon glasses of honey coloured cognac that swirls in slow motion, the dark amber climbing the sides of the glasses.

"What are you going to do with your little list?" she asks, nodding at the paper.

"Quite the dilemma isn't it? What do you think?"

She is half expecting the distant sound of sirens to draw near, hastening the inevitable demise of Fräulein Gisela Weschler, the quiet and courteous neighbour who seemed so friendly. Who would have known that she harboured a chequered past? Is she worthy of a colour spread in *Der Spiegel* that includes a damning testimony from Frau Roth, bitch-neighbour of the second floor?

Linnie takes a sip and walks to the mantel piece where she touches the carriage clock, adjusting its position.

"At first I tried so hard to put all that behind me. Not to forget, just to move on. The trouble is – the truth is – I don't want to." Now the

Meiji vase receives the same treatment as the clock. She adjusts it this way and that. "It was never about status, though God knows I had my fair share of basking in that glow. It was magnetic. You know what I mean, don't you?"

He knows exactly.

"And when I knew it was all coming to an end – we could all see it, of course you'd have had to be blind not to – I knew I couldn't let go. I had to salvage something just to stay alive."

"You could have found work quite easily."

"Not *a* living. *Living*. Life. Aldo and I watched you from the kitchen as you inventoried everything earlier, appraising each piece. When you look at my home you see Döring and Nymphenburg, Camoin and Meiji, but I don't. When I look at the glaze on this vase or the glass of the clock, I see myself reflected. Living a world in which I'm surrounded by these exquisite objects. I say to myself, 'Think how many great men have gazed upon this clock? Which great women held this vase?' Whose lips drank from the same cup?" She giggles, intoxicated, but whether by cognac or memory he isn't sure. "This is not the booty of some provincial parvenu or the hoardings of some grubby housefrau, Bruno," she says accusingly, before adding a final, defiant note. "I am their custodian. Like he was. I make no apology for that."

Lohse sits for a moment sipping his cognac. He realizes that, far from being Fräulein Gisela Weschler from the past, up here on the fourth floor, she's proudly carrying it with her.

"You're still working for him."

"I suppose I am. I never left."

"The world has changed, Linnie, you're on borrowed time. There'll be a reckoning soon. Read that crap Meinhof's writing in *konkret*. She's got an audience. The hippies are gaining ground."

"Nothing's changed, Bruno. The brownshirts are still out there, they've just had a change of costume. Violence and tragedy are still the daily diet, only now they're beamed by aeriel directly into your home, no need for cinema newsreels."

The picture on the screen is fuzzy, the signal breaks and then settles in close-up on a tall man at the window, stooping awkwardly. His hands are clasped in front of him, tied? Spitzer, the fencing coach. He's speaking to someone below on Connollystrasse. A rifle butt smashes the back of his head and he withdraws. The window closes, creating a two-way mirror that reflects the summer sun and conceals the carnage from a voracious TV audience.

"It's called legacy and memory: the next generation despises its predecessor, so it tries to obliterate it. That's legacy. But it's reactionary, swinging the pendulum towards the savagery waiting at the other end, repeating what we've all seen before. It's just a change of costume. That's memory. Or lack of memory. Or generational insomnia. So which wagon have you hitched a ride on, Bruno? Have you been clean cut and conscientious since they let you out in '50, or does the ghost of the Reichsmarschall loom as large in your life as he does in this room?" Then she adds in a whisper, "Listen carefully enough, and you can hear him."

And he believes her.

"I've not come here to expose you, Linnie. There are no police waiting in the hallway, no Wiesenthal has any idea about Gisela Weschler." He takes a long draw on the cognac, almost finishing it but not quite, deliberately saving a drop in anticipation of what's to come.

"When I followed you yesterday, I wondered what I might do. The Nazi hunting business is worth quite a bit these days. But you're no Nazi, not really. You're a pragmatist like me. So, there I was, watching Munich rattle along beside me and I remembered the letter from Schröder's." He pats his pocket. "That's *Schicksal*, Linnie – fate. It might sound silly, but in that moment I felt that he was there with me. I had his words in my pocket, after all. When I think back to those days at the Jeu de Paume, it was no secret that I skimmed a little off the top, the boss knew that himself. But *you*. Linnie, I never would have believed if I hadn't seen the inventory they compiled, seen your name. Seen this treasure trove you've got here. He's reaching out again to us both, Linnie. Reaching out from Schiller's urn."

"None of it has the value it once did," she says dismissively, shaking her head. "They're wary nowadays. It's tarnished, all of it."

"Says you. I say otherwise. I say, I have contacts. I know people. People who know when to shed a tear for the cameras there, tremble a lip here. Mutter 'Holocaust' with a sincere gulp there and write a big fat cheque. They fork out at galas and swear blind 'Never again'. Then – *then* – they call Uncle Bruno. And do you know what they say, Linnie? They say, 'Fuck the whys and wherefores, Bruno, gimme bottom dollar.' It's Göring and the boys all over again, only this time they've got a Wall Street apartment and a suite at the Georges V. It's like I always say, Nazis never die, they just change their tailor. So what do you think, shall we oil the wheels of art once again? It's what the Reichsmarschall would have wanted," he adds, patting his pocket. "What say you, Linnie?"

"*Prost.*" The balloons touch, and together they savour every last drop they can get.

Behind them, the Porta-Colour TV broadcasts the horror of memory and legacy re-emerging. Nothing says *Willkommen bei den Heiteren Spielen – Welcome to the Cheerful Games* – like dried blood on apartment walls.

From on top of her wardrobe, Linnie retrieves a dusty '33 in a paper sleeve.

Another glass of cognac becomes three and 'Let's Misbehave' crackles and spits on the grey Gebrüder Steidinger record player. Every scratch is a memory, a minute souvenir of a fondly remembered night at Carinhall etched in the vinyl. Their Golden Age.

As the evening draws in, from across the Englischer Garten, the silhouettes of a man and woman can be seen swaying gently in an apartment on the fourth floor of the Hügelhaus.

Finally, when darkness falls, Bruno steps back over the threshold. He nods to her, dons his trilby and walks slowly away.

Before shutting the door, she pauses, listening to the clip clop sound of military heels that echo alongside him, accompanying him down the grey sintered stone corridor, and she wonders if there were not three of them dancing together again tonight.

# Acknowledgements

There are a number of people I would like to thank for their sterling support and encouragement in bringing *A Mind Prone to Evil* to publication. Firstly, I am indebted to those who endured the drafting process with me and offered advice that frequently proved crucial to the development of the manuscript. Alan Lawson, Paul Malgrati and Hyw Jones gave honest and encouraging feedback as I wrestled with each chapter; I thank them for their friendship and candour. I must also thank Paul Bamlett for his overwhelming belief in the book from its inception, and for recommending the idea of its stage adaptation, *The Judas Window*. Paul's efforts on both projects have been tireless and unceasingly enthusiastic.

I am immensely grateful for the passion for the novel shown by Rose Drew, since it landed in her inbox at Stairwell Books. Her guidance and professionalism, together with that of Alan Gillott has helped me to navigate the challenges of publishing a novel. Their dedication to their authors is commendable. Susan Ronald, Catherine Chidgey and Clare Wigfall must be thanked not only for their generous endorsements but for offering advice that has helped to improve and develop the novel.

Finally, to my wife Laetitia and our daughter Camille, whom I must thank for their enduring and boundless love and support in all my madcap and time-consuming passions and projects, including spending far too long in the company of such a despicable figure as the Reichsmarschall.

Other novels, novellas and short story collections available from Stairwell Books

| | |
|---|---|
| Solstice | Ruth Aylett, Greg Michaelson |
| The Other Way | Victoria L. Humphreys |
| The Suitcase of Secrets | Julie Fearn |
| At Night, White Bracken | Gareth Wood |
| The Sunlit Pool of the Finished Image | David Hill |
| The Department of Certainty | S. C. Paterson |
| A Fistful of Ashes | Katy Turton |
| Widdershins | L.A.Robbins |
| 100 Summers | Ali Sparkes |
| Skull Days | PJ Quinn |
| The Broke Hotel | Clayton Lister |
| Equinox | Ruth Aylett, Greg Michaelson |
| Not the Work of an Ordinary Boy | Victoria L. Humphreys |
| Black Harry | Mark P. Henderson |
| Eboracvm: Carved in Stone | Graham Clews |
| Down to Earth | Andrew Crowther |
| The Iron Brooch | Yvonne Hendrie |
| The Electric | Tim Murgatroyd |
| Needleham | Terry Simpson |
| The Keepers | Pauline Kirk |
| Shadows of Fathers | Simon Cullerton |
| Blackbird's Song | Katy Turton |
| Eboracvm: the Fortress | Graham Clews |
| Waters of Time | Pauline Kirk |
| The Water Bailiff's Daughter | Yvonne Hendrie |
| O Man of Clay | Eliza Mood |
| Eboracvm: the Village | Graham Clews |
| Sammy Blue Eyes | Frank Beill |
| Poetic Justice | PJ Quinn |
| The Go-To Guy | Neal Hardin |
| Abernathy | Claire Patel-Campbell |
| Tyrants Rex | Clint Wastling |

For further information please contact rose@stairwellbooks.com

www.stairwellbooks.co.uk
@stairwellbooks